The Gambit

"As the United States attempts to neutralize Iran's march toward nuclear capability with economic sanctions and diplomacy, a battle-hardened Israeli government takes a more aggressive tactical approach. . . . There's no shortage of skillfully rendered military action, and Carlson's meticulous research into the military and political aspects of his subject matter is extraordinary. . . . This is an exciting debut effort that's certain to interest readers with a taste for contemporary political intrigue."

—Kirkus Reviews

The Gambit

By Brad Carlson

ISBN-13: 978-0-9982594-9-9
ISBN-10: 0998259497

Cover Design by BespokeBookCovers.com

To Donna, whose encouragement for this book started something I had previously only imagined.

"But over and beyond all that can be written on the subject . . . the true general must be able to take in, deceive, decoy, delude his adversary at every turn, as the particular occasion demands. In fact, there is no instrument of war more cunning than chicanery"

— Xenophon, *The Cavalry General*

"Think, too, of the great part that is played by the unpredictable in war: think of it now, before you are actually committed to war. The longer a war lasts, the more things tend to depend on accidents. Neither you nor we can see into them: we have to abide their outcome in the dark. And when people are entering upon a war they do things the wrong way round. Action comes first, and it is only when they have already suffered that they begin to think."

— Thucydides, *The Peloponnesian War*

Prologue

September 27, 2012, UN General Assembly

Ladies and Gentlemen,

I've been speaking about the need to prevent Iran from developing nuclear weapons for over fifteen years. I spoke about it in my first term in office as Prime Minister, and then I spoke about it when I left office. I spoke about it when it was fashionable, and I spoke about it when it wasn't fashionable. I speak about it now because the hour is getting late, very late. I speak about it now because the Iranian nuclear calendar doesn't take time out for anyone or for anything. I speak about it now because when it comes to the survival of my country, it's not only my right to speak; it's my duty to speak. And I believe that this is the duty of every responsible leader who wants to preserve world peace.

For nearly a decade, the international community has tried to stop the Iranian nuclear program with diplomacy. That hasn't worked. Iran uses diplomatic negotiations as a means to buy time to advance its nuclear program. According to the International Atomic Energy Agency, during the last year alone, Iran has doubled the number of centrifuges in its underground nuclear facility in Qom.

At this late hour, there is only one way to peacefully prevent Iran from getting atomic bombs. That's by placing a clear red line on Iran's nuclear weapons program.

Red lines don't lead to war; red lines prevent war.

Where's Iran? By next spring, at most by next summer at current enrichment rates, they will have finished the medium enrichment and move on to the final stage. From there, it's only a few months, possibly a few weeks before they get enough enriched uranium for the first bomb.

Ladies and Gentlemen, what I told you . . . is not based on secret information. It's not based on military intelligence. It's based on public reports by the International Atomic Energy Agency. Anybody can read them. They're online. The relevant question is not when Iran will get the bomb. The relevant question is at what stage can we no longer stop Iran from getting the bomb. The red line must be drawn on Iran's nuclear enrichment program because these enrichment facilities are the only nuclear installations that we can definitely see and credibly target.

So if these are the facts, and they are, where should the red line be drawn?

The red line should be drawn right here . . . .

-        Benjamin Netanyahu, Israeli Prime Minister

I

Tehran, Iran (Several months ago)

"Colonel, where are we at with Cyrus?" asked Said Jalili, chairman of Iran's Supreme National Security Council, referring to the most secret operation in Iran's history, even more secret than their nuclear ambitions.

"Everything is set from a logistical standpoint," replied Colonel Ashkan Rafsanjani. "All we need to do is get all of the troops in place, and I'll need a little time to do that. I've already started moving them a few at a time as I don't want a sudden and massive influx that would likely draw attention to our plans. That mistake happened before; we don't want to repeat that."

"No, we don't, this is far too important," admitted Major General Qassim Suleimani, commander of the Iranian Quds Force. "With everything else in order, and given Prime Minister Netanyahu's UN address yesterday, I believe we should step up the pace of moving your men. We really do not know how much time we have and I do not trust that Israeli pig."

"Agreed," said Jalili. "Go ahead and get them over there. There is some urgency here but we must not draw attention to ourselves—and remember, we are not the ones setting the time table here."

*   *   *   *   *

The two motorcycles appeared without notice. Dr. Zadegan, the chief electrical engineer at the Parchin military complex outside of Tehran, had emerged from his car, after his driver had dropped him off, completely lost in thought about solving the exploding bridge wire detonator problem that one of his colleagues had just discovered. He didn't even hear the motorcyclists as he walked up to the front door of his house. His driver, though, quickly switched roles from that of a chauffeur to a body guard. As he turned out of Dr. Zadegan's driveway he noticed the first assassin take out a silenced Heckler & Koch MP-5 submachine gun and lower it at his charge as the biker quickly drove past him. The two second burst fired from the assassin resulted in approximately twenty five rounds being fired at the young electrical engineer. The second assassin didn't have quite the element of surprise as the first. Zadegan's body guard noticed the second bike immediately after the first one sped past him. The second one approached so quickly, though, that all he had time to do was throw open his door in an attempt to strike the cycle as it approached his car. The impact threw the assassin off of the bike just as it began to accelerate past him. The cyclist himself completely lost control of the bike, putting it on its side, and sliding under a neighboring parked car, pinning the cyclist.

"Arielle," Jonah called to the second assassin as he sped away, completely unaware of his compatriots' predicament, "I couldn't tell; what's the status of the target?"

Hearing no answer, Jonah called again, "Arielle, can you hear me?"

No answer; "Arielle?!" Jonah called again, a sense of desperation in his voice.

"We're down; I'm pinned under a car," Arielle's driver reported. "Arielle looks to be in trouble."

Zadegan's body guard, who had lost his sidearm when his car door hit the cyclists, saw that the biker had gotten pinned under a car with his bike while the assassin had slid across the pavement and slammed against the wheel of another car. Ignoring the pinned biker, the body guard turned his attention towards the trigger puller. As the body guard charged the assassin, he unsheathed an eight inch razor-sharp double edged knife and swung at his target. The assassin, slightly dazed from being thrown off of the bike and the sudden impact against the parked car, and now unarmed as well, jumped back to avoid the guard's initial thrust with the knife only to jump back against the side of the car. Consequently, the guard's initial swing found its mark, slicing the assassin's left arm and rib cage. With the second thrust, the assassin's response caught the guard completely by surprise: as the guard took another swing with his right hand, Arielle quickly swung out with her left foot and, using the guard's momentum against him, kicked the back of the guard's knife-hand in the direction he was swinging and then immediately followed that up with another kick to guard's now fully exposed right knee, completely destroying the joint. Arielle picked up the guard's knife, now laying on the pavement as he had dropped the knife due to the sudden shock of a damaged wrist and a shattered knee, and thrust it into the guard's chest, severing the aorta. Arielle's sudden attack was over in seconds.

With the guard dispatched, Arielle grabbed the guard's car and drove the short distance to her compatriot. Running up to free her friend, she noticed he wasn't so much pinned under the car as he had a compound leg fracture below the knee. Despite her own injuries, Arielle all but carried him into the back seat of the car, secured him there, and then got back in front and took off.

"Jonah . . . mission accomplished; ahh . . . ," Arielle winced in pain, "we'll need to meet at Jericho as soon as possible"—a reference to a prearranged site where a medic is required.

"Roger that; we'll see you at Jericho in five minutes," came the prompt response.

"How'd the other teams do?" Arielle asked.

"Mission accomplished," came the succinct reply. And with that, Arielle knew that three of Iran's leading scientists, each working on different components for the development of a nuclear bomb, had just been assassinated.

*   *   *   *   *

If someone didn't know any better, the man walking out of the meeting could have been in his eighties. As it was, his aged appearance came from the news he had been anticipating, well not really anticipating in the sense that this was something he wanted to hear. No, he had dreaded hearing this news, expecting that it would be coming but still nonetheless hoping against hope that it would not. In point of fact, and try as he might, he still hadn't recovered from hearing it: Iran would have a nuclear bomb in just a couple months! This couldn't happen. The Americans had repeatedly stressed that they would never allow this. Now, given the present administration, that threat didn't look all too ominous. However, the Israelis would never allow this—and everyone in every Western intelligence agency knew that they had been practicing for just such a raid. This would not be just any normal raid, though. This could lead to the total destruction of much of the Middle East: Israel, to be sure, but also his beloved Iran. He couldn't let this happen. He knew what he had to do, and the weight of this burden almost paralyzed him. He knew that some, perhaps many, of his fellow citizens would die by his actions but in the end, he would be saving a great deal more. Getting into his car, he quietly advised his driver to take him to his home in the resort area of Bashgah-e Savarkri-e. Once there, he would make a phone call on a very secure, and very secret, satellite phone.

II

"Jim? What's up?" Thomas 'Stonewall' Jackson asked answering his cell phone. "It's got to be, what, two thirty in the morning over there?"

"Stonewall, have you left London yet?" Jim Carmichael, the head of the CIA's Intelligence Directorate asked him.

"Just about to leave for the airport; I have a ten thirty flight to Dulles and London traffic can be horrendous so I figured I'd try and give myself some extra time just in case. Looking forward to getting back home; it's been unseasonably cool and wet all week—even by London's standards. It's supposed to be summer, right; be nice to get back home to some dry weather, warm temperatures, and sunshine!"

"Well, I'm afraid you're going to have to delay that trip back home for a little while."

"What's up? I haven't heard of anything pressing at the moment. Our friends on this side of the pond really didn't have anything new on our Persian friends. We know they are pursuing a nuke but the general consensus is that they are still a couple years out. I don't believe that for a second but I don't have anything to base that on other than my gut instinct—there's just too many un-answered questions."

"Well, you're going to get that chance to prove your instincts right. I've booked you on a 9:45 British Airways flight to Tel Aviv. General Pardo just called and he's expecting you later this afternoon," referencing the head of Mossad. "Tamir mentioned that they have something really hot they are working on and wanted to know if we wanted in on it—he knew we would—I think he just wanted the chance to get me out of bed at two in the morning. I told him you'd be on the first flight out of London."

"Any idea what this is all about?"

"He wouldn't say over the phone—though we were on a secure line—which leads me to believe it's extremely sensitive. I realize you've never worked with him but he's a personal friend of mine and he was at K2 with us," a reference to Karshi-Khanabad Air Base in Uzbekistan, "in the first few months after 9/11 while you were in Afghanistan with the Northern Alliance. He knows you've recently taken over as my lead on Iranian intelligence and nuclear proliferation and I've told him that you're still active duty, a colonel with the Fifth Group"—that is, Fifth Group Special Forces, whose area of concentration is the Middle East—"so whatever they have for you, he knows you're more than qualified."

"Okay, I'm all packed and heading to check out of the hotel right now. Any idea as to who's picking me up in Tel Aviv? Someone from the embassy or one of the general's folks?"

"Her name is Danielle Yaniv and, yes, she works for Tamir, but that's all I know. Go ahead and wear your patch and she'll find you."

"Okay, will do."

"Colonel Jackson?" Danielle asked, leaning towards—and somewhat yelling through—the open passenger window, as she saw someone standing by the curb who she thought fit the description her boss, General Tamir Pardo, had given her: kind of tall, dish-water blonde, well chiseled features—and sporting an eye patch.

"Yes, Ma'am," Jackson replied. "Call me Tom."

"Hop in, Tom. I'm Danielle; call me Dani. The Prime Minister scheduled an urgent meeting with Tamir for five thirty so he told me to get you over to his office right away so he'd have the opportunity to meet you before he went in with Bibi," an informal reference to the Prime Minister. "I'm not sure what his meeting's all about but I'll get you there so you'll have a few minutes with Tamir before he has to leave. By the way, welcome to Israel; have you ever been here before?"

"No, I haven't but I'm looking forward to the visit," Jackson replied.

The tail end of Dani's pony-tail whipped across her face as she snapped her head back towards Jackson, caught completely by surprise on hearing that he had never been to Israel before. This guy came highly recommended by Jim Carmichael, a close friend of Tamir's from the CIA, yet he had never been to Israel? What was up with this, she wondered.

Jackson, seeing Dani's expression, partially obstructed by her long hair, sensed this was the wrong answer, though he had no idea why.

"Stonewall, Jim speaks very highly of you. Nice to finally meet you. You've obviously met Arielle; I trust the drive over from the airport wasn't too eventful," General Pardo added, somewhat facetiously.

"Tamir! You made it sound pretty urgent that I get him here just as soon as I could, so I did," Dani interrupted.

"Likewise, General, I'm glad to be here," Stonewall replied, somewhat surprised by Dani's interruption.

"Arielle, you won't believe what this guy did in Afghanistan. In the first few months after 9/11, the US only had a couple teams in Afghanistan; Jackson, here, commanded one of them. His team had joined the Northern Alliance up in the Panjshir region of northern Afghanistan. Remember, the US role was just getting started so the Taliban thoroughly outnumbered Stonewall's team and his allies. At one point, they came across a Taliban force of, I think, around nine thousand men bivouacked in a relatively narrow valley; Jackson's twelve man team and the Northern Alliance force amounted to something like 1,500 men. Stonewall, here, then a relatively junior captain, comes up with this incredibly bold and brilliant idea—I mean, it's Gideon out of the Old Testament all over again: Sometime in the middle of the night, something like two in the morning, he takes three hundred of his men and marches them up and down the canyon trail—with torches fully lit so everyone in the Taliban encampment can see them. The other 1,200 were set up in a blocking position at the other end of the valley. The really cool thing about this is that the three hundred men with torches—each one only marched about a couple hundred feet along this trail. Stonewall, go ahead and tell her about this."

"You see the whole trick here is about being a force multiplier. I had the men on the trail spaced out about every few hundred feet or so. I had the man at the very top of the canyon light his torches or lanterns. Each man carried two of them; he'd walk to the next one down the trail, who would then hand the lanterns to him; this man would then walk another hundred feet or so and hand the lanterns off to him, and so on. Once each exchange was made each one returned to his place on the trail. As the lit lanterns reached the bottom, these were turned off and exchanged at every hand-off of those coming down the hill so that these would go back up the hill and repeat the process. In this manner, mind you, it's about 2:00 a.m., the impression of the number of men coming down the trail would never seem to end. The idea was to panic them into thinking that a very large force was assembling and force them to run up the other end of the valley, right into our blocking force."

"How'd it go?" Dani asked.

"We destroyed the entire Taliban force."

"There's a little more to the story, though," General Pardo added. "You see, this young captain, here, was the last one on the trail, right on the valley floor and some of the Taliban decided to stand and fight."

"That they did. I had one of my weapons sergeants and my senior comms sergeant with me, along with several of the Northern Alliance guys. We set up a few claymores in the brief time we had and the few of us had every heavy weapon we could carry; we needed to give the impression that we were a much larger force than we really were. If they figured it out, it would have been a disaster. As it was, it got pretty intense and chaotic there for a while."

"I'm impressed," Dani said.

"Jim invited me to participate in the after-action debrief," Pardo added. "Jackson, and his two sergeants each received the Silver Star. It was an incredibly bold and brilliant—not to mention very risky—operation."

"I was wondering how you knew all of this," Jackson added. "I know Jim said you were over there but I never knew in what capacity."

"Well, that's our little secret. I'll have to make this brief as I can't keep Bibi waiting too much longer, but I'm curious as to the general sense in Washington regarding Iran. From over here, it seems that the current administration has lost any appetite for showing any type of leadership or involvement on the world stage. Look at the failures in Benghazi, Syria, Ukraine and the rise of ISIS—you have a bunch of amateurs running the show in Washington. In spite of these failures, your secretary

of state hasn't learned anything—she still wants to nego-
tiate with Iran and, in essence, give them an atomic
bomb. Has she lost her *mind*?!?" Pardo asked, almost
demanding an answer.

"General, there are those of us at the Agency and in
the military that share your concerns. I can assure you,
though, that if I can get something concrete that I can
take back to Jim, he'll be able to take it to Secretary Johnson and Pam McDowell," referring to the secretary of
state and the national security advisor, "to do more than
simply rely on economic sanctions and negotiations."

"You have a lot more confidence in those two than
we do." Tamir said, with more than a little degree of
skepticism. "However, I think we can help you out there.
Let Arielle, here, know of anything you want. She's
been advised to be at your disposal for absolutely anything you want—and I mean *anything*."

Hearing this, Jackson stole a quick glance at Dani.
For a brief moment, her eyes seemingly locked on his
until she looked away rather awkwardly. General Pardo,
seemingly oblivious to this, continued on.

"Also, and I believe you are aware, we've been practicing for a raid on Iran for some time now—we are prepared to 'go it alone' if need be."

"I am aware of that, and I know Jim, the Agency and
the Pentagon is as well. I just hope it doesn't come to
that."

"We shall see, Colonel. We shall see. Now, I must
apologize, but I can't keep Bibi waiting any longer."

"Nothing to apologize for, General. And thanks for
your openness; I look forward to working with Arielle
and her team."

After the brief meeting with General Pardo, Dani
took Stonewall to their operations center. Benjamin
Givon and Yoni Cohen were in a small conference room

in the middle of watching a live feed from a drone, currently flying over Iran's Parchin military facility in Tehran. As Dani and Stonewall entered the room the feed switched over to more of an urban area which Jackson easily recognized as suburban Tehran. It took a few minutes but eventually the drone centered on a somewhat remote area in western Tehran. The area looked somewhat like a park of sorts. The picture on the screen eventually focused in on a residence and then centered in on the car in the driveway.

"Looks like someone's home," Yoni volunteered.

"Zoom in on the window in the southwest corner of the house. Can you see if there's anything in the window? We told him to leave a couple plants in the window when he's home; we didn't want to simply rely on a car being in the driveway," Ben somewhat rhetorically asked Yoni, his executive officer.

"Yeah, it looks like the good doctor's home this afternoon," Yoni replied.

"Looks that way. Okay, let's get out of here. We don't want to draw any undo suspicion here at this late stage," Ben added.

"Gentlemen," Dani interrupted, "our friend from the States has just arrived. Colonel Tom 'Stonewall' Jackson, this is Benjamin Givon, our Iranian field team leader, and Yoni Cohen, our executive officer."

"The general said you'd be coming by later today. Nice to finally meet you. We've heard a lot about you, though you didn't need to go and emulate General Dayan on us," Ben added with a sly grin, referring to the black eye patch Jackson wore and which had been a trademark of the legendary one-eyed Israeli General Moshe Dayan.

"That was Jim's idea; he thought it'd be easier for you to pick me up at the airport. I've got the glass eye as well and I'm comfortable with either one. As for what you may have heard, I wouldn't believe everything you hear. I'm sure Jim embellished a few areas," Jackson said, referencing his boss at the CIA. "I have heard a little about what you all do here, though. I know that over the past few years several Iranian scientists have met with, shall we say, an 'unfortunate demise.' We also know you managed to slow the Iranians down with that Stuxnet virus. That was nice work."

"The brain drain caused by the loss of their scientists didn't slow them as much as we had hoped. Stuxnet really set them back, though," Ben admitted. "We followed that up with a Stuxnet variant which slowed them down even more than the original virus, but it didn't stop them. We knew it wouldn't; that wasn't our intent. We simply wanted to buy some time, and in that, we really succeeded."

"That's what we heard. So, tell me, just how close are they to getting a bomb?" Jackson asked the small group.

Somewhat nonchalantly, Ben simply said "farther along than you'd believe. Tell you what, where do they have you staying?"

"I guess I really don't know. I think it's a place called the Daniel Hotel, or something like that. I've never been here so I'm really not sure."

"Okay, Yoni and I have a couple things left to finish up. Let's have Arielle take you over there so you can get checked in and all, then the three of us can grab a bite to eat. Sound okay?"

"Okay by me."

"Arielle, why don't we plan on meeting you at the Accad right there at the hotel? Give us, oh . . . , about half an hour to finish up and we'll see you there."

"Yeah, that sounds good; it's new and I haven't had a chance to get there yet. We'll give him a proper introduction to Israel. You ready, Colonel?" Dani asked Stonewall.

"All set; my bag's still in your rig, so I'm ready whenever you are."

"Okay, we'll see you guys there," Dani said over her shoulder as Jackson accompanied her out the door.

"Dani, you can drop the formality; call me Stonewall, everyone else does. These days, no one's using my rank."

"Sorry, since Tamir mentioned you're still active duty I thought I'd respect the rank," Dani said as she walked to the car.

"No need to worry about that. Oh, and what's with the 'proper introduction' idea? Anything I should know about?"

"They've got you at the Daniel?" Dani asked, ignoring Jackson's question as he got into the car.

"Yeah, that's the one; I haven't even had a chance to look at it online."

"Well, I don't see a ring on that finger. Does that mean there's no 'Mrs. Jackson' or someone else in your life?" Dani had that out there before she realized it probably sounded better in her head than spoken. "Ah . . . I mean, the Daniel is one of the nicest hotels in Israel, let alone Tel Aviv. If you wanted to spoil someone, this is the place," Dani continued, noticeably blushing.

"Ah, no, there's no one else," Jackson replied. "But back to this 'proper introduction.'"

"Oh yeah; it's just the usual initiation we do for all new members of the Unit."

"Excuse me?" Jackson replied, whipping his head around to look at Dani, caught more than a little off guard on a couple different levels. As he did so, he noticed that, as she had been driving with her left arm, the left sleeve of her blouse had slipped up towards her shoulder, revealing a long scar across her arm just above the elbow.

"Relax, it's nothing to worry about, at least not too much. I mean, I've heard of the initiation some of your SEALs go through. We like to have fun, too, but that's just crazy; we won't embarrass you too much," Dani said, with a bit of a mischievous grin. "I mean, it's not like you have to drive somewhere tonight, right?"

Jackson didn't realize that the elevator opened right at the Accad restaurant. He looked around to find Dani and finally noticed her back in a corner booth. As he walked up to the booth, he realized that both Ben and Yoni had already arrived. The "initiation" to which Dani had alluded simply revolved around each of them getting to know Stonewall, and he getting to know them—in essence, more of a job interview. Dani wanted to get to know this Special Forces, turned CIA, officer who had never been to Israel before but had come highly recommended for what she knew to be a very important mission for both of their countries. Ben and Yoni wanted to size up this intelligence officer to get an idea if he might be up for this mission. So, over a very casual dinner, their "interview" began.

"So, 'Stonewall', just where did that moniker come from?" Dani began, with somewhat of an edge.

Ignoring the tenor of Dani's question, Jackson started, "It was back in '05 or '06 in northern Iraq. I commanded an A team that parachuted into northern Iraq. At one point, an entire Iraqi tank company confronted our team—mind you, the heaviest thing we had was a Humvee with a .50 caliber machine gun mounted on it—against several tanks and armored personnel carriers. We were outnumbered by about five to one. We had several of the new Javelin anti-tank missiles as well and we were facing some extreme ranges. We used them, and completely destroyed the tank company. With my name: Thomas Jackson, and the situation we faced, the colonel who relieved us tagged me with the moniker 'Stonewall', and it seemed to fit, reminiscent of the Civil War general."

"Ah, I hadn't thought of him; I can see that, now that you mention it. Tamir told me you've had quite the career with the Special Forces," Dani replied. Her use of the Mossad director's first name—again—did not escape Jackson; actually, somewhat surprised him as her tone implied more than a customary familiarity with her very powerful boss.

"As for the rest of my career with the Special Forces, I'm still active duty, just temporarily with the Agency. I can't tell you much more than what you probably already know: I've served with the Fifth Group for the last sixteen years now and along the way hit most of the countries in the region. I had a few tours in Afghanistan, a couple in Iraq, and spent some time at KASOTC," referring to the King Abdullah Special Operations Training Center in Amman, Jordan. "Serving as a CIF team commander with the Fifth Group has probably been the highlight of my career. It's been a great ride and I wouldn't change anything. I was fortunate enough to find the time to get a doctorate in Persian studies a couple years ago."

"CIF team?" Dani asked. "Aren't those relatively new?"

"The Commander's In-extremis Force team has been around since the 90's but we've honed it into a very capable unit. The idea is that whenever a situation blows up in a group's region, there's a force immediately available for the group commander, or the president, should something that sensitive develop. Every group has a team and they're permanently deployed to their region—that's how I got to KASOTC. Every asset a team commander could possibly need deploys with them, from ground transportation to air assets, be it Apache Longbows, C-130's or even half a dozen A-10's. The team can literally be wheels up to anywhere in its region—or its proximity—within half an hour. We've learned a lot from you guys, and from our own successes—and failures."

"We've both had our share of each, I'm afraid," Ben admitted.

Dani and her teammates had Jackson at a little bit of a disadvantage as they knew some of Jackson's history, given General Pardo's relationship with Jim Carmichael. She knew he had three Silver Stars, one of which could have—and probably should have—been a Distinguished Service Cross, but due to Army politics, this had been downgraded to a Silver Star. She wanted to hear how Jackson described it, if he did at all. She appreciated his modesty in leaving this out.

Jackson hadn't had the opportunity to learn much of anything about the Israeli team with whom he'd be working. Ben and Yoni looked as though they could have been part of his team with the Special Forces. They were both very well built, not overly large men as, at six two, Jackson was taller than both of them. Rather, they had a lean, rugged and confident air about them as having practiced their craft in the field rather than in the class room. Dani on the other hand, intrigued him. She fit right in with Ben and Yoni but women didn't serve in a Special Forces unit, at least not in his army. He knew women served alongside men in most Israeli army units but this wasn't the typical unit. She certainly had the athletic build and he had noticed that she moved with all the grace of a lioness on the prowl. Clearly, Dani looked as though she could certainly take care of herself.

"How about you guys; Jim sent me over here with very little advance notice."

"Both Yoni and I started out in the Paratroopers," Ben began. "I was about five years ahead of him. He was actually one of my platoon leaders when I was a battalion commander. My CO introduced me to General Pardo during some of our actions in Lebanon in the mid '90's. The general took an interest in me and, shortly after the September '11 attacks in the States, he offered me a job with Mossad working with Iran's growing threat in the region. I jumped at the chance. I had been heavily involved with the actions of Iran and Hezbollah in Lebanon, so the opportunity to work more on the Iranian connection, even inside Iran, seemed like a godsend. Several years ago, we had an opening on the team and I spoke with General Pardo about the possibility of bringing Yoni on board. He had much of the same experience I had so bringing him on board was a no-brainer."

Looking at Dani, Jackson asked, "what about you?"

Ben initially answered for her. "She's third on the team, in charge of operations. We call her 'Arielle'."

"Operations, really?" Jackson replied, clearly impressed. "And where does 'Arielle' come from?" he asked. "Just how long have you been working with these two?"

Ben replied first. "Arielle's easy; it means Lioness of God. It fits."

"So, is that what that scar's all about?" Jackson asked Dani, looking at her left arm.

"Yeah; I'm sure you've heard the adage about bringing a knife to a gun fight, right? Well, several months back, I was the number two shooter on a bike team in Tehran. We were driving through a residential neighborhood and got separated by some kids playing in the street. We were only a second or two behind but that's all it took for the target's body guard to knock me off the bike. I lost my piece and so did the guard, but he had a knife. His first—and only—swing sliced my arm and continued across the left side of my rib cage. I disarmed him with his next attempt and killed him with his own knife."

"Damn," was all Stonewall could say.

"Told you; it suits her," Ben added.

"My family's been tied pretty closely to the Israeli Special Forces and Mossad since our independence," Dani continued on. "My Dad and Tamir served together in the Paratroopers and my grandfather and Tami's father served with General Arik Sharon in the Sinai in the '67 war." For Jackson, that answered a few questions right there. "I talked with Tamir right after I finished my schooling as I wanted another challenge. Tamir offered me a chance to try out for the Sayeret Matkal"—Israeli Special Forces—"and four years later, here I am."

"What did you do your schooling in?" Jackson asked her.

"I did my undergrad work in Tel Aviv in nuclear physics. From there, I got my PhD in nuclear engineering at Texas A & M."

"Texas? Why Texas?" asked Jackson.

"A & M has a great program and I wanted to see the States. Everything I read made Texas look and feel like Israel so I applied and they accepted me. Outside of Israel, I consider Texas, my second home."

"That's cool; I hail from San Angelo. Always nice to have another Texan around."

III

Dani arrived at Jackson's hotel at six forty-five the following morning. "Hey, Stonewall, you ready?" she said into her phone.

"All set; be right down. Wasn't expecting you for another fifteen to twenty minutes."

"What's the matter? I thought you Special Forces guys were always ready," Dani chimed in.

"I'm ready; just need to put my shoes on and I'll be right there."

Jackson emerged from the lobby elevator to find Dani waiting for him—and her transformation could not have been more complete: Gone was yesterday's ponytail and tomboy image and replaced with a Giorgio Armani business suit that seriously out-classed Jackson's sport coat and tie.

"Ready to go?" She asked him as Jackson walked up to her.

"I'm not sure; just what are we doing today?" Jackson asked, noting Dani's very professional attire.

"Ah, today's an office day, so you're good."

Jackson noticed Dani's sense of style extended to her choice of vehicle as well. "Cadillac, huh? Nice car," Jackson commented admiringly as he got into her car. "A little different from yesterday's rig?"

"That was a pool car; those things are just too generic for me. I like something with a little more style."

"Well, it looks like you found it. Bet you don't see many of these over here, do you?"

"No, you really don't. I wanted something stylish yet something really sporty. The ATS seemed to fit the bill—I actually had to special order it so I picked up the ATS-V," Dani replied.

"I bet you did; this is really cool!" Jackson added. "So, what's on tap for today? Jim didn't give me any kind of agenda or any idea as to what to expect."

"Remember that sudden meeting I told you that Bibi scheduled with Tamir, just as you arrived yesterday? Well, it turns out we have a little operation scheduled for tonight."

"Really? What kind of an 'operation'?" Jackson asked.

"Well, Ben's talking it over with Tamir right now. Even though I'm Ops, I don't know all of the details on this one yet. Ben will fill us in when we get to the office."

"So, tell me about Ben. He seems like a real take charge kind of guy. I mean *he* answered the first two questions that I asked *you* last night."

"He is in command of our unit but don't prejudge him. He's very good and usually, all business. Until you get to know him, he might come off as a bit of a control-freak. Once he's had a chance to get to know someone, however, he relaxes quite a bit. Yoni, on the other hand, is much like you saw him last night, quiet and fairly reserved, but don't let that calm demeanor fool you. We've been in a few scrapes with Hezbollah up in Lebanon—there is no one, Ben included, who I'd rather have with me in a fire fight. Yoni is rock solid and seemingly knows the entire battle-scape—wherever that is—like it was his hometown."

"What are you guys doing in Lebanon? I thought this team's focus was Iran."

"Oh, Iran is, and remains, the primary focus of our team. You see, Iran supplies Hezbollah with *everything*, from ammunition to rockets—and they station several of their Republican Guards in the Beqaa Valley.   Every now and then, we get another piece of the puzzle up there."

"I can see that; just thought a different team would take care of that for you."

"When it comes to Iran, Ben likes our team to do as much of the work as possible. He wants to make sure nothing gets missed."

"Yeah, I can appreciate that."

"So, did you get your Starbucks fix in yet this morning?" Dani asked, changing the subject.

"No, I didn't. I thought there'd be one in the hotel but couldn't find anything."

"Well, Starbucks isn't in Israel. I got hooked on them when I was at A & M but had to get used to our variety back here when I came home; it's a lot stronger here. This place here's a favorite of mine."

Seeing that Dani pulled into a parking spot, rather than the proverbial drive-thru, he asked Dani, "Ah, what time are we supposed to get in to the office this morning?"

"Ben and Tamir are still working out the details for tonight's operation. They told me we didn't need to be in the office all that early, so, since you haven't been to Israel before, I thought we'd take our time this morning. Find a table and I'll get the coffee."

Jackson found a table on the street-side patio and waited for Dani. Once she sat down with their coffee, Jackson simply stated, "So, tell me about Iran's nuclear ambitions."

Tamir told Ben that as soon as Arielle & Stonewall arrived, they were to be brought into his office right away. Two hours after their coffee stop, Ben ushered them into Tamir's office.

"Stonewall, I believe Arielle mentioned that we have an operation scheduled for tonight. This will be a simple recon mission that will last about a day and a half. Would you be interested in tagging along as an 'observer'? We'd love to have you along for the ride."

"I'd love to. Jim didn't give me much in the way of instructions so, yeah, let's go."

"Excellent. While this is a recon mission, we still want to get you checked out. What do you carry for a sidearm?" Tamir asked Stonewall.

"I carry either an H&K VP9 or a Sig P226," Jackson responded, suddenly piqued by the nature of this "recon" mission.

"Good, we have both. Yoni will take you out to the range and check you out. Ben and Arielle will go over the mission while you're out with Yoni. Once you get back, we'll fill you in on all of the details."

Two hours later, Jackson joined Tamir, Ben, Dani, & Yoni in the conference room where he initially met Ben and Yoni. Ben began the briefing letting Jackson know that they would be flying to Baku, Azerbaijan, that evening and from there they would drive to Tehran.

"We kind of figured you'd be going," Ben added, as he handed Jackson his false documents. "We'll have the rest of the gear you'll need when we get to our destination."

"I'm not even going to ask you how you put these together so quickly."

"That's okay; we wouldn't tell you anyway," Ben added with a big grin on his face. "Okay, when we're done here, Arielle will take you back to the hotel to get some sleep. She'll pick you up around nine o'clock tonight, grab some dinner and get you to the airfield."

Jackson knew that every Israeli served in the military in some capacity. However, he had as yet to fully accept the exact capacity in which Dani served. She'd clearly been in the field before; that much was obvious. However, given her position in Mossad, the operations officer of this team, and her education—a full-fledged PhD in nuclear engineering—he fully expected her to be more of a rear echelon-type who would be monitoring events via satellite in some highly secretive operations center. When they arrived at Tel Nof Air Force Base around midnight, though, Jackson was somewhat surprised to see that Dani would be joining them.

"You're going to?" Jackson asked.

"I'm the operations officer for this unit; I kind of need to go."

"I'm sorry, I guess I just figured . . ." Jackson started.

"What? That since I'm a woman, I'm not a full member of the team?" Dani interrupted, with both a bit of an edge but also knowing she had something over on Stonewall.

"It's just that I'm not used to women serving in a Special Ops unit."

"Well, this is Israel, not the United States. I can hold my own, I think I've demonstrated that. And, besides, on this little excursion, we'll be traveling as a couple— once we get to Iran, you'll be my husband."

"What?!?" Jackson blurted out.

"Ben didn't tell you that, huh?" Dani said with a bit of a laugh. "Relax, we both speak perfect Farsi and I've been over there several times. It'll be a walk in the park, as you Americans fondly say."

Upon landing in Baku, they taxied over to a large hangar at a far corner of the airport completely out of sight from the rest of the terminal. The pilot actually taxied the plane into the hangar and, once inside, the doors of the hangar closed and the pilot shut down the engines. Poking his head out of the cabin door before deplaning, Jackson noticed several things seemingly all at once: the hangar was far larger than it needed to be for this little plane but it also housed four other planes, each presumably Israeli though there were no markings on the planes. As he walked down from the plane, Jackson noticed that each of the planes in the hangar sported large, conformal bulges—clearly electronic warfare aircraft—and quickly suspected that something else was in the works.

"Ah, Dani, what's going on?" Jackson asked as he got off the plane.

"What do you mean?" Dani quickly responded.

"Dani, you're Ops; unless I'm mistaken, you've got four EW planes parked in here as well as the plane we just flew in on. Is there something else in the works that I'm not aware of?" Jackson asked.

"Nah, we keep these guys here to keep a close eye on Tehran. It's a lot closer than flying from any of our bases back home, which means they can spend more time in the air over here. Obviously, we have a pretty tight, and secret, agreement with Azerbaijan." Dani went on, hoping to sound somewhat reassuring.

"Uh huh. . . ." Jackson replied, not entirely convinced. "We knew you were working with them and had rights to use the air field, in an emergency—or so we thought—but didn't realize they allowed you to base your EW craft here."

"Well, we haven't advertised it but this airfield has come in quite handy. Looks like our ride is here," Dani added, quickly changing the subject.

Jackson hadn't noticed the two Toyota SUVs that pulled up behind him while he had been talking with Dani. Both vehicles were registered in Astara, Azerbaijan, so as not to raise any undo suspicion: they would not be in Iran very long and would appear to be nothing more than tourists traveling in Iran for a few days—it was the height of the summer tourist season, after all. The six man team, now broken into two teams—Jackson and Dani in one vehicle and the other four in the second SUV—proceeded to the Astara border crossing, which was the only open crossing as the Azerbaijanis had recently closed the crossings at Bileh Savar and Julfa due to a border incident involving Iranian border guards firing at a farmer working the river bank separating the two countries. Ben had planned on hitting the border around 7:00 a.m., ordinarily one of the busiest times of the day at the border crossing as it was; now, the increased border traffic at Astara greatly eased the infiltration as the border guards here, like low level bureaucrats everywhere, were seriously overworked and underpaid.

Getting into their SUV, Jackson looked at Dani and, somewhat facetiously said "Well, 'Mrs. Jackson', just how long of a drive do we have?"

"Careful with that, Cowboy," Dani replied, after all, he was a Texan Dani thought to herself. "Ben wants to hit the border crossing around seven o'clock. It's what, oh . . . something like 185 miles and it's a little after three right now so we should make that as planned. From the border, it's about another 320 miles or so. As long we're in Azerbaijan, I can help you with the driving but once we cross the border, you'll need to do all of the driving as the Iranians don't like their women driving."

IV

Back in 2012, when Prime Minister Benjamin Netanyahu made his UN speech drawing a "red line" in the sand, he also made an estimate as to when the Iranians might be able to produce a nuclear bomb. The Prime Minister had followed up his 2012 UN speech with another one to the same world body just a few days ago and this one specified, in rather great detail, as to when the Iranians would have a nuclear weapon—in just a few months. This was incredibly sooner than anyone in the agency, let alone the world, had expected. Most everyone in the agency—and the world, for that matter— simply assigned this, understandably, to regional paranoia. No other intelligence agency in the world, not MI6, not the DGSE, hell not even the KGB, believed Iran was this far along. However, Jackson thought there might be something to this and the opportunity to join Dani and her team on the recon mission into Iran looked like a golden opportunity to see whether or not the Israelis and his own agency were operating from the same intelligence—or if the Israelis had a source unknown to the CIA.

"You realize what he's telling us, don't you?" Grand Ayatollah Khameini said to Said Jalili who sat across from him in his office.

"Of course," Jalili responded rather smugly, "Netanyahu's telling us that he knows how close we are to achieving a nuclear bomb. We have a leak."

"Not only that, but he's essentially daring us to find his source. He's betting everything that we won't be able to find the leak."

"Even Netanyahu wouldn't be so cynical as to burn his own source. He either doesn't think we'll find him, or her, or . . . ."

"They are attacking. . . ." Khameini finished Jalili's sentence for him. "They are attacking . . . . They wouldn't dare; not alone." Khameini couldn't believe what he had just said. On the one hand, it made sense, but on the other . . . they wouldn't go it alone. They couldn't; they didn't have the means. Neither the Saudis nor the Jordanians would allow the Israelis to violate their air space. The Turks, well, they might, Khameini thought to himself, but that would be the longest route for them to take and the Israelis simply did not have the logistical means to do something this ambitious. No, Netanyahu clearly thought they would never find his source. That arrogant pig Khameini thought to himself.

"Said, you need to find our leak. That arrogant pig is daring us to find his source. He doesn't think we can find him. I want you to put your best people on this. We need to plug this leak immediately. We have come too far to let it all slip away at this point."

"I'll find the leak and I know just who should handle this," Jalili said. Unlike the Grand Ayatollah, though, Jalili knew that he also needed to get ready for an attack. Khameini could delude himself all he wanted to, but Jalili fully believed an attack would be forthcoming. He'd had plans in place for this for a little while but he never expected he'd have to find a mole. No, that stunned Jalili more than the prospect of an Israeli attack. He knew he could handle—and survive—any attack the

Israeli's threw at him. However, the prospect of a mole, a *spy*, infuriated him to no end—and since he had no idea where to look, he had no idea the damage this spy could inflict.

*   *   *   *   *

Dani and Stonewall followed Ben and the rest of the team in the lead car. Once the team crossed the border in to Iran, he noticed a particular change in Dani that he had usually only seen in his Special Forces teams—it was not one of fear but more of recognition, and acceptance, of their very real danger. They knew they were on a dangerous mission but they also knew their experience and training made them more than ready for anything they might encounter. For his part, Jackson had no idea as to what the nature of this "recon" mission was. He'd conducted all kinds of recon missions with the Special Forces but something about this one just seemed different. He'd been a part of teams that had been hastily organized where no one knew more than half the team, so being new to this team did not faze him. He knew that as the chief of operations, Dani knew their mission. However, it was her inherent contradictions that really intrigued him: this relatively tall and attractive woman, who defined Class and Style, also served as one of the toughest commandos in the IDF!?! Women were not allowed in any type of Special Forces in the US military; SEALS, Delta, the Rangers, or the Special Forces. Yet, he was sure Dani could qualify for any one of them: She appeared to be incredibly physically fit and she had a distinct air about her that exuded an uncompromising tenacity. Clearly, this was not Dani's first time in indian country.

"So tell me, just how did you get to be a part of this team? You already mentioned your family ties to General Pardo but this team would appear to rival any of our Special Operations teams. I didn't realize women could be a part of the Israeli Special Forces."

"Zivah and I are the first two women who made it into the Sayeret Matkal. You'll meet Zivah later today. After I finished my doctorate, remember I was still in the IDF, I looked for another challenge, and I found it. I asked Tamir if he could get me into the program, and, reluctantly, he did. Zivah and I were in the same class and I couldn't have gotten through it without her—that's the hardest thing I've *ever* done, but it's been very rewarding: How many women do you know who serve in a Special Forces unit who also have a PhD in nuclear engineering?"

"Ah . . . you would be the first."

"Yeah, well as Iran's progress with its nuclear program became more pronounced, I was a natural fit with Ben's team. Ben's been doing this for close to ten years now; I'm on my fourth with the team."

"I kind of thought you'd been over here before."

"Yeah, I've lost track of the times I've been over here. Often enough that we know some of the border guards by name. That being said, we still compartmentalize the nature of each mission—only Ben, Yoni, and myself fully know the nature of most of our missions. Obviously, since I'm Ops, I usually know the nature of each mission but Ben's in charge—he can change the mission as he sees fit."

"Just when does Ben plan on telling the rest of us what we'll be doing?"

"He usually fills everyone in at the last possible moment. We're all exceptionally well trained and we've been working together for the last four years. Zivah and I were the last two to join the team and having two women on the team adds to our cover—the Iranians would never suspect two women would be part of a Sayeret Matkal team, after all, you didn't," she said with a smirk that screamed "Gotcha."

"Yeah, you got me there. So, just what all do you do when you're not 'lockin' horns with the Iranians?"

"'Lockin' horns,' huh? I see where this is going. I may be Israeli but I'm not *that* far removed from A & M—see this ring here?" she asked, referencing her Aggie ring, as she held out her right hand ring finger. "I'm still an Aggie."

"What? Everyone knows there's only one real school in Texas."

"I know, and it's in College Station. I mean, have you ever been to Austin? That's one of the drabbest and dullest places in Texas; even their school colors reflect the community: a dried up, burnt up orange."

"Yeah, well at least those of us in Austin knew we were at a university; we didn't need to name the community after the type of school we were at, just in case we forgot."

"Touché. Well, to answer your question, I do a lot to stay in shape; I do a lot of jogging and swimming, when I can. I read when I get the chance, a lot of non-fiction, Mideast history for the most part, and I really enjoy playing the piano. The piano is probably my favorite; it's just so relaxing, I can totally lose myself in it."

"So, in addition to being a full-fledged PhD in nuclear engineering and a highly trained commando, you're also a concert pianist?"

"I didn't say that I'm a concert pianist, just that I really enjoy the piano," Dani replied with a sly grin. "Though, I am pretty good," she added.

"I bet you are, and, after knowing you for only a couple of days, you seem to be one that, no matter what you do, you do it to excess. I mean look at it: You received your PhD in nuclear engineering from a fairly prestigious university, you're in the highly specialized Sayeret Matkal, you drive an exceptionally nice car, your sense of style is incredible; shall I go on?"

"Think you have me pegged pretty good, huh? But doesn't the old adage say that 'if it's worth doing, it's worth doing to excess'? But no, I'm not a concert pianist—that would be my sister; she's incredible. She studied in New York at Julliard. She's a couple year's older than me and has played in some of the finest orchestras in the States and here in Israel. She's the one who really got me interested in the piano."

"So, is your whole family a bunch of over achievers?" Jackson asked.

"There's just the two of us, and my parents, of course. But we are very competitive; we both just hate to lose, at anything. I think we feed off of each other."

"Yeah, I can believe that. How did everyone feel about you signing up for Sayeret Matkal?"

"My sister thought it was pretty cool; my folks were dead-set against it. My dad, being a former paratrooper, has obviously seen his share of action and he definitely did not want his little girl trying out to be an elite commando but he knew he couldn't stop me. I'm sure he talked with Tamir ahead of time to try and discourage me, and I did speak with Tamir, but he was very fair with everything. Like I said, that was the toughest thing I've ever done. But what about you? It seems that I'm the one doing all the talking."

"Who, me?" Jackson replied. "There's nothing special about me."

"Right. You appear to be rather young for a full bird colonel and, from what I understand, you have, what, *three* Silver Stars? Then there's your eye patch, and with one eye, you still managed to requalify for the Special Forces—there's gotta be a story behind that."

"Nah, no real story, stuff like that kind of happens when you're too close to an Iraqi mortar. As for the rest, I guess that's what you get when people exaggerate about some of the things you've done."

When Jackson and his fellow team members arrived at the safe house, he was more than a little surprised that Dani walked right in the front door without bothering to unlock the door in some manner or to alert anyone who might have been inside. Dani had been to this house before and took more than a little pleasure in showing Jackson all the "amenities" this house provided—starting with the entrance. Jackson had used safe houses before in his career with the Special Forces, and was rather surprised at the apparent lack of security as the door seemed to be unlocked as Dani had walked right in. Playing off of his amazement, Dani took Stonewall back out front and had him try and open the door, only to find the door completely locked—and very solid. Dani, then, simply opened the door for Jackson to let him back in the house. At this point, Jackson began to realize just how sophisticated this safe house really was.

"Oh, this is good; this is really cool. Is there some sort of facial recognition key that automatically unlocks the door?" Jackson asked.

"Close; there's a biometric sensor at the door that picks up on both facial recognition and behavioral analytics to function as the 'key'," Dani replied. She could see that Jackson was suitably impressed—and she loved showing off.

For his part, Jackson had used safe houses before, but nothing like this—this "house" was more like a small fortress, complete with an eight foot wall around the perimeter: to all but the most trained eye, each window could stop a 7.62 bullet; he didn't see any cameras but he knew they were there as well, both inside and out. Dani took him to the basement control room where he realized just how thorough the camera surveillance really was: multiple cameras had every square inch of the property—and its approaches—thoroughly covered, with multiple redundancy; if someone tried to sneak up and disable even half a dozen cameras, there were still more. Dani showed Jackson the "armory" next; in addition to the usual small arms, this arsenal had enough hardware to take out a battalion of tanks and to take down a small squadron of fighters—even an aerial assault could be met with fierce resistance. Jackson had been so taken in by Dani and the "amenities" of the house that he had totally failed to realize that there were three inhabitants of the residence. Ben, and the rest of Jackson's new Israeli friends, did not fail to, good naturally, remind him of their presence!

"So, Arielle, who's General Dayan, here?" Zivah asked Dani as she sized up Jackson. Turning to Stonewall, she simply commented, "You don't work out much, do you?" Jackson had been wearing a loose fitting cotton Oxford, which felt pretty good in the cool morning air up in Baku, but had removed this due to the intense afternoon heat in Tehran. The fitted Under Armour T-shirt he now wore accented his sculpted torso, which Zivah admiringly noticed.

"I usually run about five miles a day and then do a little work in the weight room; I spend more time on the cardio than on the weights."

"Well, don't change a thing! It's working for me; you fill that shirt out in all the right places!" Zivah commented admiringly.

"Dani, he's a keeper!" she continued.

"Zivah! I can't believe you!" Dani exclaimed, noticeably blushing. "Stonewall, this is Zivah—and watch out for her. She's our electronics and comms expert—

she has 'ears' everywhere! Next, this is Ayal, he's our explosives expert. Finally, we have Jonah, who pretty much lives here."

"Nice to meet you all," Jackson replied.

"I assume there's a story behind the 'Stonewall' name?" Ayal asked.

"There is. Suffice it to say that a colonel I worked with a while back thought something I did reminded him of our Civil War General Thomas 'Stonewall' Jackson; my name is Thomas Jackson, so the handle fit."

Once the complete team, now nine members strong, had been fully introduced to Stonewall, Ben set about explaining the exact nature of their little mission. From the first, Jackson suspected that this little mission they were on had to be something big—and he was not disappointed.

"Recently, Prime Minister Netanyahu spoke at the United Nations and drew a red line advising the world body that Iran was extremely close to achieving a nuclear bomb. What he did not tell the world was that we have a source within the Iranian government that has been leaking highly classified information to us and that, within that speech, was a coded message for our source to get ready to leave Iran as we would be coming to get him—we are that mission," Ben advised.

"My God; you guys are . . . Ah!" Jackson exclaimed as he received a powerful elbow in the rib cage. "What was that for?" he asked Dani.

"Just shut up; we'll discuss this later," she quietly responded.

"Our source, is none other than Dr. Ali Bagheri Kani, the deputy secretary of Iran's Supreme National Security Council," Ben continued. "Bagheri knows we are coming but he does not know exactly when or how we will be picking him up; there is simply no way of getting that information to him. He currently lives in a residence in the resort area of Bashgah-e Savarkri-e, not too far from here in Tehran. The resort is part of the National Botanical Gardens, and there are only two entrances—one on the west and the other on the east side of the park. We know he is home as Jonah and his team here, have had him under surveillance for the past week. The plan to get him out is relatively quite simple: We'll grab him tonight and head immediately for Astara and the border," Ben said with a smile. Jackson knew, as did everyone else, that it wouldn't exactly be that simple.

After Ben's briefing, Dani took Jackson aside.

"You're pretty quick," she told him.

"Well, it's pretty obvious. You tell the world that the Persians are on the verge of a nuclear weapon, you have four EW aircraft forward deployed and now we're over here to smuggle out your source before everything hits the fan—you guys are attacking." A simple statement; no question implied. "Dani, don't get me wrong, I'm all for it. Some folks in Washington might not be but we'll have to cross that bridge very soon."

"Tamir said you were a quick study. You put that together very fast. I don't need to tell you: don't let this out, and for that matter, the decision really hasn't been made. Zivah, Jonah, and Ayal don't know how soon we might be attacking, though you are correct—if this mission is a success, we'll probably be attacking as soon as we get back."

"Dani, don't worry. Your secret's safe with me. I've been around the block a time or two. It wouldn't surprise me if the raiding party already has their engines warmed up by the time we land back in Tel Aviv."

Bagheri, who was Said Jalili's chief deputy, found himself in a unique position: each member of his family had been killed in service to the Islamic Republic: one son had been killed by an Israeli air strike in the Beqaa

Valley in Lebanon helping Hezbollah with some advanced long range missiles; another son had been killed in the US air strike that had also killed Abu Musab al-Zarqawi in Iraq; and, his wife and first born son had been passengers on Iranian Flight 655—something which would have no meaning to any American but had been etched into the psyche of every Iranian since that fateful day in July, 1988, when the *USS Vincennes* had shot down Iranian Flight 655 in the Persian Gulf, killing all 290 passengers on board. Bagheri thoroughly detested everything about the United States and its arrogance. However, he, perhaps more than anyone else also clearly saw the direction that Iran was heading with its pursuit of nuclear weapons, and he also clearly saw the only possible outcome that could become of such an objective— and he loved his country more than he hated the Americans, which was why he had decided to aid the Israelis in their desire to keep Iran from obtaining a nuclear weapon. The fact that his family had been destroyed by both the Israelis and the Americans put him way beyond reproach—no one would suspect him of helping the hated Zionists and their ally, the Great Satan.

Stonewall already knew that this wasn't Dani's first rodeo but he still felt a little odd going into a combat situation with her. He didn't think of himself as "old fashioned" and he could tell that Dani certainly knew how to handle herself. Rather, he simply blamed this "odd feeling" on the fact that women did not serve in the Special Forces and he simply wasn't used to it. Dani could sense his discomfort and tried to put him at ease, calling this a very simple routine mission. However, Stonewall had been around long enough to know that there was no such thing as a "routine" mission.

As sunset drew near, the nine man team (seven men and two women, actually) set out for Bagheri's residence. The team broke up into five vehicles; Ayal drove a relatively larger box van type of truck; Jonah had another in which he drove separately; and Zivah and Levi had the coms vehicle, each of which would actually enter the gardens from the west entrance; Dov and Yoni would be in a fourth vehicle and Ben, Dani and Stonewall would be in the fifth. On the way out of Tehran, Bagheri would be riding with Dani and Jackson. The photos that Ayal's advance team had provided the actual assault team appeared to show a relatively lax security arrangement—and driving through the gardens gave Jackson a firsthand look, and confirmation that the security lacked the detail he would expect from a more professional force. Either the detail team did not think there was much of a threat to Bagheri, or they were not all that professional of a detail, or a combination of both. Bagheri lived alone in a modest single family residence located on one of the main streets that leads straight through the gardens. About a quarter mile from the house a relatively wide entrance way allowed some cover for Ayal's, Jonah's and Zivah's vans. Zivah stayed in her van and monitored all of the electronic jamming gear to make sure no outgoing calls could get through while Ayal, Jonah and Levi proceeded to Bagheri's house to take out the guards before Ben, Jackson and the rest of the team pulled into Bagheri's driveway—they wanted to make sure the outside guards had been dispatched prior to their arrival. As expected, both of the guards covering the exterior of the place did not pose any problems for Ayal's team. When Ben pulled into the drive way—Dov stayed quietly along the roadside with his lights out—it was obvious from the disturbance inside that Bagheri's guards were not expecting company this evening, though it was still relatively early.

Ben and Dani had teamed up and both were at the door and announced that they were looking for Dr. Bagheri as Dani explained that while visiting the gardens that afternoon, she thought she overheard someone mention that he lived around here. She went on to explain that she had Dr. Bagheri as a professor at Tehran University and, as long as she was back in the area, she wanted to look him up if this was where he lived. The guard that answered the door seemed rather nervous, looking over Dani's shoulder to see why his guards had not intercepted this couple, and gruffly insisted that there was no Dr. Bagheri here, which is when Ben pulled out his 9mm silenced Sig P226 and put two rounds into the guard's chest. At this point, Dani and Ben rushed through the door, followed closely by Jackson, Dov, and Yoni. Dani and Ben took the left side of the house; Jackson and the others, the right side. In the kitchen, Dani surprised another guard preparing dinner and quickly dispatched him. Bagheri's office was at the end of a long hallway that led right from the front entrance. Jackson found another guard here with Bagheri himself and quickly took him out as well. Three guards, plus the two outside, were all that Ayal's advance team had expected and after a quick search of the house, Yoni announced the all clear. With the assault completed, Ayal went back to where he had parked his truck, brought it into Bagheri's driveway and parked it immediately adjacent to the house.

Ben immediately met with Bagheri and introduced himself as his escort out of Iran. Introductions were made all around, and Bagheri was surprised to hear that a US Special Forces member was on the team as well. Jackson admitted that he, too, was surprised to be a part of the team but indicated that he would not have had it any other way. With the pleasantries completed, Ayal advised Ben that the security detail had been cleaned up and hidden away so that no one should be finding them until they intended. Zivah had gathered up all of the computer equipment—the guards had a laptop, as did Bagheri, along with a desktop and cell phone and she took these to her van. She returned with two old laptops and an old desktop to replace those she had just taken. To Bagheri's amazement, Yoni and Jonah grabbed the guard's body they believed to be the detail lead and put him into one of the vans which would remain in Tehran—on the way back to the safe house, the body would be hidden in a very secluded place along the Tigris River.

Ben now advised Bagheri of their plan to park a large truck bomb next to the house and detonate it early in the morning—prior to the changing of the guards. Ben told him that "we simply want to cause as much confusion regarding your disappearance as possible. If they find you missing and all of your guards have been killed, that's going to raise some suspicion. However, if we can thoroughly demolish the house and the authorities find you and the team leader for your security detail missing; that's going to create some confusion as to what really happened. Hopefully, they'll think you and your detail here have been assassinated. They may even think that the two of you have fled and have been unable to make contact. In any case, in the time it takes for them to try and figure out what actually happened . . . well, let's just say, hopefully, it won't matter. We'll be heading straight for the Azerbaijani border and traveling all night; four of the team will simply return to our safe house. The plan is to arrive at the border before 7:00 a.m. tomorrow morning—just when the traffic crossing the border will be at its peak—and also at about the same time the truck bomb should be going off—if all goes according to plan." Ben explained that he wanted to take advantage of the overworked guards at the crossing as they were always the easiest to distract as well as the ones that would often simply let things go without taking the time to ask a lot of questions—especially when there was a solid stream of cars and trucks wanting to cross the border. Ben specifically requested that Bagheri ride with Dani and Jackson so that Jackson could get a firsthand account of just how close Iran was to achieving a nuclear weapon. He also had given Dani a recorder so that the conversations they had for the next eight hours on the way back to Baku would be recorded. For the next several hours, then, both Jackson and Dani got an earful of the sophistication of the Iranian nuclear weapons program—something Jackson had long suspected but only now began to fully appreciate the implications of their program—with a bomb just a couple months away—and of Israel's impending attack.

At the border, Ben and his team found the crossing as expected—a line of cars proceeded for close to a kilometer ahead of him. By the time his car got close to the border, he could tell that the guards were getting pretty lax in their duties—as he had expected. Ben's car was the first of the two and passed through the security without any difficulties. Dani, Jackson and Bagheri were a little nervous, wondering if Bagheri's detail had been discovered and an alert issued but everything was in order. Bagheri was a little surprised that the fake passport Ben had given him had an entry stamp, the same as the rest of the team. He wasn't sure how Ben had accomplished that feat but he did not pursue it; he was just thankful that he was able to cross the border into Azerbaijan without any difficulty.

The rest of the trip proved rather uneventful for the entire team. They still had a three hour drive from Astara to the Baku airbase. From there, it was a relatively short flight from Baku back to Tel Aviv. However, Bagheri had spent most of the past five hours spelling out the details of Iran's nuclear program, including the development of a previously unknown fuel reprocessing facility at Arak and long suspected, though unconfirmed, details about testing at Parchin. Both Jackson and Dani were completely surprised to learn that the actual testing of an Iranian nuclear weapon was just over a month out. Once past the border, and with the adrenalin from the tension for the past several hours spent, Bagheri collapsed in the back seat of the car.

The plane on which the team had arrived only a couple days before had remained in the hangar at the Baku airbase. Ben had radioed ahead to let the flight crew know they were on their way and they needed to get back to Tel Aviv just a soon as possible. By the time the team arrived, the flight crew had the engines warmed up with the preflight checklist completed—all that remained was the team and their guest.

Once the team was airborne, Jackson immediately asked Ben about the possibility of notifying his superiors in Washington. The communications gear their plane had rivaled that of Air Force One so gaining a secure link would not be a problem. Both men knew the urgency of getting their information back to Washington so Jackson did not have a hard sell with this; Ben ordered the call made at once.

V

Said Jalili knew he had to act right away to find the source of Netanyahu's information. He thoroughly detested the Israelis, but he had a great deal of respect for them, and he did not believe for a minute that Netanyahu would be so callous as to discard a source which had to be extremely reliable, and important, without so much as making an attempt to get him out of Iran. The trouble was, he had been out of the country when Netanyahu gave his speech. As a result, he was getting a late start. His first call was to Colonel Ashkan Rafsanjani. Colonel Rafsanjani reminded Jalili of himself twenty years ago: extremely intelligent, relatively good looking and very ambitious and, even though he was the youngest colonel in the Quds, he had recently been appointed as the operations officer for the Supreme National Security Council by Major General Qassim Suleimani, the leader of the Quds Force. Together, Jalili and Suleimani had already tasked him with Operation Cyrus, one of the most secret and boldest operations in Iranian history. However, now they needed him to plug the Intelligence leak as well.

Operation Cyrus had kept Colonel Rafsanjani extremely busy at his office out at the Bidganeh Republican Guards base. Jalili's call interrupted a hectic afternoon and he immediately thought the secretary was requesting yet another briefing on Cyrus. However, he knew otherwise after Jalili mentioned he had another urgent task for him—and that he should report to the Ministry just as fast as he could get back into Tehran. One hour later, Rafsanjani walked into Jalili's office to find him staring out his fifth story window. The secretary motioned for him to take a seat and, as he did, Jalili—still staring out the window—casually asked him if he had heard Netanyahu's speech.

"I did, and I noticed that his estimate for us finally getting a bomb is quite accurate," stated Rafsanjani.

"It is, and that is what I want you to look into. Just how is it that the Israelis know precisely how far along we are in building a nuclear bomb? Netanyahu's estimate is the same one I received from our own Atomic Agency Commission. We obviously have a leak and I want you to look into this right away."

"Right away? What about Cyrus?"

"I still want you to pursue that. If I know the Israelis, they won't be sitting on their laurels. They will attempt to get him out of the country as soon as possible. For all we know, they might already have a team here to pick him up. Obviously, I do not expect this search to last all that long. You have an executive officer; delegate the operation to him while you pursue this traitor. I wouldn't expect this to be much more than a week long endeavor."

"Do we have any leads whatsoever?" asked Rafsanjani.

"You know as much as I do," replied Jalili.

"So we have nothing," more of a statement than a question.

"We have nothing at all."

"Well then, I guess I'll start with the borders. Maybe we can get lucky and catch both the traitor and an Israeli team trying to smuggle him out."

"Just keep me appraised of what you find out," and with that, Rafsanjani took his leave.

Back at Bidganeh, Rafsanjani called in his executive officer, Major Farrok Zarin, to discuss Jalili's new assignment.

"So, you need to find a grain of salt on the beach, huh?" asked Zarin.

"So it would seem. I'll be starting with the borders in the north. The Astara crossing is already the only crossing from Azerbaijan so we'll double the guards there. We'll also beef up the Bazargan crossing at the Turkish border. This is really going to hurt things in the north but I don't expect it to last all that long. We won't be closing the border but it is definitely going to take a lot longer to cross it. The Iraqi border is pretty well covered; we've had that managed pretty well since the Americans invaded back in '03."

"What about the coast? Israel has a number of submarines and it wouldn't take much for a submarine to surface in the middle of the night and have a few Israeli commandos come ashore to smuggle someone out."

"That is the hardest part. We only have 1,700 kilometers of coast line to guard," Rafsanjani added rather sarcastically. "However, the Bushehr reactor is right on the coast. I'll have the navy saturate the surrounding area with patrol boats so no one could get through. We also need to check and see if any 'surprise' inspections show up here in the next few days or if anyone is making an unscheduled trip to Bushehr."

"What do you think about Afghanistan and the eastern borders? I can't see the Israelis going this far out: we don't have any nuclear facilities in that direction and it's a long way to travel if they want to pursue this route."

"Yeah, I agree with you there. It just doesn't make sense. I'll alert the border guards but aside from that, I don't see it out there."

"What about actually looking for the traitor? Any ideas there? From what I understand, it seems to be some pretty specific information that has been leaked. There can't be all that many people with that kind of knowledge."

"Yeah, I've thought about that. We can't put everyone under a microscope—that was done when each of these people was hired in the first place. We'd essentially be looking for something that doesn't exist. No, the source of this leak is going to be someone beyond reproach. And, if we start investigating the secretary of the Supreme National Security Council or the head of our Atomic Agency Commission, I'm liable to end up in front of a firing squad. However, I think we should look at each of these respective offices, and others, and see if there are any junior staff members who are planning on taking any unscheduled trips, with or without their superiors."

"You realize the trouble with this idea, though, is that irregular travel is the norm for these people—and their staffs. What you'll need to look for is irregularities, within the irregularities: is there a staff member who hardly ever travels, but is taking a trip now? What about phone calls and email correspondence? Have there been any phone numbers called in the past few days that had not been contacted on a regular basis? Were there any staff members who had family all of a sudden 'vacationing' abroad?"

"You know, Jalili suggested letting you take over our original project. However, you seem to have a pretty good grasp on how to conduct this search. Why don't you take over the search—use my name whenever you need to—and I'll continue with Cyrus?"

"That's fine. I don't think this will last all that long, either, and then I can get back to work around here. Besides, I personally think our original assignment is a little more important and your talents would be better used on

Cyrus than trying to find this traitor who is probably on his way out of the country as we speak."

"Good. Since we both expect this to be a relatively short lived assignment, why don't you swing by my office every afternoon before you leave for the day and let me know how things are going?"

"Will do; see you tomorrow." And with that, Zarin dismissed himself.

"Good morning, Amir," Colonel Rafsanjani greeted his driver. Amir had been driving for Rafsanjani for a couple years now.

"Good morning, sir. Where to this morning, the office or out to Bidganeh?"

"Bidganeh, Amir. Major Zarin is working on a small project for me and I'll need to see him later this afternoon so let's just head to the base."

The drive to the base took about half an hour longer than to where Rafsanjani had his office at the Ministry of Intelligence in Tehran so he came prepared for the ride: Rafsanjani already had his new iPad open and began trying to get caught up on several items he had hoped to get done yesterday. Jalili's call and new assignment had taken up his entire day, leaving him a day behind on his latest project.

Amir interrupted his concentration as they approached the halfway point to the base. "Colonel? Excuse me, sir. Major Zarin is on the phone for you. He said something about an explosion over at the Botanical Gardens."

"The Botanical Gardens? There's nothing over there; who wants to blow up a bunch of trees? Give me the phone. Major, what's going on? Amir mentioned something about an explosion over in the Botanical Gardens. There's nothing over there."

"Sir, Dr. Ali Bagheri lives over by the gardens. Would the Israelis be targeting him?"

"Amir, turn around and let's head over to there. Farrok, get me Bagheri's address. We are on our way over there now but it'll take us forty-five minutes to even get in the general area—the traffic is awful. Send me a text with Bagheri's address as soon as you can."

"Will do, sir; I'll get it to you right away."

"Here you are, sir. Bagheri currently lives in a resort area of Bashgah-e Savarkri-e, which is actually a part of the National Botanical Gardens."

Rafsanjani could tell that the explosion had come from the resort area of the gardens as they passed through the east entrance. The remnant wisps of a heavy smoke plume rising from that area, as Farrok had indicated, clearly indicated a massive fire had raged here. The local police already had established a cordon about a quarter mile from Bagheri's residence, or what remained of it. However, being a colonel in the Quds Force has its privileges. One of which is ready access to catastrophic scenes such as that posed by the horrific scene of what once was Ali Bagheri's residence and surrounding yard—there was nothing left of the house but a huge crater and scattered and charred debris of what once was the residence of the Islamic Republic's Deputy Secretary of the Supreme National Security Council. The incident commander had already relayed that two bodies had been discovered though identifying who they were would require contacting a few dentists. There simply wasn't enough left to visually identify the bodies. Rafsanjani inquired about any other corpses and the commander indicated that they had only found the two but, given the extent of the devastation—and the still smoldering fire amongst the vegetation—there was no telling if they would ever know just how many might have been at the home. Clearly, Dr. Bagheri had been assassinated, Rafsanjani thought, as no one had heard from him as yet and at this hour of the morning, he should have either been at his office or have been in contact with someone from his security detail. He did not need the commander's expertise to tell him that this was not an ordinary explosion: the size of the crater, and its location immediately adjacent to the house, clearly implied something other than an accident. The list of suspects would not be a long one. It would take time to determine just who had assassinated the deputy secretary, though he had a good idea who would be at the top of the list.

"Major, I want you to start your search with the deputy secretary's office," Rafsanjani said over his cell phone.

"Surely you don't suspect the deputy secretary?" replied Major Zarin.

"No, the deputy secretary is dead; there is no way anyone could have survived that blast, and not even Netanyahu would be cynical enough to kill his source. However, this is the only unusual or irregular thing to occur that is really out of the ordinary. We need to track down any loose end that might come out of Bagheri's office, no matter how remote the possibility could be—you said it yourself just yesterday: did anyone in the office make any calls to a totally different number, even if they turned out to be a wrong number? What about email correspondence? Are there any emails that might look like SPAM or junk emails? Is anyone in the office planning a family vacation out of the country—I want you to track everything down no matter how small it might seem. I'm sure the Israelis are involved in this in some manner; the only question is how. I'm going straight to the Ministry to see Secretary Jalili. I'd expect to be out to the base later today and will talk to you then."

Rafsanjani quickly realized that there was no point in his hanging around what used to be Ali Bagheri's residence. They had professionals already assigned to dig through the rubble and search for any remaining bodies. Rafsanjani did not need to take part in that. He told Amir to head immediately to Said Jalili's office at the Supreme National Security Council's office downtown. He knew Jalili would demand an update from him even though he had absolutely no jurisdiction in the assassination. However, he already had Major Zarin chasing down any leads from Bagheri's office personnel to see if his assassination could be connected in any way with Netanyahu's speech. He really didn't see how, but he knew that is exactly the situation that would arise in their search for the traitor, whoever it might be.

Rafsanjani found Jalili completely shocked by Bagheri's assassination—and furious—Bagheri was his deputy. "Colonel," Jalili began, "just how bad is it?"

"The devastation could not be more incredible. They used enough explosives to bring down *this* building."

"Any chance of survivors?"

"None; there's no way anyone could have survived that blast. The local fire officials found two bodies so far and I think they were lucky to find them. It's too soon to begin looking at reconstructing this but we'll begin that tomorrow if we can, certainly by the day after, and that will give us a better idea of what actually happened. Do we know if there had been any threats towards Bagheri? I mean, taking him out serves absolutely no purpose."

"Ali Bagheri was our leading negotiator with the West regarding our nuclear ambitions. To think the Europeans would be involved in this?—totally ridiculous; certainly not the Russians or the Chinese. The Americans right now are simply out of the picture on the International front. That leaves the Israelis, who incidentally are not a part of the negotiations. I can easily see them trying to derail the negotiations to try and prove a point but even for them, this would be an extremely dangerous game."

"Okay, well, I'll get back over there tomorrow and see if we can begin to get to work reconstructing this thing to see just how powerful this bomb was, where it came from, and all that. I'll keep you posted as things develop."

"Do that. For the next few days, this is your first priority. Turn over everything else to Major Zarin."

"I've already done that; see you tomorrow."

VI

Several thousand miles away, Jim Carmichael received a phone call at home from his signals people. "Sir, we are receiving word of a detonation just outside of Tehran. From the looks of it, this happened within the hour."

"Do we have any details on this as yet?"

"Sir, it's conventional, but it's huge. Brigadier General John Anderson out at Cheyenne Mountain called in the initial report. If they picked it up, it had to be big. Looks like someone took out an entire city block on the outskirts of Tehran. Preliminary reports are saying that the Israelis just took out Ali Bagheri."

"What?!? He was leading their negotiating team in Bern. Why would they do that? What the hell are they thinking? Okay . . . Stonewall Jackson is supposed to be in Tel Aviv. Try and raise him. It's what, about 5:00 a.m. over there? Keep trying until you get ahold of him. I'll be in early in the morning, unless something else develops; keep me posted."

"Yes, sir."

Jackson had not been with the Agency long enough to have the clout to call up the Director of National Intelligence (DNI), and since he had seriously exceeded his orders, he figured he'd be better off starting with his own superior—and friend—James Carmichael. He had known Jim Carmichael for more than fifteen years now, dating to September of 2001. Jim had lead a CIA team—the Northern Alliance Liaison Team—that entered Afghanistan very soon after the assassination of General Ahmad Shah Massoud, known in Afghanistan as the Lion of Panjshir. Massoud commanded the Northern Alliance and had been seeking the CIA's assistance in fighting the Taliban for a number of years. The combination of his assassination on September 9th, 2001, and the attacks in New York and Washington D.C., two days later, ironically, cemented the deal for this assistance. Indeed, the afternoon of September 11th, the director of the CIA ordered the establishment of a team to support the Northern Alliance with all means necessary to defeat the Taliban and root out and kill Osama Bin Laden and his Al Qaeda cohorts. The Clandestine Services Division jumped into high gear: Word quickly went out to the Army's Special Operations Command looking for anyone from the Special Forces' Fifth Group who would be willing to join the team—they'd still be active duty, just temporarily attached to the Agency. Thomas Jackson, then a bright, young and eager captain in the special operations community, had signed up as soon as word went out for volunteers. Two weeks after the World Trade Center collapsed, Carmichael, Jackson and the rest of the team was in Afghanistan and working in the Panjshir valley.

Stonewall knew his little trek into Tehran had stretched things more than a little but he also knew that Jim was not one to dwell on technicalities when one obtained the desired results—and Jackson knew he had just delivered. Now, he needed to get those results to those who could actually act upon them.

"Stonewall, where have you been? We've been trying to get ahold of you for the past several hours. Do you have any idea as to what is going on over there? It seems the Israelis have just assassinated Ali Bagheri, the deputy secretary of their Supreme National Security Council."

"Jim, back up a bit. Ali Bagheri is out of the picture as far as Iran is concerned—because he just defected to the Israelis. I've been on the mission to pick him up in Tehran—I'll tell you more about that later. The bombing you've seen was designed to make the Iranians think that Bagheri is dead; in fact, he's sitting right here with me now."

"Wait a minute; you were in Tehran?"

"I'll explain later. The real issue is just how far along the Iranians are to achieving a nuclear bomb. Jim, they'll have the bomb in the next couple of months. If I was a betting man, now that the Israelis have their source out of the country, they'll be attacking any time; they may already have the strike force warmed up. They already have the EW planes forward deployed to Baku. Jim, the Israelis are attacking—it's just a question of how soon."

This was a lot of information all at once, even for someone as experienced as Jim Carmichael.

"Are you sure of this? This is way off of what we've predicted. And the Israelis; Tamir hasn't even dropped a clue to me."

"Sir, I've spent the last several hours talking with Bagheri. His information all checks out. There is no way any of this is disinformation; not from him. We grabbed his laptops, desk top computer and cell phone to verify everything but, sir, everything checks out. You'll need to check with the Pentagon to see what assets we have in the region. As soon as we touch down in Tel Aviv the Israelis are going to be free to attack as they feel they have nothing left to lose."

"Well, the extent of what we can or will do is beyond our call, but I'll be getting this information up to the DNI, the national security advisor, the secdef, and the

president as soon as we hang up. We have some resources in the area—we've kept a carrier in the gulf since
'03 and I know we have something in the Med, I'm just
not sure what all we have there. Give me a call after
you've landed and have had a chance to talk with Pardo.
I know the Israelis have not been sitting on the sidelines
diplomatically should they decide to attack on their own.
No one in the region wants the mad mullahs of Iran to
have the Bomb and all are content to let Israel do the
heavy lifting. I know they have had some discussions
with the Turks and it sounds like you know more than
the rest of us about their relationship with the Azerbaijanis. Aside from that, I don't know of anyone who would
actually assist them with an attack but most in the region
will certainly look the other way."

"Okay, will do Jim. It's about a two hour flight so
I'll give you a call later this afternoon or early evening
my time; that should be right about noon on the east
coast."

"Okay, I'll be expecting your call. Let me know
what Pardo is thinking and just how soon the Israelis
might go."

"Sir, if I read this right, they're already locked and
loaded."

"Yeah, that's my thinking too. Let me know what
you find out. I'll set up the meetings with the White
House, the national security counselor and the rest of the
national security team for later this morning; if you can
call back before, say five this afternoon your time, I'd
have a little time to go over everything before I brief
them."

"Okay, I'll get back to you as soon as I can."

"Ben, I know you probably don't know the answer to
this question, for obvious reasons, but just how soon do
you really think the IDF will launch their attack?"

"Well, we should be landing in around two hours. They'll want a little time to debrief Bagheri, say about three hours, and that puts it right around 6:00 p.m. our time. Given the complexity of the attack, I would assume that the Air Force would prefer to launch and refuel in daylight—that's just a guess, not being an airedale myself. As such, I would expect them to launch about twelve hours later, or six in the morning . . . but that's just a guess."

"Okay, that's kind of what I suspected; no reason to wait now."

As soon as the team's plane landed, Dani and Ben escorted Jackson in to see General Pardo. "So, Stonewall, what did you think of your little trip?" Pardo asked him.

"I have to thank you for the opportunity to join the party; it was quite the trip. I must say, it was not quite what I expected when you offered it to me."

"Well, I couldn't exactly fill you in on all of the details but I'm glad you were able to go. I realize you don't know the disposition of your fleet, but could you relay a message for us? You see, now that we have Bagheri, all of our assets are safe; we can attack at will. We've already positioned several of our tankers and EW aircraft along the route; in fact, you may have seen some of them in Baku. We aren't looking for any assistance from you with the strike; we believe we can handle that on our own. In retrospect, our strike on the Syrian nuclear site of Dayr az-Zawr actually served as a nice practice run. However, we would really like to know if we could at least count on US support in some manner. We know you have one carrier, the *Roosevelt*, I believe, in the Mediterranean and another in the Persian Gulf, the *George Washington*, with a third, the *John C Stennis* on the way to relieve the *Washington*. We are not sure what other ships might be accompanying these carriers but we are not asking for help with your navy fighters. Rather, we'd like to know if we could count on your navy's support should any of our pilots have to ditch either in the gulf or the Mediterranean. Also, if in the unfortunate circumstance, any of our pilots were to be shot down, would your navy be available to go in and rescue them? I know that is asking a great deal but it would be a nice gesture if the United States government could do this."

Left unsaid was the simple fact that, in all likelihood, the Iranians would lash out at the American fleet in the gulf and try to hit one of their vaunted carriers with the new Sunburn missiles Russia had provided them. The Sunburn is a radar-guided anti-ship missile, capable of being fired from the air, land or sea, making it an extremely versatile—and dangerous—weapon. The Russian version of the Sunburn had a range of one hundred miles—no one knew if the Iranians had modified this—carried a powerful 750 pound warhead, and flew very fast at Mach 3—at that speed, it could travel the hundred miles in less than three minutes! Any anti-missile defenses the navy had would have a very limited time in which to respond. The French made Exocet missile, by comparison, which the Argentinians used in the Falklands War back in the 80's, only carried a 350 pound warhead, and flew at less than half the speed of the Sunburn. However, the Argentines still managed to sink two British destroyers with the Exocet. Clearly, the Sunburn posed a very clear threat to any vessels in the gulf—and an American carrier posed a very tempting target.

"Well, sir, it would seem that you know more about our fleet's disposition than I do, but I will most definitely pass this on. Actually, if you'd have a secure phone, I'd like to call my boss right away and fill him in on everything."

Pardo handed Jackson the phone; he was not too surprised to hear that the phone was already ringing.

"Tamir, is that you?" asked Jim Carmichael, having General Pardo's number in his speed dial.

"No, sir, it's me, Stonewall. Jim, how soon can we get the *Roosevelt* through the Suez Canal and into the Arabian Sea and the *Stennis* to the gulf? Tamir has shared their operational plans with me and it seems that all assets are in place—and like I mentioned earlier, their EW aircraft are already forward deployed. I can't get into a lot of detail for obvious reasons but Tamir told me to tell you to remember Dayr az-Zawr in Syria. Jim, the Israelis are ready to rock; they'll be airborne before first light. Tamir isn't asking for any assistance in the attack—he believes they can handle that themselves—but, ostensibly, he would like to know if he could count on any CSAR"—Combat Search and Rescue—"support from the carriers both in the gulf and the Med if any pilots are shot down during the raid. Plus, the *Washington* needs to be ready for any retaliation from Iran—and they will retaliate."

"This is for real, right? I mean, this isn't a hypothetical thing, is it?"

"No, sir; this is the real thing. They'll be launching in about twelve hours or so. They're ready to rock."

"Okay, this is what I need. I'll be briefing the president and the rest of the national security team in half an hour. The vice president, though, is out of town at the moment. Tell Tamir 'thanks for the heads up' on this one. Oh, . . . and Stonewall, the next time you decide to join a raiding party in a hostile country, at least let me know what you're up to; you don't need to necessarily ask permission, but it would be nice to tell your next of kin that you at least died in the line of duty."

"Okay, will do sir."

"Well, Tamir, I guess we wait and see," said Jackson, turning to General Pardo.

VII

Washington, D.C.

This was not Jim Carmichael's first visit to the White House; over the past few years, he had made several visits here and had given several briefings as well. However, this one was different. The current administration had based their entire Iranian policy on their preconceived notion that economic sanctions would completely solve the nuclear issue. As the chairman of the CIA's Intelligence Directorate, Carmichael knew otherwise—and had repeatedly said as much; it was the politicians who didn't want to listen, or really believe, what was really happening. He had given his boss, Felix Jones, the director of national intelligence, a heads up on this morning's meeting—essentially a condensed *Reader's Digest* version—though he had not fully briefed him as yet on all of the details. He knew he was going to get some push-back—especially from State and the White House—on their, read "his", failure to really determine just how far along the Iranians were on their nuclear ambitions but all that was a mute-point at this stage of the game.

Jim rode in the DNI's limo on the way to the White House and briefly updated Jones on the latest developments from Stonewall.

"Here's the latest: I just heard from Stonewall; the Israelis will be attacking tomorrow. I guess for that matter, their planes will be taking off in about ten hours. I already let 'Axe' know"—referring to Eric Axelsson, the secretary of defense—"that the Fifth Fleet should be expecting some company very soon. I didn't give him any specifics—didn't really have any at the time as this was before Jackson's latest call—but the Pentagon's been put on notice. Axe and the chairman will be at the White House so they'll receive the latest information at the same time everyone else will."

"Jackson's sure this is the real thing, right? I mean, State's going to come unglued that their ambassador hasn't been clued in on any of this."

"Well, we've warned them about the deteriorating conditions with our relationship with the Israelis. This is exactly why I sent Stonewall over there—he's essentially my personal representative to Tamir. I had a feeling something was coming down and they weren't comfortable enough with State to let them know. I didn't think it would amount to their attacking Iran, but I had a feeling something was in the works."

"Well, let's go," Jones said as their limo arrived at the White House. "Don't be surprised if both State and the chief of staff hit you up on failing to pick up on Iran's nukc program."

"I'm expecting that. The real issue here is the Israeli's pending attack; I won't let them diverge from that."

"You do that, and I'll be there as well to help you out should one of them try and get you off track. After all, we weren't the only ones who underestimated the Iranians: MI6, the KGB . . . hell every intelligence network not named Mossad missed this."

"Yeah, but we're supposed to be better than all the rest, right?" Carmichael responded.

"Keep telling yourself that," Jones replied. "Remember, the other . . . ."

"I know, I know . . . the other guy wants to hide his activities as much as we want to figure them out."

As they walked into the White House, Carmichael noticed that they were the last ones to show up—everyone else's limousines were already in the lot.

"Off to a great start already—looks like we're the last one's here."

"Yeah, I noticed that, too. Well, might as well get the show started," Jones added as they approached the Situation Room.

Sure enough, Carmichael noticed: everyone was here, that is, everyone except President Barre . . . and the front podium was empty. Jim walked right to the podium and Jones took his seat at the middle of the conference table. No sooner had he gotten his briefing outline pulled up on his iPad than the president walked in and took his seat.

"Good morning," President Barre said to those seated around the table. "I understand we have something pressing so I won't take up any of your time Jim; you can proceed whenever you're ready."

"Thank you, Mr. President," Carmichael replied. "I received a call from Colonel Tom Jackson first thing this morning. Tom's an assistant of mine that is acting as a liaison for me with General Tamir Pardo, the head of Mossad. It seems that the Israelis have had a very high level asset in Tehran. This morning, they managed to smuggle him out of Iran. We all know him, or at least know of him, as it's none other than Dr. Ali Bagheri, the deputy secretary of Iran's Supreme National Security Council and the man who led their negotiation team in Bern."

"Ali Bagheri is Mossad's source on all of this?" asked Secretary of State Andrea Johnson.

"That's correct. Jackson called me from Baku just as they were flying back to Tel Aviv. The team set off a car bomb in Bagheri's driveway to cover their tracks—and completely took out both the house and the garage—there is literally nothing left. In fact, NORAD actually picked up the detonation so the explosion had to be massive. Obviously, the Israelis want Tehran to believe Bagheri is completely out of the picture. However, what is more important is that Jackson also noticed that the Israeli Air Force has prepositioned four of their advanced EW aircraft at Baku. I called Axe as soon as I got off the phone with Jackson and let him know that things could get real hot for our folks in the Persian Gulf."

"I let Admiral Fischer know of the possibility of any action and I've ordered the *Teddy Roosevelt* to make best possible speed to the gulf," interjected Axelsson.

"Good, because we're going to need the firepower," Carmichael replied. "Jackson went straight to General Pardo when he arrived back in Tel Aviv. With their asset now cleanly out of Iran, the Israelis will be attacking at dawn tomorrow morning. In fact, their planes will be taking off in roughly ten hours or so."

"What?!?" Tom Fleming, the White House chief of staff, and Secretary of State Andrea Johnson blurted out in unison.

"You've got to be kidding?" added in Pamela McDowell, President Barre's national security advisor.

"I wish I was," Carmichael replied. "You see, the Iranians are only a couple months away from fielding a nuclear bomb—if even that long. Jackson managed to discuss Iran's nuclear ambitions with Dr. Bagheri for several hours; they are much farther along than we thought possible. The Israelis wanted to get their asset out before they attacked—and they just accomplished this so the attack will commence as soon as practical."

"How did you miss this?" McDowell demanded.

The "you" of McDowell's question did not escape Carmichael, nor Jones.

"Damn near everyone missed this, except the Israelis. We'd been reporting that the Iranians were probably farther along than we expected, though we did not think they were this close," Jones immediately replied.

"You also told us that the economic sanctions would work!" Secretary of State Johnson interjected.

"No, we said that the sanctions would work as *part* of an overall strategy. However, you have instead allowed the sanctions to be our *entire* strategy—and we told you, this would not work," Jones emphasized. "Our diplomatic strategy, aside from the sanctions, has been pretty weak. We've always warned that the Iranians were going to pursue the bomb regardless of any sanctions. A bigger stick was needed rather than simply relying on sanctions."

"And just how do we know that your assistant, Colonel Thomas Jackson, is reliable? The Israelis haven't said 'boo' to our ambassador in Tel Aviv. It would seem to me that if they haven't bothered to tell our ambassador, and go through our official channels, they are simply trying to embarrass us."

"Andrea, they haven't told our ambassador as you wouldn't believe them even if they did," Jones shot back.

"Ambassador Richards is a very trusted supporter of the president, and has been so for years," added Fleming. "If the Israelis are really serious about this planned attack, there is no reason they couldn't have notified him."

"Tom, even if they had told Ambassador Richards, not only would you not have believed him, this administration is so tuned into economic sanctions that we probably would not have even listened. As for Jackson—he's as reliable and trust-worthy as they come," Carmichael interjected. "He's been a member of the Fifth Group, Special Forces, for many years—three of those years he led the CIF team for the group—and has his doctorate in Persian studies. He's been monitoring the Iranians for several years. Finally, he was a part of the mission to grab Dr. Bagheri and get him out of Iran."

"Wait a minute! We had US troops on the ground in Iran?!?" Pam McDowell demanded.

"No, we had one Special Forces officer accompany an Israeli Sayeret Matkal team on the ground in Iran."

"Who authorized this? Eric, did you authorize this?" Tom Fleming demanded of the secretary of defense.

"Jackson has been on temporary assignment to the CIA for a little while, so, no, I did not know about it."

"Colonel Jackson is one of very few men we have suitable for just such a mission," interjected General Stan Kaufman, chairman of the Joint Chiefs. "Jackson has served with the Fifth Group for more than fifteen years and has served several tours in both Iraq and Afghanistan. Between his military training and his academics, he's as qualified as anyone for a mission of this type."

"So then, Felix," Fleming asked turning to the DNI, and totally ignoring the general's comments, "did you authorize this?"

"Actually, Tom, I'm the one who gave Stonewall his orders—and I gave him a wide degree of latitude to pursue his objective," Carmichael answered before his boss had a chance to say anything. "However, the issue here is not who may have exceeded their orders or to pronounce the eulogy of a failed policy. Rather, the Israelis will be launching their raid in something like ten hours from now. We need to be ready."

"Eric, what's the disposition of the Navy?" President Barre asked.

"I put the Fifth Fleet on notice as soon as I received Jim's call. We have the *Washington* currently in the gulf and the *Stennis* in the Arabian Sea on the way to relieve them. The *Roosevelt* is in the Med on its way to the Suez

Canal. They can be in striking range in just a few days. In addition, we have an Amphibious Ready Group in the gulf as well, centered around the *San Antonio*. Unfortunately, we've allowed our forces at Al Udeid to dwindle quite a bit. All we have there are a couple squadrons of drones and an F-15 squadron. For the moment, the Eagles will be on standby to assist the *Washington* in the gulf and essentially guard their rear flank as the *Washington* Battle Group heads towards Doha."

"Can the *Washington* take care of herself? I don't want to hand the Iranians any PR victories by having them put a hole in one of our carriers," President Barre asked.

"Sir, once the missiles start flying, it's a whole new ball game. However, that being said, she can take care of herself, even in the narrow confines of the gulf. And with two carriers, and a third on the way, we'll be able to assure the world that the Strait of Hormuz will remain open."

"Okay, get word out to the Fifth Fleet."

"I'll do that, sir, but what are the rules of engagement?"

"Each officer has the authority to do what is necessary for the safety of his command. The Iranians are going to be thoroughly pissed and I'm sure they will strike out at the fleet. If we need to take out the entire Iranian Navy and Air Force, then that is what we need to do."

"What about offensive operations, sir?" Axelsson followed up. "Can I tell Admiral Fischer that he can conduct any operations inside Iran? The gulf is exceptionally narrow for defensive operations. I'd like to let Fischer and Admiral Ramsey, the commanding officer of the Fifth Fleet, conduct operations inside Iran if they even get a hint of possible action against them. If they have to wait until a threat extends beyond Iran's territorial waters, their options will be seriously restricted."

"Mr. President," Andrea Johnson interrupted, "if we invade Iran's air space, we will have lost all deniability on the world stage, and it will look as though we were actually behind this attack. I'm sorry but we cannot allow the Navy to attack Iran. This is an Israeli operation and we should have no part of it. If the Navy stays by Doha they should be out of range of Iran's capabilities and be perfectly safe."

"Mr. President," Axelsson interjected, "we do not know the extent, or range, of Iran's capabilities. Andrea's notion that the fleet should be safe at Doha could be right—but we missed on their nuclear ambitions. I wouldn't want to bet the safety of our fleet on our intel on the exact ranges of their defense capabilities in the gulf. The fleet needs to be able to defend itself. Furthermore, if they launch on our ships—and at this point, I am assuming that they will—we should have every right to defend ourselves—and that should include taking out any threat before it materializes. Remember, we did not start this."

"Tom," President Barre said, turning to his chief of staff, "set up a meeting with the Speaker and the rest of the Congressional leaders for seven tonight. Jim, you said the Israelis would be taking off in what, about ten hours?"

"That's right; it's now about twelve thirty in the afternoon here so that makes it about 7:30 p.m. in Israel. Colonel Jackson thought they'd be launching around six in the morning, local time."

"Okay, six tomorrow morning over there would be 11:00 p.m. our time. By seven tonight—that'll be just four hours before they launch—we should know if anything else has developed. At that point, I'll let the Speaker, the Senate Majority Leader and the rest of the Congressional leaders know that Israel will be launching their attack and that we expect hostilities with Iran in the gulf and that if that arises as expected, the Fifth Fleet will have authorization to take out any naval and air threat they deem necessary—including operations within Iranian territory. However, actual offensive operations will not be authorized at this point. Is that understood Eric?"

"Yes, sir."

"What about the Strait of Hormuz?" General Kaufman quickly added. "Tehran has long boasted that they would close the strait should something like this happen."

"The same goes for the strait. It is a vital interest to this country—and we will defend it as such. Let Admirals Fischer and Ramsey know that both the fleet and the strait are to be defended, and that includes operations within Iranian territory, though again, no offensive operations."

"Very good, sir. I'll let them know."

VIII

USS *George Washington*

"CAG, come on in," announced Captain Noel Roberts, CO of the *George Washington,* to his commander, Air Group.

"Sir, what do we have?" replied the CAG.

"We have just been advised by the Pentagon that the Israelis will be taking out several of Iran's nuclear sites. They'll actually be launching in about eight hours; that's about 6:00 a.m. their time in Jerusalem."

"Nice of them to give us some warning," the CAG remarked acidly. "So, where does that place us? Did the *Stennis* get the same warning?"

"Are you familiar with the term 'Like shooting fish in a barrel'? Well, we're the fish and this lake we're in is the barrel. We're too far north to make a run for the strait to try and get out of here. We'll head to a little pocket between Doha and Abu Dhabi. Russia supposedly has supplied the Iranians with a pretty good supply of Sunburn missiles. However, by the time everything kicks off, we should be out of their range—if they haven't modified those things. If they have, well we'll have your Hornets out there to knock down anything that flies as well as anything that even looks like it might be ready to fire at us. The *Stennis* received the same warning as we did; they'll remain in the Arabian Sea. Their

Hornets will need to pair up with buddy stores to help us out should we need it. In addition, the *Roosevelt* is on its way as well and should be transiting the Suez Canal as we speak and, at full speed, could be here in a little more than three days."

"I'll keep two Hawkeyes up and double the CAP," referring to the Hornet's combat air patrol over the fleet. "I don't want to do too much to tip off our friends for tomorrow morning but I want to get as much up and still not raise too much suspicion. The Israelis will be launching at six, figure it will take them three hours to get to their targets, so we'll start launching everything we have about eight thirty, or two and a half hours after they've launched."

"Once they're airborne, I want them on station north and east of us. Any plane that gets past the Iranian coast line needs to be warned to back off immediately. I don't want any unidentified aircraft within 150 miles of us so if they don't back off, shoot'em down. If by chance they have some Sunburn missiles from the Russians, we'll need to keep them at least one hundred miles from the fleet; I don't want to take the chance that they might have modified these and extended their range."

"Do we have any other assets in the region?" asked the CAG.

"Not as much as we did just a few years ago. There's a squadron of Eagles at Al Udeid as well as a couple squadrons of Wraiths and Reapers. The Eagles will be guarding our back door as we head south. The Wraiths and Reapers will be airborne over several of Iran's nuclear sites so when the Israelis hit them, we'll know about it right away. A few years ago, the Iranians actually hacked into one of the Wraiths and brought it down so if they happen to see one snooping around, it shouldn't raise too much suspicion."

The following morning, twenty-five F-15I Eagles and seventy-five F-16I Vipers took off for Iran. Each of the F-15's were loaded with two GBU-28 five thousand pound bombs while the F-16's each carried two GBU-27 two thousand pound bombs. In addition, each of the fighters carried their own complement of air-to-air missiles: the Eagles each carried four missiles while the Vipers carried two each. Jim Carmichael had been right in that the Israelis had not been idle on the diplomatic front. The pilots were going to need to refuel in flight and both Turkey and Azerbaijan had granted the Israelis permission to base their tankers and other support craft out of their respective air fields; in Turkey, the Diyarbakir airfield practically sat astride the route the Israelis were flying so the tankers would fly out of here. In addition, the Azerbaijanis had granted use of the Baku airbase as Jackson had noticed, and the Israelis would base their G-550 EW "Eitam" craft out of here. The Eitams would meet up in flight as the strike fighters made the turn to enter Iranian airspace.

The Israeli G-550 EW, that is, electronic warfare, aircraft first made a name for themselves when the Israelis took out the Syrian nuclear plant at Dayr az-Zawr. The Israelis managed to crash Syria's entire air defense system allowing its fighters unfettered access to their target. It seems that some enterprising graduate student at MIT had caught on to the notion that a significant part of any radar system is to *receive* data. He figured that if a way could be designed to capture the signal frequency of the radar unit and, instead of simply jamming that frequency, actually hijack the frequency and send data back along the frequency—that is *any* data—you could literally do anything you wanted to the enemy's radar and, potentially, their entire air defense network. In the case of the Israeli raid on the Syrian nuclear facility at Dayr az-

Zawr, the Israelis had actually shut down Syria's air defense network—for the entire country!

As soon as the raiders met up with the G-550's they split up into three main groups: ten of the F-16's and one of the G-550's headed to the heavy water nuclear reactor at Arak and ten more Vipers and an additional Eitam headed towards the Esfahan Nuclear Research Center. The remaining two Eitams accompanied the fifty-five F-16's and the twenty-five F-15's that headed towards the Natanz and Qom/Fordow uranium enrichment facilities. One of the Eitams, thirty of the Vipers and fifteen of the Eagles ultimately veered off towards Qom/Fordow leaving the remaining Eitam, twenty-five of the Vipers and the ten Eagles for Natanz. It was a brilliantly coordinated attack: At both Natanz and Qom, for over twenty minutes, every thirty seconds another two tons of high explosive projectiles penetrated the earth. In each case, the Eagles went in first with their heavier bunker buster GBU-28's softening up the targets for the lighter GBU-27's carried by the Vipers. At both Qom and Natanz, the Eitams earned their pay as the Iranian SAM search radars were non-existent. However, the Iranian Air Force had obviously been alerted. The Eagles, having been the first ones in were now free of their heavy ordnance, reverted to their original purpose—an air superiority fighter. In the forty year history of the F-15, not a single plane had been lost in aerial combat—and this day would pose no exception. Every one of the Iranian defenders that rose to challenge the raiders went down in flames. As in the Dayr az-Zawr raid, the destruction was complete—by the time the raiders had left, the Iranian nuclear program had received a blow the likes of which no one in Iran had dared contemplate: its nuclear program was in tatters and its Air Force had been ravaged.

*   *   *   *   *

Ever since the 2008 US presidential election, the Iranians had been boasting of their ability to close the vital Strait of Hormuz should they be attacked by either the Israelis or the United States. The subject of the Iranian nuclear program had gained more and more headlines in the US elections with each presidential candidate promising that they would never allow a nuclear Iran. Said Jalili knew that Iran needed a response and literally everyone expected a response in the strait—after all, the strait was the doorway to the Persian Gulf—*their* gulf! However, America presented Jalili with a huge problem: the Great Satan was the most powerful empire the world had ever known. They based their Fifth Fleet in Qatar, and while no ships were permanently assigned to the Fifth Fleet, the US maintained a constant presence in the gulf with either an Amphibious Ready Group, a Carrier Battle Group—usually the case—or both. Even if the Israelis were to attack on their own, Iran would still have to contend with that American fleet. He knew that any attempt to close the gulf would be a gamble. Iran had a stockpile of Russian made "Sunburn" anti-ship missiles, but they had never been used in combat and he'd only seen them tested on a stationary target. In addition, once they fired their first salvo, the Americans would have at least a couple airborne warning aircraft up—probably an Air Force AWACS or, more likely, a Navy Hawkeye, or maybe even some of their new Predators, Wraiths, or Reapers, each of the latter three could also be armed—watching for any activity that could even be mistaken for preparations for a missile launch. Once detected, attack aircraft from Al Udeid or a Navy carrier would be on them in seconds leaving little chance to launch a second salvo. Obviously, then, their first shot would possibly be the only one they were going to get, so it needed to be a good one.

However, if these missiles worked as advertised, they could certainly give the US Navy a black eye, and maybe a little bit more. Jalili still remembered the *USS Stark* incident back in 1987 when an Iraqi fighter fired a couple French made Exocet missiles into the *Stark*. The frigate did not sink but it was badly damaged and thirty-seven sailors were killed. The Sunburn missile far surpassed the capabilities of the Exocet so just maybe, they could at least make the Americans pay for playing in their pond. One thing was certain: they would not want for targets as the US Navy had both an Amphibious Ready Group and a Carrier Battle Group in the gulf. It would be a gamble but it was one worth taking and, perhaps, they just might get lucky.

Jalili's real plan, though, used the expected attack in the strait merely as a diversion. His real plan had been in the development stage since clear back in 2008 and Colonel Rafsanjani had advanced this to the point that it could be implemented immediately. Jalili believed that as mighty as the United States was, it had its vulnerabilities. Al Qaeda's attack on September 11, 2001, demonstrated that the United States was not invulnerable; indeed, those attacks actually exposed a vulnerable side of the United States that was not expected, and many still did not fully recognize. What he needed, Jalili reasoned, was to present to the United States a response they expected to see, and then hit them hard with something totally unexpected. Many a commander had been lulled into a false sense of security by seeing his opponent do exactly as expected, only to find out that his enemy was actually delivering a devastating blow somewhere else that was totally unexpected—and Jalili knew just where to strike, and he would strike with all the force of a mailed fist. First, he would strike—as expected—in the

Strait of Hormuz—it would be a gamble, a gambit really, as he fully expected to be sacrificing the best of Iran's naval and air forces in this, his opening move, but it could pay huge dividends, and, after all, he intended this to be a diversion anyway! The vaunted Quds Force, commanded by Major General Suleimani, would actually deliver the decisive blow with Colonel Ashkan Rafsanjani in the van.

IX

The Israeli raid had actually caught the Iranians completely by surprise. No sooner had Deputy Secretary Ali Bagheri been assassinated than the very next day, Israeli war planes took out their nuclear facilities at Arak, Esfahan, Natanz and Qom/Fordow. In spite of Netanyahu's warnings and all of the talk in the international community about keeping Iran from obtaining a nuclear weapon, the Iranian political leaders never really believed Israel would attack, especially acting alone. As a result, the Iranians were caught more than a little off guard. Not so, the Americans. Stonewall Jackson's call to Jim Carmichael had enabled the Pentagon to put the Fifth Fleet on alert that the Israelis would be attacking. Admittedly, the alert only gave the navy a couple hours' notice, but it was enough for the fleet to get out of harm's way and increase their patrols.

No sooner had the dust settled at Natanz than the orbiting E-2D Hawkeye radar planes from the *USS George Washington* picked up a number of Iranian F-4 Phantoms and F-14 Tomcats taking off from several airbases in the region. They also detected a lot of surface activity around known—and suspected—missile battery sites. *Washington's* CAG already had all but one of his squadrons in the air and the last one would be airborne within five minutes. The Hawkeyes—the eyes of the fleet— were already directing the first two squadrons of F-18's to the missile batteries that had been detected; the rest of the squadrons would handle the incoming fighters. *Washington's* Aegis missile equipped battle group would concentrate on any missiles they managed to launch—but if any of the missile batteries fired the suspected Sunburns, the Fifth Fleet could be in a world of hurt. They needed to take out these missile batteries right away.

The Hawkeyes focused on the missiles first; the planes came second. The airborne battle control officer aboard one of the Hawkeyes vectored in the first of the two squadrons at the land based missiles as soon as they received a launch indication; they were too late to take out those missiles which had already been fired but they could take out the launchers and any missiles stockpiled adjacent to their respective launch sites—and these were eliminated in seconds. The Iranian Phantoms and Tomcats—both of which had been retrofitted to carry the Sunburn missile: the F-4 Phantoms could carry two while the Tomcats only one—received the attention of three Hornet squadrons while the *Washington* was still shooting off the last of the Hornets. Both the Phantoms and the Tomcats were early versions of much older American Navy and Air Force fighters; consequently, defeating these posed very little problem for the Hornet pilots. However, the first salvo of the Sunburn missiles posed an acute problem for the *Washington* and its battle group.

"Vampire! Vampire! In bound missile attack! Commander, we have forty-eight incoming missiles, range 115 miles, bearing 010 to 015, speed Mach 3.4."

"Ok, Wick, let 'er go," Commander Andrew Jones said to his radarman, Petty Officer Robert Wickersham, referring to let the computers governing the powerful Aegis class cruiser to go into a fully automatic mode.

Commander Jones served as the Force Anti-Air War Coordinator (AAWC) aboard the Aegis cruiser *USS Chancellorsville.* The Force Tactical Action Officer (TAO), who technically commanded the aerial battle, served aboard the *Washington,* but as the ranking anti-air warfare officer aboard the Aegis cruiser, Jones essentially controlled the air battle. In addition, the *Chancellorsville* had recently received the upgraded Baseline 9 version of the Aegis missile system which networked the entire fleet defense so the defense of the entire fleet could be controlled by one ship—in this case, his ship.

"Yes sir, missiles away!" replied Wickersham, and with that, the *Chancellorsville* and her sister ship, the *USS Antietam,* went into a fully automatic mode and began launching their SM-6 surface to air missiles (SAMs). The first salvo consisted of forty-eight SAMs launched from each ship for a total of ninety-six missiles—the two ships would average four missiles fired every second—truly an impressive display—but it still took twenty-four precious seconds to fire the entire first volley. In that time span, the incoming missiles had a fifteen mile spread from those targeted at the beginning of the volley to those at the very end of the first salvo.

"Hit!" yelled out Wickersham, "another hit! and another! Miss, hit, another miss . . . ."

"Sir, range is now fifty-two miles, thirty missiles remaining; launching a second salvo, now," reported Wickersham rather apprehensively.

"Keep it going, Wick, let her go."

"Hit! hit! and another, . . . miss! . . . damn, another miss . . . ."

"Range is now twenty-four miles, nineteen missiles remaining! Launching a third salvo, now!"

"Oh, sweet baby Jesus!" Wickersham heard someone pray in the background.

The third salvo of the SM-6 missiles did not fare as well; for some reason, the accuracy of the Standard missiles suffered at the much closer range.

"Range is now *19,000 meters*, sir! Fifteen missiles still in bound," Wickersham called out, sweating profusely, his uniform now thoroughly soaked. "RAMs away!" he announced, referring to the Rolling Airframe Missiles aboard the *Washington* and two of her destroyer escorts.

"ECM, where are we?" Jones asked his electronic counter measures officer, with a remarkably controlled voice thought Wickersham. Jones knew he was down to about nineteen seconds before the first missile hit one of their ships.

"Almost ready . . . ."

"We're running out of time."

"Hit! . . . hit! . . . miss! . . . another miss! . . . hit! . . . ."

"Sir, range is now seven thousand meters; seven missiles remaining, sir!"

At this range, all the fleet really had left were the Phalanx CIWS—Close in Weapons System—which amounted to a radar guided Gatling gun firing depleted uranium slugs—and her electronic counter measures. The use of the CIWS truly amounted to knife-fighting range at the speed with which these incoming missiles traveled—approximately *one thousand meters per second*! At that speed, even if the CIWS hit every one of the remaining missiles, the kinetic energy of the missile could seriously damage or even sink a destroyer. The *HMS Sheffield*, which had been hit by an Exocet missile in the Falklands war, had suffered all of its damage simply from the kinetic energy of the missile as the warhead had actually failed to detonate. Ironically, the electronic countermeasures aboard the *Chancellorsville* were very similar to the countermeasures the Israelis used to shut down the Iranian air defense network as they attacked their nuclear sites. The Sunburn missile uses an active radar guidance system—which means it transmits its own signal and is guided by the radar returns it receives. The electronic warfare computers aboard the *Chancellorsville* had never encountered this missile so it had taken about 165 seconds—seemingly an eternity for the powerful computers aboard the cruiser—to locate the frequency used by the missiles' guidance system.

"*ECM!?!*" demanded Jones.

"Just a second . . ." he responded, furiously typing.

"We don't have many seconds left!"

". . . *Now!*" yelled out the electronic warfare officer as he hit the last stroke of the key board. And with that, all seven of the remaining missiles suddenly turned twenty-five degrees to starboard away from each of the targeted ships. Once the *Chancellorsville* identified the frequency used by the Sunburn missiles, the ECM officer hacked into it and began transmitting the false returns thereby redirecting the remaining missiles away from each ship. A few of the sailors on board the *Washington* actually saw one of the remaining missiles skirt past her fantail, missing by less than a hundred yards!

"ECM, that . . . was *close*! Nice work, Wick," Jones added, with a huge sense of relief.

The two orbiting Hawkeyes had been monitoring both the missile attack as well as any further activity along the Iranian coast and inland. All five Hornet squadrons had been given targets based on previous intelligence reports and had taken out every known launch site or vehicle that posed an immediate threat to the *Washington* and the inland side of the strait. The *Stennis* had been monitoring the missile attack and had launched its own Alpha Strike against the known and suspected missile sites in the Arabian Sea. Despite the Iranian's best efforts, the Strait of Hormuz remained open.

"How bad is it?" Jalili asked General Suleimani.

"It's bad. We were able to get forty-eight missiles off—and then the American's pounced on us as if they were waiting for us. A few of our radars remained active long enough to determine that they shot down several of our missiles. All of the batteries, radars and our inventories were destroyed within minutes, if not seconds, of our launch. Like I said, the Americans were waiting for us."

"Did we score any hits?" Jalili asked.

"We don't know. None of our radars remained active long enough to find out, but I have my doubts. We also lost every one of our remaining F-14s and most of the older F-4s—we've managed to rescue about half of the air crews. It's amazing we didn't lose every fighter. Those that survived could not even get close enough for their own search radars to tell if we scored any hits. My guess is this was a total fiasco."

"Well, we suspected something like this would happen; that's why we've made additional plans. I don't think they'll be waiting for what comes next. Colonel," Jalili said, now addressing Rafsanjani, "just how soon before you and Major Zarin can leave to implement Cyrus?"

"Sir, our bags are always packed; we can leave as soon as you give the word," Rafsanjani responded.

"Okay, then; the word is given: *Initiate Cyrus!* I want the four of you heading out on two different flights—commercial aviation only. As the rest of your unit has flown out, catch a flight from here to either Karachi or Islamabad; from there head west, the Peninsula, Kenya, South Africa, or something along that sort and then to Buenos Aeries to Mexico City. I really don't care the routes you take but I want you over there just as soon as possible. Speed is of the essence, but so is security. Once you leave here, I do not expect to hear from you until you are on your way out—and even then, we will need to maintain strict operational security. Our ambassador in Mexico assures me that everything is set on his end. I know you are aware of that but all of the properties we have purchased are operating as they are intended and no suspicions have arisen of which we are aware. You should have no problems. That being said, and I know you don't need me to tell you this, but be on constant alert. This is the most secret and daring operation anyone has ever attempted. As soon as you arrive over there, strike immediately; do not wait for anything. Do you have any questions?"

"No, sir; everything seems to be going as we have planned it. As far as I know, the Americans do not suspect anything at all."

"Colonel Bukhari, I want you heading back to Beirut. You are to organize a Hezbollah response in attacking Israel. As soon as the third attack is completed you are to unleash Hezbollah on Israel. We have given them thousands of advanced rockets; now is the time for them to use them."

"Good luck, then, Colonel," Jalili said to Rafsanjani. "If all goes well, I hope to see you back here in a week or so. We'll be releasing a statement to the world press and in the UN condemning the Zionist's unprovoked attack and calling for the world to punish the American lackey in the strongest terms."

With that, Colonel Rafsanjani left for his base. He did not want to call Major Zarin en route just in case the Americans might be eavesdropping on the call. Once he arrived, he had his orderly get four flights out of Mehrabad airport; one of the flights went to Karachi and the other to Islamabad. Major Zarin would travel with his aid as would Rafsanjani with his; of course, all four would be traveling under false names using fake Indian passports.

X

Tel Aviv

Jackson, Dani, Givon and the rest of the team were busy in their "ready" room trying to glean as much information as they could regarding the raid that they all knew was currently underway. Jackson had done some rough calculations and about the time he expected the pilots to be on their return leg he asked Dani if she could get him back in to see General Pardo.

"Stonewall, do you really think he has time for you with all that is going on? I mean, I know you have connections back in Washington but don't you think he is a little busy right now?" Dani asked.

"Oh, I think he'll make time for me," Jackson replied. A few minutes later, Dani received word from General Pardo to bring Stonewall into see him. Dani could not believe it; she knew Jackson had connections but in the midst of the biggest raid in her lifetime, that Tamir would take time for Stonewall completely amazed her.

"General, how are things going?" Jackson asked.

"We hit every target we intended but, as you know, it's too soon to tell just how badly we hurt them. Every one of our pilots made it out as well—and that somewhat surprised me. I had high hopes but never really believed we'd come out of this without losing a single plane or pilot."

"That is very good news, sir," Jackson agreed.

"I understand the Iranians are causing quite a stir in the gulf as well. It sounds as though your Navy is quite busy."

"That does not surprise me; and, thanks for the heads up on this. We really appreciate the warning."

"Not a problem; we appreciate all of the support you have given us. So, tell me Stonewall, just how long will you be with us?"

"I just spoke with Jim. It sounds like they'd like me to stay over here for a while, especially since things have really heated up over here. Jim would like me to hang around and keep my ear to the ground so to speak."

"That sounds like a good idea; we'd love to have you."

"Obviously, I'd really like to speak some more with Dr. Bagheri. We knew he had the most up to date information on their nuclear program but I'd be curious to know if he had any information on their retaliatory measures. We all know that the Iranians have boasted about their plans to shut down the Strait of Hormuz. However, I'd really be curious if they didn't have something else in mind. Shutting down the strait is an obvious response, almost too obvious."

"I agree. We've been trying to see if either Hezbollah or Hamas has any plans to retaliate against us, or any intel we can glean from them, but so far, we haven't had any luck. We were hoping that Dr. Bagheri could shed some light on this topic as well. We shall both see what we can find out. We've let him rest up from the last couple of days but we'll be talking with him this afternoon. I presume, you'd like to be a part of it?"

"Absolutely. I would think that being the number two man in their national security council, he'd be privy to some intel regarding any retaliatory plans they had."

The Israelis had kept Dr. Bagheri at their Mossad headquarters in Tel Aviv. The Spartan nature of the quarters didn't really anticipate someone the stature of Bagheri but these were only temporary, though he didn't fully realize that; events had kind of taken on a life of their own. That afternoon, General Pardo, Stonewall, Benjamin Givon and Dani began a rather soft interrogation of Dr. Bagheri.

"Dr. Bagheri," General Pardo began, "we obviously know you had up to date information on Iran's nuclear program, and we appreciate the sacrifices you've made to help us with this threat. Our main interest right now, though, is what you might know or have over heard, regarding any retaliatory measures Said Jalili might have planned. We know your government threatened to close the Strait of Hormuz, but we're thinking there might be something else planned as well. Do you have any ideas as to what, if anything, that might be planned?"

"General Pardo, I don't know of any specifics but I know that Said had something planned. He has been working on a very secret operation with General Qassim Suleimani. Colonel Ashkan Rafsanjani, a rising star under General Suleimani, is a part of our Supreme National Security Council and the three of them have been working on something, very, very secret. Mr. Jackson, Colonel Rafsanjani is not unlike your Colonel Oliver North under your President Reagan's National Security Council—if you remember what happened back then. Colonel Rafsanjani is a very capable young officer, and very ambitious."

"Yeah, I remember Colonel North," replied Jackson. Bagheri was referring to the arms for hostages deal that

Colonel Oliver North headed up outside of his office within the National Security Council.

"As do we," replied Pardo. "Do you have any idea as to what these three had planned?"

"I really don't. As I said, this was a very secret operation, kept strictly on a need to know basis. I simply didn't need to know. However, that being said, I know Rafsanjani was working on something. I overheard them mention something about sneaking in somewhere through some very secret tunnels, though I do not know where. My guess would be they are planning on getting something in through some tunnels from either Gaza or Lebanon into Israel. I do not know just what they have planned but, as I said, Rafsanjani is a very capable officer. I would keep track of him, if you can, and once located, do not let him out of your sight."

"You don't know of any travel plans Colonel Rafsanjani might have? Or any aliases he might use?" asked Pardo.

"I really don't. I don't know the colonel that well and we never met together socially."

"Okay; that is a huge help, though. Both of our governments will see if we can't locate him and then keep him under a microscope. We have already discovered several new tunnels from Gaza into Israel in our last little adventure in Gaza. We'll start with our Hamas contacts and see if we can learn anything from them. We suspect that Hezbollah has tunnels up north as well so we'll crack down up there as well. Is there anything else you can think of at the moment?" asked General Pardo.

"Nothing comes to mind. I didn't hear where the tunnels were, or where they led to, or what the plan was so I don't know what more I can add. I will say this, though. Do not underestimate either Said Jalili or Colonel Rafsanjani. They are both extremely capable. Jalili has been the architect of Hezbollah's, which is to say, Iran's, guerrilla war in Lebanon and he fully understands the concept of 'asymmetrical warfare' as I'm sure you can attest, General. Colonel Rafsanjani has been a very apt student of Jalili's, having served in Lebanon on multiple occasions over the years. Jalili's greatest strength, and perhaps his greatest weakness, is that he is very sure of himself. Oh, and on a completely different topic, just what do you have planned for me? I haven't led an extravagant lifestyle but I would like a few more conveniences. I realize I'm not at liberty to walk around freely, and I accept that, but a few more creature comforts would be appreciated."

"Yes, I realize that. We have a safe house for you but events of late have taken on a life of their own, so to speak. We'll get you moved out in a day or two. And, there will be more amenities for you; don't worry about that." With that, Dr. Bagheri left with one of Ben's team members.

"Ben, I want you and your team down in Re'im and operational in the morning. Stonewall, are you interested in joining them once again? This trip might be a little on the boring side of things compared to your last trip—that is if Ben keeps you out of Gaza—but it might be beneficial."

"Of course, I'd love to join them. However, I need to contact Jim as soon as possible and let him know what we've learned, and let him know where I'm headed."

"Naturally; Ben can give you a secure phone."

"Thank you, sir, I really appreciate it."

"Don't mention it; you're practically one of the team now."

"Jim, we've been talking with Dr. Bagheri and trying to find out if he has any information regarding any retaliatory plans the Iranians might have planned for us. He really didn't know anything other than some tunnels he believes the Iranians had ordered either Hamas or Hezbollah to dig from either Gaza or Lebanon into Israel. As you know, the recent Israeli action in Gaza turned up several of these."

"Yeah, we heard about those. They made headlines all over the world, and we all know Hamas had them built but do we know for certain Iran was behind these tunnels? And if so, what do the Iranians have planned?"

"That's the million dollar question; no one knows. Bagheri didn't have any ideas. Mossad doesn't have any information either. I'm headed down to Re'im with the same team I was on before to see if we can't get any more intel on what the Iranians might be up to. I'll keep you posted as we learn of anything."

"Isn't Re'im down by the Gaza Strip?"

"That's the place; I'll keep my head down."

"You do that; talk to you when you get back to Tel Aviv, if not sooner. In the meantime, I'll get with our friends in the Puzzle Palace and see if they can't look back at some of the data they may have picked up with Epsylon and see if they haven't picked up on something out of Tehran. It's possible they've picked up something and didn't have a complete picture as to what they were looking at. Viewed with this information, we might be able to put something together. I'll let you know what, if anything, we find out."

XI

Colonel Rafsanjani knew that time was of the essence. As a result, he had his orderly book four flights on a flight from Tehran to Mumbai, India. However, from there, they diverged. He had Major Zarin and his aide follow Jalili's recommendation by traveling from Mumbai to Doha, UAE; from Doha to Mexico City via Nairobi, Kenya to Johannesburg; Sao Paulo, Brazil; Panama City to Mexico City. All told, it would take Zarin and his aide a couple days just to reach Mexico City. From there, Zarin still had to catch a flight to Juarez, opposite El Paso, TX on the US/Mexican border. Rafsanjani and his aide, though, took a more direct—and risky—route—and one that placed them directly on the west coast of the United States. He took a direct KLM/Royal Dutch airline flight non-stop from Mumbai to Amsterdam. From there, he grabbed another nonstop flight, this one on United Airlines. Rafsanjani and his aide, traveling on an assumed Indian name and passport, arrived in San Francisco the day after Israel hit Iran's nuclear facilities. Hertz was only too glad to rent him a full size pickup; of course, Hertz never realized they would never see that truck again.

From San Francisco, Rafsanjani immediately left the airport and picked up I-80 and headed towards Reno where the two of them spent the night, booking a room

at the Peppermill Casino. The following morning, Rafsanjani and his aide drove to a twenty thousand acre
ranch outside of Tonopah, NV, that had been purchased
in 2009 by a shell corporation that had been organized
with the help of the Mexican authorities.

Shortly after the 2008 presidential election in the
United States, Said Jalili and General Suleimani began
working with their ambassador to Mexico to put together
a number of agricultural corporations within the United
States to purchase a number of ranches in the extreme
western US. Beginning in 2009, and over the course of
the next two years, these ranches, purchased by legal US
corporations and operated by Iranian intelligence officials through a Mexican liaison, were actual working cattle ranches, but served another purpose entirely. These
ranches, usually running ten thousand to fifteen thousand
acres, or more, each served the dual purpose of a working
cattle ranch as well as a training and staging area for an
assault force, all members of the elite Quds Force of
Iran's Revolutionary Guard. Ultimately, there was one
big ranch purchased outside of Tonopah, which served
as the base headquarters in NV, while two others in NV,
one outside of Silverpeak and another outside of Round
Mountain, served as auxiliary bases. Four ranches were
established in Oregon, a twenty-three thousand acre
ranch outside of Princeton served as the base HQ in Oregon, while three subsidiary bases were established outside of Fields and Riverside. Rafsanjani established another one based outside of Marathon, TX, though this
one was smaller and served a totally different purpose.

Once the ranches were purchased, select members of
Iran's Quds Force gradually began leaving Iran and making their way to Mexico City via various International
routes, leaving from Bandar Abbas, Shiraz or Tehran and
taking various routes via Sanaa, Yemen; Nairobi, Kenya;
Johannesburg, South Africa; Buenos Aeries, Rio de

Janeiro, etc., and ultimately ending up in Juarez, via Mexico City. Everyone, though, stayed away from any, and all, European airports as security in Europe tended to be far greater than most other African and Latin American airports. Once they arrived in Mexico City, Rafsanjani had made arrangements with the Mexican Sinaloa drug cartel to infiltrate the US along their very porous border in the Arizona desert. All told, roughly an *entire battalion* of the Quds Force successfully infiltrated into the US. Once successfully across the border, each soldier proceeded to his previously assigned ranch in either Oregon, Nevada, or a very select few, to Texas. Smuggling an entire battalion into the US took time. However, within a year and a half, an adequate—and extremely capable—force was ready.

On the ranches, preparing for a huge influx of men presented more than a small logistical problem; housing the men was not much of a problem as bunkhouses on these cattle ranches were all over the place. Feeding them, though, gradually became an issue; there was plenty of beef, obviously, but other food stuffs were needed and, though still remote, the ranchers did not want to raise suspicion. Everyone remembered the ranch in Bly, Oregon that the blind sheik had established, only to have a few observant neighbors become suspicious and blow the whole ball game.

Outfitting this force with weapons did not pose a problem at all. The Sinaloa cartel who smuggled the men in through a few tunnels in both AZ and Texas supplied the men with the weapons that they needed. The rest of the weapons and supplies needed were readily available throughout the West: monstrous outdoor sporting goods stores like Scheels, Sportsman's Warehouse, and Cabela's in Reno and Salt Lake all had seemingly limitless supplies of ammunition, black powder, and even night vision gear. Even Home Depot and Lowes offered supplies the unsuspecting thought completely innocent. In short, from Cabela's and the Sportsman's Warehouse to Home Depot and Lowes all of the material needed to wreak havoc were readily available, if one just used the imagination—and Colonel Ashkan Rafsanjani had a very vivid imagination!

As Rafsanjani's men began arriving, their task of gathering other kinds of supplies dramatically increased: the Nevada ranches stockpiled fertilizer high in ammonium nitrate while the Oregon ranches gathered all kinds of Aluminum, iron oxide, and magnesium as well as a few other chemicals. The ranch outside of Marathon, TX simply worked as a working cattle ranch—until they received word that their mission was changing.

Rafsanjani had company commanders at each of the ranches and he had made arrangements with each of them regarding the timing of their separate operations. Communication with each of his commanders would not be easy due to the sheer distance between each of the ranches. The Round Mountain and Silver Peak ranches were each an hour away from the Tonopah ranch—in opposite directions. The Oregon ranches were at least a full day's drive away on top of that. As such, Rafsanjani had each of his company commanders establish separate Gmail accounts under relatively innocuous names that would not draw any attention. Once Rafsanjani had received word to launch their operation, he would send an email out to each of them advising them of "his summer plans to visit Yosemite National Park"—an iconic National Park in California that Rafsanjani believed would generate thousands of hits should anyone in the US government try to search for a coded message. Once this message was received, each commander knew the operation would commence.

While Rafsanjani and his aide made it to San Francisco in less than twenty-four hours, Major Zarin and his aide had considerable more difficulty. Zarin's initial flight out of Nairobi had mechanical difficulties—a not uncommon occurrence in this backwater region of Africa, Zarin thought to himself. He knew time was of the essence but other than getting completely irritated at the local mechanics, he knew he was powerless to do anything. Nevertheless, Zarin couldn't help but think of the irony of his position. Rafsanjani had assigned him to the Marathon ranch in extreme west Texas. Marathon—the ancient battle where the arrogant Greeks defeated his Persian ancestors, whom the "civilized" Greeks referred to as "barbarians!" Well, now he was marshaling his force once again at another Marathon—and this time, he and his men would be delivering the *coup d'grace* to the proud, and equally arrogant, Americans. The delay in Nairobi, while it only took a matter of hours to fix the plane—again, this is Nairobi, a spare plane could not simply be inserted into the schedule—it caused him to miss his connecting flight in Johannesburg. Zarin arrived in Johannesburg a little after 10:00 p.m. local time. The next available flight to Brazil—or anywhere in South America—did not leave for another ten hours! Fortunately, or so he thought, Zarin found a flight to Mexico City, via a connecting flight in Amsterdam on a KLM Royal Dutch Airlines that left Johannesburg a little before midnight. The only drawback to this, he realized, is that it still took more than twenty-five hours to reach Mexico City; he would then need to find another flight to Juarez, right on the Texas border opposite El Paso. He knew he was way behind schedule, and incredibly frustrated at the incompetence of the mechanics in Nairobi. At this point, it would take him at least two full days to reach the ranch in Marathon!

Re'im, Southern Israel

Ben, Stonewall and Dani arrived at Re'im late in the afternoon, several hours after the last of the Israeli attack planes had landed. They had plenty to do: in the last IDF incursion into Gaza, the IDF discovered at least thirty-six tunnels leading into Israel; they knew some of them existed but had no idea as to the full number nor the extent of the tunnel network. The network consisted of tunnels that were so sophisticated that the Hamas leadership actually had a complete war room interconnected with tunnels that spanned the entire length of the Gaza Strip. Ventilation shafts, food stocks, and, of course, complete armories with stockpiles of missiles and rockets were found throughout the tunnel network. Benjamin Givon's team simply had to find out if there was an Iranian thread from General Suleimani involved in this tunnel scheme and, if so, what that might be.

Upon arriving in Re'im, Ben immediately looked up an old friend of his, Amos Yaakov, who happened to be another Mossad team leader temporarily based in Re'im. Amos' team specialized in interrogation and his team had been busy of late due to the latest IDF incursion into Gaza.

"Amos, understand you've been a little busy of late, huh?" asked Ben.

"You could certainly say that. We have interrogated literally hundreds of local Palestinians, all with ties to Hamas. Most of these guys are simply foot soldiers who don't know anything more than what they are told. We've come across a few officers in their organization who know a little bit more but not much more. They have done a good job compartmentalizing the knowledge of each officer level so that if they are captured, they can't reveal too much information. However, we've been able to piece a few things together: we knew Hamas had several tunnels leading into Israel but we didn't know where they ended; we also knew they had underground bunkers where they could both hide and store their rockets; we've found many of these as well. We know Hamas is tied to Iran but we have yet to learn of any specific or combined operations which they might have in the works."

"So, you haven't uncovered anything that would lead you to believe Hamas has any combined operation with Iran planned for any retaliation of our bombing their nuclear sites?" asked Ben.

"Nothing yet, though we are really pressing these guys, especially the leaders we've captured. None of them seem to know anything about any contingency plans that may exist for any retaliation effort on their part," Amos replied.

"Have any of your operatives ever heard of an Iranian Quds officer named Colonel Ashkan Rafsanjani? He's a key figure in the Quds Force and their intelligence operations. We believe he has been planning some highly secret and catastrophic operation with General Qassim Suleimani and the only possible lead we have is that part of Rafsanjani's operation involved tunnels, presumably with either Hamas or Hezbollah. We don't have any idea what it involves, where he'd be hitting or, for that matter, where he even is; it seems he's dropped off the face of the earth. My guess is that as soon as we can locate him, we'll have a better idea as to what is planned."

"When I was working up north, I heard a little about him working with Hezbollah in the Beqaa Valley, but that was a few years ago. He was already making a name for himself then, but I don't think that had anything to do with a long range plan to retaliate for what we've just done. You might want to check with the group up north but we haven't seen or heard anything that would lead us to believe there is anything in the works down here."

"Okay, I'll leave part of my team here and take Arielle and Stonewall up with me. Let me know if you find anything at all. Something is in the works; I'm sure of it. I just can't believe that Jalili would limit himself to something so obvious, and poorly executed, as to try and block the strait; he's much more cunning than that."

* * * * *

Rafsanjani arrived at the Tonopah ranch the evening of the day after Israel's attack on his country; his arrival at the ranch surprised no one. Quite the opposite: His company commanders knew that the colonel took a "hands-on" approach to everything—and he would never delegate something this important to a subordinate. "Where is Captain Turani?" he asked the soldier who met him as he got out of his pickup truck. Captain Bashir Turani was Rafsanjani's leading Company commander in this entire operation.

"The captain's doing a final run-through with everyone. Based on the news reports, Captain Turani believed we'd get the word to go as soon as you arrived, which he believed to be anytime. He's making sure the troops know their targets—which they all do—but, more importantly, are prepared for any contingency, should anything unexpected arise. We've noticed that the routes to some of the targets have detours due to some recent highway construction projects and we want to make sure that everything is coordinated to go off at the same time."

"Excellent. Please take me to them; I'd like to listen in. I don't want to interrupt what he has going on."

"Right this way, sir."

"Finally, for those of you heading to Torrance and Carson," Captain Turani continued with his briefing, "the California Department of Transportation has announced a night-time construction project on State Highway 91 in the Cerritos/Paramount area. As such, plan on taking Interstate 405 instead. This route may be a little longer but it should avoid any delays. We don't want any of you sitting on the highway when everyone else is hitting their targets. Any final questions?" Seeing none, and expecting none—the men had been over this several times—Captain Turani was about to dismiss the group when Colonel Rafsanjani walked in."

"Well done, Captain," said Rafsanjani.

"Thank you, sir. We were kind of expecting you, though we didn't know exactly when you'd arrive. Based on all of the news reports, we kind of expected that we'd be heading out any time."

"That is correct. Since we want each of you at your targets at precisely 2:00 a.m., you will all be leaving tomorrow afternoon. I know each of you already has the schematics of your route planned out. Get a good night's sleep tonight; spend the morning making any last minute preparations for your trips. And remember, secrecy remains paramount. We are on the verge of something truly remarkable; something that has never been done before. The American people believe that the September 11th, 2001, attack on their World Trade Center in New York was the worst thing that could have happened to them. Well, we are here to show them otherwise. Your actions tomorrow night will bring this country to its knees in ways no one in this country thought imaginable. Each of you should be proud of the role you are about to take in it." Each member of the two companies present knew that there were others taking part, but they did not know where they were coming from nor did they know any of the other targets, though it did not take much of an imagination to figure out. Moreover, no one knew anything about the operation headquartered in Oregon or about the Marathon, Texas, operation as well. Rafsanjani made sure that the operational details were as compartmentalized as possible. Even Captain Turani did not know the specifics of the Oregon operation and he did not know anything of the Marathon operation. That part of the operation was limited to Major Zarin and the Company commander in Marathon—no one else knew of that part of the operation. As soon as Rafsanjani dismissed Captain Turani, he sent out an email to his commanders letting them know of his summer vacation plans to visit Yosemite National Park.

About an hour later, four pickups, each with an accompanying travel trailer, left the ranch outside of Marathon, Texas, and headed up towards I-10 and their long journey east.

XII

On the drive up to Kiryat Shmona, Stonewall got to thinking about Dr. Bagheri's comment regarding the tunnels. "Dani," Stonewall began, "just exactly what did Dr. Bagheri have to say regarding the tunnels he overheard Jalili and Rafsanjani discuss? If I remember correctly, he simply indicated he overheard them talking about tunnels to gain access to somewhere; he simply assumed this to be about either Hamas, who he thought more likely, or Hezbollah. Everyone knows that Hamas has tunnels into Israel. Are there other places in Israel where either a tunnel or tunnels could provide access that are not nearly so obvious?"

"There are tunnels under various parts of Jerusalem but these are all highly guarded," replied Dani. "Getting past the guards would be possible, but it would take more of an assault force to get past these guards; it is not something that could be done quietly. Once past the guards, any attacking force would be somewhat limited in the amount of explosives they could use."

"What about one of the reported older suit-case type of nuclear bombs from the old Soviet Union?" Stonewall asked. Something like this could be brought in relatively quickly once an assault force had disabled any number of guards."

"The problem with that idea, though," interjected Ben, "is that you wouldn't need to get particularly close to the target. Even those small nukes had a relatively large blast area where the devastation would be complete. A tunnel wouldn't serve any purpose. I still think Bagheri's original idea is the correct one: these tunnels were used to gain access to something or somewhere; more of a means to an end rather than an end in and of itself."

"If that is the case, and I'm not discounting it," replied Stonewall, "have you ever uncovered any tunnels into Israel from Lebanon used by Hezbollah? I've never heard of them but that could be the very reason to look up here."

"Hezbollah has used tunnels in the past, back in the '90's, but we haven't heard of any reports of them lately."

Once the trio arrived at Kiryat Shmona, Ben went right to see David Eitan. Eitan and he had served together in the IDF Paratrooper brigade several years before both applied for the Mossad. They both received their selection to Mossad ten years earlier. David specialized more with the Syrian/Hezbollah terrorist connection while Ben spent his time working more with Iran and the Persian Gulf region. The two of them worked relatively closely from time to time as the tie between Hezbollah, Syria, and Iran grew increasingly closer. Over the years, Iranian intelligence and Quds Force members made repeated visits to the Beqaa Valley region of Lebanon. Ben hoped that his old friend had stumbled across any puzzle pieces regarding Rafsanjani that he didn't realize were part of a bigger picture. When Amos Yaakov mentioned that he had heard Rafsanjani frequented the Beqaa Valley years earlier, he hoped that his friend could possibly add to this puzzle and hopefully fill in some pieces, admittedly, some rather large pieces but they needed to be filled and he hoped Eitan could do this for them.

"David, have you ever heard of a colonel in the Iranian Quds Force named Ashkan Rafsanjani?"

"Yeah, I've heard of him. He's made a few trips up to the Valley. He's in pretty good with our Hezbollah friends up here. Why? What's he up to now?"

"We think he is involved in some type of retaliatory mission after we took out their nuclear sites yesterday. We have some fairly good intel that he is involved in some type of operation and some type of tunnels would be used to gain access somewhere. We originally thought this would be down in Gaza as we recently discovered over thirty new tunnels that Hamas had dug; some were pretty sophisticated but nothing has come up as yet. Amos is obviously keeping his eyes and ears open but he suggested I come up here as he had heard that this Rafsanjani had been in the Beqaa Valley a few years ago."

"He's been up there a few times, and relatively recently, though we haven't heard of any special operation he might have going on. We have some pretty good humint up there," referring to human intelligence, "so if they had something special going on, we should have heard something but we haven't heard anything like this. The real danger up there is in a growing Al Qaeda-type of organization that you folks seem to have over looked," Eitan commented—referring to a group calling themselves the Islamic State in Levant, or ISIL—looking directly at Jackson with some displeasure.

Jackson had to agree. "We've been aware of them for some time, though we don't see them involved in this in any way. Actually, we're thinking that the Iranians might oppose these guys about as much as everyone else in the region. I'd like to believe that Rafsanjani's presence up here has more to do with trying to combat this militant variant of Islam than working with Hezbollah to further antagonize you folks."

"However, that still begs the original question: Where are these tunnels? What is Rafsanjani's role in all of this, and for that matter, just where is this Iranian colonel?" asked Dani.

"So, we don't even know where he is?" asked Eitan.

"That's correct," replied Ben. "We lost track of him a couple days ago. It's as if he has dropped off the face of the earth. We are convinced he has a retaliatory strike in the works; we just don't know where."

"But the use of tunnels of some kind seem to be a part of this operation?" Eitan asked once again.

"That's about all we know at present. Our electronic wizards back at the NSA have pulled every disc they have of every conceivable conversation taking place in Tehran that we know of to see if Jalili, Suleimani or Rafsanjani himself might have let something slip in a cell phone conversation or an email but as of yet, they are coming up blank as well," Jackson added. "If they have something in the works, and we believe they do, they have been very, very quiet about it—and, that's more than a little disturbing."

"Okay, now that we have a clear focus—both on who and on these tunnels—I'll have my crew press every one of their contacts to see if we can't turn something over. If there is something planned up here, we should be able to sniff it out. This might take a few days, though. We haven't known about this angle but we'll get right on it."

"David, I can't over emphasize the importance of this enough, and the urgency of this. We need to find Rafsanjani, and right away. My suspicion is that his disappearance means only one thing," Ben added, "he's already given the go ahead to launch his operation—whatever the hell it is."

Half a world away, the day was just beginning in Oregon and Nevada. Rafsanjani's men were busy making their final preparations as, if everything proceeded as planned, this would be a day like no other in American history. Four pickup trucks from the Princeton, Oregon, ranch and twenty-six more from the Nevada ranches were each loaded with ten 55 gallon oil barrels. Each of the barrels contained ammonium nitrate fertilizer; seven of which were topped off with diesel fuel; the remaining three would be topped off with nitromethane as the drivers got closer to their targets. Once the four trucks at the Princeton ranch were loaded with the barrels, they headed out, along with two additional pickups for an escort, and a ride home—Rafsanjani did not intend for this to be a suicide mission. These six pickups had the farthest to go and they did not want to get caught in traffic as they passed through Seattle. The operators from the Nevada ranches had a little more time to spare; they still had a long drive of their own—each averaging more than four hundred miles—and they, likewise, had to be concerned with traffic as several of them would be passing through the Los Angeles area. However, each driver had made practice runs to his assigned target so each driver had an idea of what to expect. By mid-afternoon, thirty-nine pickup trucks had left the Nevada ranches—twenty-six of them carrying a very deadly cargo—and another six had left the Princeton, OR ranch.

Captain Reza Sassani, based in Princeton, OR, commanded the second wave and he began preparations for his teams as soon as he received Colonel Rafsanjani's email. His teams consisted of the balance of the Princeton, OR, ranch plus the three ranches outside of Riverside and Fields. The second wave consisted of the remaining pickups at the Princeton ranch as well as every pickup from the three remaining ranches outside of Riverside and Fields for a total force of forty pickups. At each ranch, these trucks were loaded with as many apple crates as they could carry without drawing any undue attention to themselves. Each apple crate contained relatively innocuous plaster castings, which, ironically, were about the size of a large apple. By late afternoon, Captain Sassani's teams headed north for their targets.

*   *   *   *   *

"Ben, its David. Sorry to wake you at two thirty in the morning, but we found something you and your team needs to see right away, especially Jackson."

"Okay, I'll get them up right away. We'll be right over."

"Hey Arielle, Jackson," Ben yelled as he knocked on their doors. They were staying in what amounted to a small dorm on the base at Kiryat Shmona so Ben only had to knock on the two doors next to his to wake up his two cohorts. "David's got something—and Stonewall, David specifically requested you join the party. It sounds like something involving you guys more than us. I told David we'd be right over. Get dressed and let's go."

Five minutes later, the three of them met David in his office; he clearly had not left his office since they left him there the preceding afternoon. "I think we may have found something for you, though I don't think it's what you were expecting."

"Why's that?" asked Ben.

"Well, one of my colleagues came across a Hezbollah operative who did some drug running in Beirut. Turns out, he has some connections with some of the cartels in Latin America, the Medellin cartel in Colombia and the Sinaloa cartel in Mexico. This guy mentioned that he heard that these cartels were contacted by what he described as 'a couple Arabs' awhile back to smuggle about five hundred men—soldiers mind you—into the United States via a tunnel system between Juarez and El Paso, Texas. He didn't know what they were up to, and didn't ask."

"What?!? Did he give you an idea as to what either of these two guys looked like?" asked Jackson.

"He said one of the guys was pretty domineering, and wasn't afraid to make demands of either of the cartels—and that's saying something as both of these cartels can be incredibly ruthless," responded David.

"That sounds like it might be our man," replied Jackson. "Rafsanjani is not one to be trifled with and he is not intimidated by anyone. So, if Rafsanjani is smuggling five hundred or so soldiers into the US—we're talking the Quds Force; something really big is in the works. I need to get on the horn right away. Do you have a secure line to Washington?"

"My XO's office is right across the hall; the phone is on the desk. All of the phones in here are on secure lines so no need to worry about anything."

Jackson suspected that Carmichael would be at his home by this time. It was now 3:00 a.m. in Israel; that put it at 8:00 p.m. in Washington. Jim put in a lot of long hours but he figured he'd be home by now. "Hello," Jim answered, with some hesitation in his voice; he didn't recognize the number calling him but knew only a few people had his number.

"Jim, its Stonewall. We've got a big problem. We've uncovered some evidence over here and it seems that the Iranians have been working with the Medellin and Sinaloa cartels to smuggle a sizable Quds force into the United States through a series of tunnels from Juarez to El Paso. The operation appears to be led by a Colonel Ashkan Rafsanjani; he's a rising star in the Quds Force and is a member of their Supreme National Security

Council. We don't know just how sizable of a force this might be; our source simply mentioned 'five hundred or so' but we're thinking that number is a bit of an exaggeration but even if 250 got in, we have a serious problem."

"What?!?" Carmichael cut in. "Are you telling me those mad mullahs have smuggled a battalion of their Quds Force into the United States?! Stonewall, are you serious? Do we know anything else? I mean, just how solid is this?"

"Jim, this is as solid as anything we have right now, and granted, we don't have much. However, this is a solid contact Ben's Mossad friend has used over the years. He simply said that a couple Arabs contacted the Sinaloa cartel 'awhile back' to smuggle around five hundred soldiers into the US—we don't know how long ago this may have been or anything else. We don't even know the objective of this operation of theirs but with a significant number of Quds Force members running loose in the US, we've got a serious problem. I'm working with Benjamin Givon over here to see if I can't get a plane straight to Fort Bliss. He'll have to get Pardo to approve it but I don't see that being a problem right now. Jim, the intel on this is solid. We just learned of this about twenty minutes ago. We met with the Mossad chief for northern Israel this afternoon. He's an old paratrooper friend of Ben's. He said he'd get right on it, and he sure did. I'll get as much of the details as I can regarding the location of the tunnels and then forward them to you. We'll need to contact the El Paso Border Patrol office and give them the location information once we have it. I would assume that this tunnel, or tunnels, are still operational. If so, the Border Patrol folks need to camp out on the exit of this tunnel and any other tunnel they know of, and see if we can find out if it is still being used and if so, by who and see if we might just be able to follow someone and see where this leads. As soon as

Ben has some more detailed information, I'll relay it to you. Maybe we can learn something from one of these guys if we can catch them."

"Okay; good work, Stonewall. I'll contact them, Homeland Security, and the DEA here in Washington and see if they can't get some of their agents in on this as well. The cartels over here aren't exactly known for keeping secrets. When you are as ruthless as they are, they rely on intimidating others to keep silent. I'll have the DEA put a full court press on their Mexican counterparts to see if we can't stir something up. I'll let you know what, if anything, we develop. In the meantime, get on a plane to Fort Bliss as soon as you can. I want you there working with the point man for the FBI. I don't know who that will be but I'll contact the director and let him know you'll be there tomorrow and then relay that to you en route. They'll obviously have jurisdiction on this but you know the guy we're after; we need you on the ground out there."

"Roger that. I'll talk to you later." With that, Jackson disconnected the call and hollered across the hallway.

"Ben, can you get me on a plane to Fort Bliss, Texas?! I need to leave right away! Also, any chance Dani can join me? You'll want a liaison with me anyway and, given the international aspect of this, having someone along from the Unit could be a big help. Besides, she went to school at College Station, so she's somewhat familiar with the territory."

"Jackson, you got your plane. Arielle, make sure you're packed and ready to go."

"Ben, the bag's always packed—you know that; I'm ready whenever Stonewall is."

"Okay, we'll get the two of you on a G-650ER out of Ramat David; there's practically one on stand-by round the clock. This will get you all the way to El Paso without having to stop and refuel."

"You've got one of those on standby? Those things can fly forever," Jackson marveled.

"So it would seem. You realize the Viper is made in Fort Worth, don't you?" Ben replied, referring to the F-16. "We're flying there at least once a week. I think we can shake one loose for you."

"Cool! How soon can we leave?"

"Grab your bag and you can leave as soon as I can get you a driver. Arielle, keep me in the loop!"

"Absolutely; thanks, Ben!"

"Okay, you two, get on your way. It will still take you about an hour before you can get to the base and get airborne. In the meantime, we'll continue with the interrogation of this fellow and email you with all of the details regarding the tunnels used, locations, etc. Best of luck over there."

"Thanks, Ben; I really appreciate all of this."

"Don't mention it; I'll see you two later."

*   *   *   *   *

"Bob," Jim called out, slightly louder than he needed to as he had the secretary of homeland security, Robert Harmon, on speaker phone. "I got some bad news—and extremely urgent—regarding the Iranians plans for retaliating due to the Israeli airstrikes yesterday. The word is that it seems Iranian intelligence operatives have been working with the Sinaloa cartel to smuggle close to a battalion of their Quds Force into the Southwest through a series of tunnels from Juarez to El Paso. We don't have much to go on, other than that El Paso seems to be the entrance point for getting into the US."

"You've got to be kidding!? A battalion?!? That seems kind of farfetched, doesn't it, Jim?"

"Bob, the intel on this is as solid as we have right now. We believe the Iranian's attempt to close the Strait of Hormuz was more of a diversion than anything else. We fully expect them to try something else, we just don't know what, or where."

"Jim, are you sure of this? I mean, this isn't a ploy by the Republicans to try and discredit the president, is it? They've been screaming for enhanced border security throughout the duration of this administration. You sure this isn't some plan of theirs to take advantage of this situation?"

"Bob, like I said this is solid. It's coming straight from Mossad."

"Okay; does the president know of this yet?"

"No, I wanted to let you know right away. I just found out about this right before I called you."

"So, all we really know at this point is that there are supposedly some tunnels from Juarez to El Paso the Sinaloa cartel has used to smuggle in a small battalion of Iranians, right?" Harmon asked, still not really convinced of this latest intelligence.

"That's correct," Jim replied, catching the drift of Harmon's tone. He had to remind himself that, though Bob was qualified for the job, he really was a political appointee. "I know it's not much to go on but I thought the DEA or the Border Patrol—or both—might either know of a tunnel like this or should at least be made aware of this."

"I'll give them a call right away; they might even still be in the office as it's still right around six out there in El Paso. I'll also let Tom Fleming know as well. No real reason to call for a meeting at the White House but I think we need to keep them in the loop on this."

"Agreed. No reason for any type of meeting at this point—we simply don't know very much. Once we learn more—and we will—I'll let everyone know and let either Tom or Pamela," referring to the White House chief of staff and Pamela McDowell, the national security advisor, "convene a meeting, probably with the NSC, for some time tomorrow."

"That sounds good, Jim."

As he hung up, he knew sending Jackson to El Paso was the right call. He knew Harmon did not take him seriously and, consequently, they'd need someone on the ground who knew what was at stake—and clearly, no one from Homeland would answer this call. He just hoped it wouldn't be too late.

*   *   *   *   *

Dani and Stonewall made it to Ramat David Airbase a little before 4:00 a.m. The G-650ER looked everything as Jackson had dreamt it would be—and more. Upon boarding, and walking into the main cabin area, a complete and fully stocked galley greeted him. Behind this sat a small table and a couple chairs on each side of the aircraft. As he walked down the cabin, a small but very adequate lounge area unfolded with a couch on one side with a couple lounge chairs and a table on the other side, complete with a forty-three inch TV, capable of either DVD's or streaming internet. Behind this, a doorway walled off the sleeping cabins: two on each side of the aisle, each approximately two and a half meters long, and could berth up to eight people. Finally, in the middle and at the very rear, Jackson found the commode, complete with a shower as well.

After Dani gave him the tour of the aircraft Jackson returned to the cockpit; he needed to know what their anticipated arrival time in El Paso would be. "It's about four in the morning here; what time will that put us in at Biggs airfield at Fort Bliss?" Stonewall asked the pilot.

"Well sir, it's about a fifteen hour flight and El Paso is eight hours behind us, so that would put us in right around eleven this morning, sir. If you don't want a serious case of jet lag, I suggest the two of you sack out right away. I believe Arielle just showed you the amenities this little beauty has to offer."

"That she did, and it's very impressive. We'll do that. Wake us up if you hear anything."

XIII

Los Angeles, CA

Amanda Freitag had had a busy afternoon. She had been planning this vacation for the past year. After all, she reasoned to herself, what better way to celebrate their twenty-fifth wedding anniversary than by taking a three week trip back to Italy where they got engaged? Scott, her husband, had been stationed at Naples as the HAZ-MAT/Safety officer for the base's fire department while she had been working for a government contractor there on base. Twenty five years later, it seemed like the perfect opportunity to return. Only this time, they'd be taking a cruise around the Mediterranean: they'd be stopping in Sicily, Malta and several stops around Greece. They both loved Italy but they had never taken this cruise. She couldn't wait to get over there and, while Scott didn't let on as much, she knew he couldn't wait to get on the plane either. Their flight was scheduled to leave at 6:55 a.m. It was now well into the evening and Scott hadn't returned from the station. She knew he probably had a lot of last minute items that needed his attention but she couldn't find their passports.

"Honey," she asked over the phone, "I know you've got some last minute things to finish up but I can't find our passports."

"I locked them in the top left desk drawer in the office."

"What are they doing there?" she asked rhetorically. "Okay, I'll grab them. Everything else is packed. Want to meet for dinner over at Fish Bonz? It'll probably be your last chance to get a decent Cajun Ahi tuna dinner for a few weeks."

"Yeah, that sounds like a good idea. Give me about fifteen minutes to finish up here, so, should be there in what, half an hour, forty five minutes?"

"It's a date. I'll see you there."

"Was that Amanda?" Dave Ramirez, Scott's assistant—and best friend—said walking into his office. "Don't worry about a thing. Go ahead and get out of here. I'll finish this stuff up for you."

"You sure? I'm just finishing up this report for Division that I wanted to get off before I left."

"That's all you're working on? I can take care of that for you. Get going and meet your bride, okay?"

"You're sure?" Scott asked once again.

"Yeah, I'm sure. You and Amanda deserve a trip like this. I'm really excited for the two of you. When you get back, Lori and I want the two of you over for dinner the first Friday night you're home—you can tell us all about it. I'll provide the steaks, you bring the beer. Okay? Now go!" Dave said, with a great deal of encouragement.

Scott and Dave had met about twelve years ago when both were lieutenants with the Los Angeles Fire Department. Scott had been a new lieutenant fresh out of the Navy. Many people do not realize that the Navy takes firefighting very seriously. After all, one of the last things a commander at sea wants to hear is that there is a fire on his ship. Scott received his first duty station on board the USS *John Hancock* upon graduating from the Naval Academy. Soon after leaving port, on his maiden voyage, a fire erupted in the engine room and quickly spread to several other parts of the ship, including the CIC. Scott learned real quickly that there is more to fighting a fire than simply putting wet stuff on the red stuff! There's a real science to fighting a fire in confined spaces and he loved it! Thereafter, he spent as much time as he could learning all he could about fighting fires, either aboard ship or on base. After twenty years in the Navy, Commander Scott Freitag left the fleet and walked right into the lieutenant's position with the Los Angeles Fire Department.

Dave Ramirez had been with the department for just a couple years when Scott came aboard. That first summer—and ever since, for that matter, their families spent practically every other weekend at the other's place grilling steaks or salmon on the BBQ. Amanda and Lori Ramirez hit it off just as Scott and Dave had. Though Dave "outranked" Scott in actual service time, Scott clearly outranked him in experience—and about five years in age—and he quickly rose through the ranks. Since their time as lieutenants, both had advanced through the department from one battalion or another. Four years ago, Scott—now the battalion chief for Battalion Six—had been looking for an assistant battalion chief and he knew who he wanted right away, Dave Ramirez. For his part, Dave was only too happy to be reunited with his friend.

Forty minutes after hanging up with Amanda, Scott pulled into Fish Bonz' parking lot. Amanda's Mustang sat by itself in one corner of the parking lot so Scott pulled in next to her car. As he walked into the restaurant, he noticed Amanda placing their order for the two of them. He could tell Amanda was more than a little excited about their trip as he slipped into the booth across the table from her: she had a glow about her that just radiated excitement. He was excited, too, but he thoroughly enjoyed seeing his wife so excited—just one look at her and even a perfect stranger could see it in her eyes.

The secret got out very quickly that Scott doted on his family and he just loved the sparkle in the eyes when he could surprise someone. This same joy extended to his work family as well—he had worked with most of them for the past several years. When any of them had a special event in their personal lives, Scott, and Amanda, always found a way to help his "family" celebrate the occasion. When it came to a true "family" celebration, like the birth of a child or some other special occasion, Amanda and Lori usually teamed up to plan the event. Firefighters were a fraternity, a true brotherhood and Scott lived it out every day.

*   *   *   *   *

The hardest part for any commander is the waiting. Rafsanjani had given the order and every one of this men were now en route to their designated targets. There was nothing he could do now but wait. The men were well trained; he had made sure of that. He had seen evidence of this with Captain Turani. Nevertheless, he feared that somehow the Americans might have learned of his operation. He had absolutely no reason to suspect that the Americans knew what was about to happen and he was sure he hadn't made any mistakes regarding operational security. But, this was the biggest operation in the history of his country. If he could pull it off for just a few more hours . . . .

About eleven that evening, along various rest areas and service stations along I-5 in both California and

Washington, a number of vehicles pulled over and began the final stages of their operation—that of adding the nitromethane to the remaining fuel barrels in the back of their truck beds. At this point, each driver only had a few hours left before reaching their targets and the chance of having to drive over an unmaintained road was remote at best.

At precisely 1:53 a.m., Captain Turani pulled off of Rosecrans Avenue into a south entrance of the Chevron oil refinery in El Segundo, California; the largest refinery on the west coast. One of Turani's lieutenants followed right behind him. Turani followed Chevron Refinery Way for perhaps a quarter mile with a small part of the tank farm on his left. He proceeded past a small rail yard, made a very tight turn and found himself directly between two extremely large, and very tall, refining towers. He parked his truck there, set the fuse, and both he and his armed escort retraced their path on foot back to Rosecrans Ave. Turani's lieutenant parked his truck in the tank farm whereupon he made his way west to Highland Avenue where he and his partner awaited pickup. At precisely 2:00 a.m., the bombs in both trucks detonated. The bombs were essentially clones of the one constructed by Timothy McVeigh when he bombed the Alfred P. Murrah Federal building in Oklahoma City, only these bombs were twenty-five percent smaller. Nevertheless, each of these bombs, detonated at an oil refinery, had significantly more potential for wreaking havoc due to the very premises in which they were detonated. The resulting fireballs, and secondary explosions, could be seen for miles. Over the course of the next five minutes, this same scenario played itself out in Carson, Torrance and Wilmington in Southern California; in Bakersfield in Central California and in Benecia, Martinez, Richmond and Rodeo in Northern California and in Anacortes and Blaine, Washington—in the span of less than five minutes, the thirteen largest oil refineries on the west coast had been completely destroyed.

"Hello?" Scott said groggily into the phone. He knew it was sometime in the middle of the night and he also knew that his phone should *not* be ringing—not unless it was a dire emergency.

"Scott? It's Dave. We have a problem."

"What's up?" He knew that Dave of all people would not be calling unless there happened to be something seriously wrong—rivaling the attack on the World Trade Center type of wrong.

"I'm down at the station. We're receiving reports that the six large refineries here in the LA area have been rocked by explosions. From the station here, I can see the fireball over at the Conoco refinery to the west of us and then there is a massive glow in the air over what has to be the Tesoro, Valero and Shell refineries some four miles north of us. I think we can handle the Conoco fire. We've called everyone in and as soon as everyone gets here I'm taking them up to the Tesoro and Valero refineries—that looks to be a firestorm up there; they're going to need all the help they can get. I hate to tell you this but the chief said to get you in here right away. Sorry about that."

"I'm on my way; I'll be there in about ten minutes."

"Was that Dave? What's going on?" Amanda asked, now wide awake herself.

"Yeah, turn on the TV. Dave said that six of the large oil refineries here in LA have been rocked by explosions. Even though it's a little after two in the morning, this has to be hitting the local news. Sorry, honey, but I need to go in."

"Oh, WOW!!! Look at that!!!" Amanda shrieked. She had skipped the TV and ran out on the deck off of their bedroom that overlooked much of the LA area, to-tally oblivious to the fact that she was completely naked. "The entire sky's aglow!!! What happened?"

Scott looked out at Amanda on the deck, noticing her toned body silhouetted against the orange glow from the fires and knew this was going to be bad. "Dave didn't say; I don't think anyone really knows for sure at this point but my guess is it's pretty obvious; something like this doesn't just happen by itself."

"Honey . . . be careful. I know the trip is off—or at least delayed . . . but be careful. This looks real, real bad." Amanda said as Scott turned and headed out the door.

He reached the station in less than ten minutes; at two fifteen in the morning even Los Angeles traffic wasn't that bad. Dave was just heading out as Scott pulled into the station.

"Any word on what's going on?" Scott asked.

"Nothing, but with all of these explosions, I think we both know the answer to that question."

"Yeah, I'm afraid so.   Okay, where are we at?"

"I've sent stations Seventy-nine, 101, 110 and 111 to County; everyone else is here, over at the Conoco fire. I'm heading up to join the 101st at the Tesoro fire."

"Okay, I'll head over to join our guys over at the Conoco fire. Be careful over there; this could get real bad, real fast."

"Roger that."

As Dave drove up SR 47, he could see the Tesoro refinery towers—or what used to be towers—to his right completely destroyed and a massive fire raging through what used to be the refinery. The tank farm to the north was a raging inferno as well. A captain from the 101st had set up the command post at a large vacant lot at the corner of E. Lomita and 47. As the assistant battalion chief, Dave took command upon arrival. From this location, they could see the Tesoro Fire immediately to the east of them and the Valero fire immediately to the north just beyond the tank farm.

The blast which took out the Valero refinery had the unfortunate result, and in a very rare fluke, of sending the shock wave through several of the refinery pipes rather than simply destroying them. Consequently, the pipes acted more like wind tunnels than fuel pipes. The actual force of the blast jammed the valves which were intended to prevent any back-flow of fuel from the tanks in the tank farm from returning back in to the refinery. The corresponding result led to the fire at the refinery having a near limitless supply of fuel flowing back from the tank farm. Unbeknownst to many, the Valero tank farm did not store fuel for extended periods. Rather, Valero only stored fuel long enough until it could be shipped out to its corresponding service stations. By 2:00 a.m. that morning, a few of the smaller tanks in the farm had almost emptied their contents to the nightly train of semi tanker trailers that delivered gasoline throughout the state. When the blast traveled through the pipes and jammed the back-flow valves, a couple of these smaller tanks quickly drained the last of their fuel. Now, with the tanks devoid of fuel and the pipes leading from them no longer feeding the refinery fire, all that remained was vapor, which now allowed the fire to travel back up the pipes. The resulting explosions set off a chain reaction throughout the tank farm as shrapnel from the first exploding tank ruptured the tank next to it, which then exploded sending shrapnel into other tanks and so on, and so on.

Dave Ramirez noticed the first explosion across Lomita Boulevard. By the time the second tank exploded, he realized—too late—that they needed to evacuate their command post immediately. He reached his command

SUV just as the fifth—and largest—tank exploded sending a wall of flame and shrapnel through what used to be the command post for stations Seventy-nine, 101, 110 and 111. An already chaotic situation was now punctuated with the PASS alarms of the entire incident command staff.

One of the lessons both Said Jalili and Colonel Rafsanjani learned from the September 11, 2001, attacks on the World Trade Center in New York was the impact the attacks had on the entire US economy. The grounding of the American airline industry for just the very few days in which it lasted sent the entire economy into a recession. They fully realized that the US economy represented one of its greatest weaknesses. Two incidents on the US west coast gave a little hint of that vulnerability, and reinforced in their own minds the "rightness" of the operation and the vulnerability of the American economy: in the summer of 2012, the Anacortes refinery was down for routine maintenance—a not uncommon occurrence. However, shortly after Shell Oil shut down this refinery, Chevron's oil refinery in Richmond, CA, had a major fire, shutting this refinery down for several months. The combination of the closing of two refineries on the west coast brought gasoline prices to record levels throughout California, Oregon and Washington. At the time, the American public vociferously complained to their Congressmen about price gouging by the oil companies, but the American public has a notoriously short memory: once both refineries were back on line, fuel prices gradually dropped, though not to the levels they remembered, and all was good. Life could return to the normalcy everyone remembered.

However, for Rafsanjani, this little incident in 2012 reinforced his idea that taking out the largest refineries on the west coast—a combined 2,031,000 barrels of oil per day—would bring the US economy to its knees. Indeed, the Cherry Point refinery in northern Washington alone provided eighty-five percent of the fuel for Sea-Tac International Airport in Seattle. At the root of who Rafsanjani was, he was first and foremost a soldier. He was not a killer, as such, and did not enjoy killing merely for the sake of killing. No, Rafsanjani wanted to punish America as a whole. The World Trade Center attacks had killed a lot of people, but only those nearest to those who were killed really suffered. However, by taking down the US economy, Rafsanjani theorized, the entire country would suffer. The bombing of the west coast refineries, though, only amounted to the beginning of his operation.

XIV

32,000' above the North Atlantic

"Colonel Jackson, Colonel Jackson?"

Stonewall wasn't sure what he heard first, the knocking on the door or the co-pilot calling out his name. They'd been on the go for a few days and this had been his first real chance to get any kind of rest.

"Yeah, what is it?" he replied.

"Sir, we have an incoming call for you," the co-pilot advised Jackson.

"Okay, do you have a phone somewhere in the cabin up there?" Jackson asked.

"There's a phone by the table, mid-cabin, sir. Just pick up the phone and the connection will be made. It's on a secure line so no need to worry about that."

Putting on a pair of cargo pants and leaving his shirt and eye patch on the bed, Jackson walked out of his berth and out into the cabin interior and found the phone as described. "Jackson, here," he said.

"Stonewall, Jim here. We found out at least part of what Colonel Rafsanjani is up to. It appears that several of his troops pulled a Timothy McVeigh on us and bombed several of the larger oil refineries on the West Coast. It is still very early in the morning over there, something like two forty-five or so, so we aren't sure of the exact damage, or even the extent of it, but if the reports coming in are in any way accurate, this is going to be a disaster rivaling September 11th. Obviously, it is still too soon to account for casualties, and there are some, but the more significant impact is to the refineries. I'm not discounting the casualties in any way, but the impact this will have on the country is going to be huge; we've never seen anything like this in our history."

"Damn!" Jackson elicited in frustration. "I'm not sure where we're at right now—probably somewhere over the North Atlantic. Do you want us to continue on to El Paso or should we plan on taking a detour to Andrews first?"

"When are you expecting to land at Biggs?"

"It sounds like right around eleven this morning; maybe earlier if the pilot steps on it."

"No, go ahead with the original plan and head straight to Fort Bliss. You know as much about this guy as anyone and we know precious little as to how they did this. We know some of the perpetrators were killed in the explosions but we have not captured any of them. We need to pin down how they got into the country, how many of them are here, is there anything else planned, etc. We've got a lot of work to do yet. The sooner you can get there, the better off we'll be. Don't worry about any jurisdictional issues. I'll get that ironed out on my end. The ATF is really going to want the lead on this given the nature of the attack and, for that matter, every Federal and State agency will want in on this but the FBI's going to have the lead—they simply have the most horsepower to deal with a case like this. The ATF is going to cry foul over that but that's just too bad. However, you have one advantage over all of them: we know who did this and you know him better than anyone."

"Okay, we'll continue straight on to Biggs. Let us know if anything else arises."

"I'll do that. In the meantime, I'm sure I'll have a meeting at the White House sometime this morning, probably first thing. We still don't have a lot of intelligence on just what happened, or how, but we'll need to give the president some options on how to proceed, even though we'll be working on really limited intel. If you and Dani learn anything—anything at all—let me know right away."

"Will do, sir. I'm sure we'll be talking to you later."

"That was Jim?" Dani asked as soon as Stonewall hung up the phone.

"That was Jim, and it sounds like we've learned what at least part of Rafsanjani's plan was—it appears he just bombed several of the larger refineries on the west coast, Timothy McVeigh-style. It's too soon to even speculate on the extent of the damage but this could be bad, real bad."

"Are we still headed to El Paso?"

"Yeah, we know Rafsanjani better than anyone and Jim thinks we'll be more useful there helping the FBI than anywhere else."

"Good, that was the original plan, anyway," Dani added, echoing Jim's comment to Jackson.

"Well, I think I've had about seven hours of sleep—you look like you've had a lot more than that"—Jackson began, good naturedly, changing the subject. Dani had emerged from her cabin wearing a stylish Under Armour sports bra, revealing a generous hint of cleavage, and a pair of loose fitting sweats with her long black hair mostly pulled back into a pony tail—she clearly felt very comfortable around Jackson. She looked sexy as hell and he suspected this would get a rise out of her, and he wasn't disappointed.

"Thanks a lot! You sure know how to make points!" Dani commented as she threw one of the couch pillows at him and then proceeded to charge him and pummel him with a few well-placed slugs to the shoulder. It was at this point that she noticed several scars he had on his left chest, shoulder and arm.

"Say, what happened here?" she asked him regarding the scars on his left shoulder and chest.

"Ah, just a reminder of a bad day we had in Iraq a few years back."

"Seriously, what happened? Is this related to your eye injury?" she asked, genuinely interested while also noticing a nasty scar on his left temple leading to his eye socket.

"It's a long story but suffice it to say that we—my team—got placed in a location that Intel thought would be relatively safe—famous last words, right? We were assigned to occupy a major intersection in northern Iraq. Three or four different main roads converged on this one spot and we were tasked with occupying this junction. A battalion from the Eighty-second was on call if we needed immediate support but they were quite a ways away. You've heard of Bastogne, from World War II and the Battle of the Bulge? This would be its equivalent in our endeavor in Iraq—don't get me wrong, we weren't surrounded like those guys were but we were heavily outnumbered and had to hold a key highway junction. Every one of us on the team got shot up, some more than others, though we held the cross roads until the Eighty-second arrived to reinforce us and I could get my men out. I took a mortar blast pretty close in; took several shrapnel shards in the left shoulder and arm and one little piece cut across my left temple and eye socket. I obviously couldn't see at the time—I thought it was because of so much blood—head wounds bleed like crazy—but it was actually a combination of blood and the fluid in the eyeball. . . . We've had better days. . . . Well I can't sleep now and we still have several hours to go before we land. What's there to eat on this plane?"

"The galley usually is stocked pretty well," Dani answered, recognizing Stonewall wanted to change the subject. "Let's go take a look," she continued as she walked past him. "Let's see, we've got quite a variety of fresh fruit, eggs, a few veggies, an assortment of meats and cheeses, . . . kind of looks like mostly fresh items so we can throw something together rather than any processed stuff."

"Okay, this looks pretty good; what would you like?" Jackson asked turning to Dani.

"What, you're going to cook?" she asked, looking at him somewhat surprised.

"Yeah, I can hold my own in the kitchen," he commented as he looked over the galley to see what they had for pots and pans, a coffee pot and possibly a blender. "It's about breakfast time, right? You up for an omelette and some fresh fruit?"

"Sure, I'll try one; go ahead and surprise me with what you put in it."

"Okay, just remember, you asked for it."

Twenty minutes later, Jackson had four, three egg omelettes prepared—one each for the pilot and co-pilot—of which Dani quietly took notice of his consideration for the flight crew. As for the breakfast, he completely surprised her as to the flavors he had managed to pack into a relatively simple, and often overlooked, breakfast staple.

"This is really good!" Dani exclaimed. "Where'd you learn to cook like this?"

"It's largely been trial and error. After spending so many years in the Army and eating simply for the caloric intake, I decided that when I had the chance, whatever I cooked would be packed with as much flavor as I could cram into it. It's been a lot of fun, and I've gotten to be a pretty good cook."

"I guess you have. Sure glad you didn't let me do the cooking; that would have been a huge disappointment!"

"Oh, I don't know about that. I'm sure you can handle yourself in the kitchen. But, aside from the culinary arts, what else do you do in your free time?" Jackson asked.

"I try to catch up with my sister every weekend that I can. She travels quite a bit; it seems she's on tour either in Europe or the States for weeks at a time. We both live in Tel Aviv, though she's married now."

"Sounds like you two are pretty close. Does she know what you actually do? I mean, given your family connection to General Pardo."

"We're real close but no, she has no idea what I do. She knows I'm in the Unit and that I'm a nuclear scientist for Mossad, but aside from that, she really doesn't know anything. I'm sure she suspects a lot more but that's about it. How about yourself?"

"I'm in the Special Forces as I really enjoy the lifestyle, and the challenge. I love the outdoors. One of our training missions paired our team up with one from Fort Lewis. They took us on a seventy-five mile trek through the North Cascades in northern Washington—that was a great trip. I actually took a couple weeks off to ride out there and back from Fort Campbell."

"Oh, wow; that'd be an awesome trip! I'd love to do something like that! What do you have for a bike?"

"I've got a Harley, Touring edition. Do you ride, too?"

"Not really; I mean, I've got a bike but it's just not the same here as it is in the States. When I was in Texas, I kind of got spoiled; there's just so much open space. Here in Israel, we're so small, you can cover the entire country in a single day."

"Yeah, that's what I like about back home, there's so much to see. I'm also a big sports fan and a huge Dallas Cowboys fan. I do some reading—history, the classics, and some thriller-type of novels, stuff like that."

"No family to speak of?" Dani asked.

"Two brothers and a twin sister; my folks are still in San Angelo."

"You have a twin sister? That's awesome!"

"Yeah, it was kind of neat growing up. It was pretty cool when she got accepted at the Air Force Academy and I went to West Point—two kids from the same family going to one of our Academies in the same year—that doesn't happen every day!"

"Wait a minute; backup a bit. I thought you went to Texas?"

"The academy first; did my graduate work at Texas. UT is a bit of a tradition in our family. My sister and I kind of broke that but I came back and did my graduate work there. My sister went to Johns Hopkins SAIS for her graduate work. We're pretty scattered now: I still have a home outside of Fort Campbell, even though I'm temporarily attached to the CIA; one brother's in Boston and the other's back in Texas with the folks; my sister's in the Air Force, currently stationed at Ellsworth in South Dakota—she's a B-1 pilot."

"Your sister's a B-1 pilot?!? How cool is that!?!"

"Yeah, but she's only a lieutenant colonel—I kind of remind her of that whenever I see her."

"I'm sure you do—just like any loving brother would do!"

"I'm sure she's flown over me a few times on some of our missions—don't know that for sure but we have both been deployed to the Middle East at the same time and the B-1's been key to a lot the air support we've had. I actually stopped by and saw her on the trip out to Fort Lewis."

"Oh, that's nice."

"It's always fun to catch up with her. Since we're so scattered, we don't get to see each other that much."

"So, what's your read on Rafsanjani's attacks out west?" Stonewall continued.

"I don't think he's done. Our source indicated that around 'five hundred' men were smuggled across the border. It wouldn't take that many to do what he's just done. There's more to follow, and I'd be willing to bet we'll find out pretty soon. I don't think he's one to stretch this out over weeks or months. I think he'll hit, and hit hard, over the next forty-eight hours—and if he has that many men, I would guess he has a host of targets. Think about it—you're SF, what could your team alone do in the States, and that's just twelve men. Now, imagine *forty teams!* They could wreak havoc from one coast to the other. He's not done yet, not by a long shot."

"Have to agree with you there. Problem is, there's no real way to anticipate what's next."

XV

Back on the west coast, more specifically, the Pacific Northwest, elements of Captain Sassani's second wave roamed the Columbia River Basin. The single greatest exposures up here are obvious: the multitude of dams along the Columbia and Snake rivers. The greatest of these, the Grand Coulee Dam, is monstrous. To this day, there is only one larger concrete structure in the world. The volume of water that this dam holds is literally mind boggling. If this dam were to fail, the impact it would have throughout the entire Pacific Northwest is unimaginable: Virtually all of the irrigation for the *entire* state of Washington east of the Cascades comes from this dam. Without the water from the dam, most every farmer in eastern WA would be out of business. In addition, the power plants for this dam alone generate over 6,800 megawatts of electricity—more than three *times* the amount of electricity generated from the Hoover Dam! Electricity from the Grand Coulee Dam alone is supplied to eleven western states: Arizona, California, Colorado, Idaho, Montana, Nevada, New Mexico, Oregon, Utah, Washington, and Wyoming!

Clearly, for Rafsanjani, Grand Coulee Dam posed a tempting target all by itself; putting a hole in the Grand Coulee would make a huge statement. However, this dam in particular, is exceptionally well guarded, and especially would be in the wake of the first attacks on the west coast refineries. The armed guards here are not shy about brandishing their automatic weapons and reinforcements would not be far off. A separate assault force would be needed to carry the entrance to the dam and then they would need to hold it while a tremendous amount of explosives were set within the dam. His men could easily do this, and it *would* make a huge statement to the world, but there was a better—and an easier—way and one that would have an even larger impact.

* * * * *

Thermite; sometimes called TH3.   According to chemists, thermite is a chemical composition of metal powder, fuel and a metal oxide that, when ignited, undergoes an exothermic reduction oxidation reaction. To the common lay person: thermite is a combination of rust and aluminum powder that, when properly formulated and ignited burns extremely hot—four thousand degrees hot! Add in some plaster to cast the metal powders and an igniter and a thermite "grenade" of sorts is the result. Thermite, however, is generally not considered an explosive; rather, it is an incendiary and is usually considered very stable.   Moreover, it can be made quite easily in any backyard garage in the country as all of the components are readily available at any hardware store. Since thermite burns so incredibly hot, the proper placement of a thermite "grenade", or charge, will easily cut through steel that is more than three-eighths of an inch thick.

Each of Captain Sassani's forty individual teams consisted of a one ton pickup truck, two passengers, and a full load with apple crates stocked full of thermite plaster charges, each roughly the size of a large apple; a select few others had smaller ANFO charges as well. Rafsanjani had selected thirteen dams and Captain Sassani had teams assigned to each one of these. He had tasked seven teams to the Grand Coulee Dam and six more to the Chief Joseph Dam, both of which were clear up in north central Washington. Sassani took five teams with him as he had a special target.

For Sassani, though the Grand Coulee Dam presented an awesome target, and he assigned his executive officer, Lieutenant Mahdi Akhtar, to that task, another of the dams provided its own unique opportunity, though not nearly as well known. The Dalles Dam, located at The Dalles, OR, offered a very unique target indeed, known locally as "Big Eddy." Big Eddy, officially known as the Celilo Converter Station, serves as the northern terminus of a 3,100 megawatt high voltage direct current power line; the southern terminus is located just outside of Los Angeles. This line carries enough electricity to serve close to three million households in LA and, at peak summertime capacity, provides almost half of LA's Department of Water and Power's electricity!

Sassani's team of five trucks headed up US 197 through central Oregon. He pulled his team over at a view point outside of Tygh Valley for one last review with his team. At two thirty in the morning, he knew there would be very little traffic so he wasn't too concerned about being noticed by anyone.

"As we approach The Dalles, there will be a sign indicating the route to the Celilo Converter Station. There'll be a locked gate here but no guards. Lieutenant

Nazari, Sergeant Abedini and Sergeant Kadivar will follow my team. Nazari's team and mine will park our
trucks inside the Big Eddy complex." Unlike the rest of
Sassani's team, Lieutenant Nazari and his own truck
were loaded with four 55 gallon barrel ANFO bombs—
the same type of bomb used by his compatriots to take
out the refineries.

"Abedini and Kadivar, you and your men will set
your charges amongst the towers surrounding Big Eddy.
Once you've set your charges, come back and pick us up.
Sergeant Pahlavi, you will need to continue on the highway for about a kilometer until you see Columbia View
Drive; it should be the second right after we get off of
the highway. This will take you through a small residential area and will eventually take you away from town.
As you proceed up the hill, you will see the towers—
some of these will actually be right alongside the road.
In all, there will be approximately fifty towers your three
teams should target. Work quickly and remember to use
the night vision goggles; we need to work in total dark-
ness. There shouldn't be any guards but we don't want
to raise any suspicion. At precisely 4:00 a.m., we'll blow
the two trucks at Big Eddy. Once the rest of you see this,
blow your charges as well. Sergeant Pahlavi, once you
and your team are done, meet us where you turned off of
the highway. You should be finished first as there are
only about ten towers where you are headed. Turn in
behind us once you see us pass the turnoff. Three of us
will take the freeway to make our escape; I don't want
all of us to retrace our route on the way back. Sergeant
Abedini, you and your team will retrace our route and
will follow up this attack and place your remaining
charges on the towers outside of Maupin. Any questions?"

"Okay, very good. We'll be there in about an hour."

Soap Lake, WA

"What was that?" Lieutenant Akhtar asked.

"Blowout. We must have hit something," replied Sergeant Mokri.

"I thought you checked everything before we left," the lieutenant demanded.

"I did," Mokri replied. "Sir, these are rural highways and all kinds of farm tractors and vehicles travel these roads. Let me check what happened . . . . As I suspected, sir, looks like about a 10cm spike."

"Great! How long is it going to take to change the tire? We don't have any time to lose."

"I know that, sir, but it's going to put us about twenty minutes behind schedule."

"Hossein, try and raise the others while Mokri and I change the tire. Let them know what has happened and that we are running about twenty minutes late. They are not to wait for us; we still have sixty miles to the target so if we are lucky, we might still catch up with them."

"Ah, sir, didn't Captain Sassani order total emcon? (emission's control)" Hossein replied.

"Yes he did, but at this point, I don't think it will matter. Go ahead and try to raise them."

"Will do, sir," Hossein replied, "but I don't think we'll be able to reach them. They're in the midst of this canyon that we're just entering and there's only about a twenty minute window where we'll be able to reach them as they emerge from this canyon south of Coulee City; sir, just as we get this fixed and get back on the road again, we'll be entering this canyon as they'll be coming out of it. Once we start coming out of this one, they'll be entering the Banks Lake gorge, and we won't be able to reach them there, either. Lieutenant, I think we're on our own at this point."

"Damn it. At least we have three other ANFO charges in the group. Lieutenant Darvish knows that if we get separated, he's to assign someone else to take the primary target along with him. Let's just hope he does that. Once we get back on the road, we'll take the secondary one if he has followed the plan."

"It's three twenty; let's pull off at Steamboat Rock up here and get organized; it looks like we're missing one vehicle," Lieutenant Darvish told his driver.

As Darvish's pickup pulled into the wayside, five others quickly followed. "It looks like we're missing the lieutenant," Darvish told his little group. "Sergeant Abbasi, in the lieutenant's absence, you and I will take the 500kV switchyard up by Fiddle Butte. Sergeant Lajani, you will take the secondary switchyard just north of town, as will Lieutenant Akhtar, if—or when he arrives. If he doesn't catch up with us, we hit it anyway. The rest of you know your targets; nothing has changed there. Any questions?"

Seeing none, and expecting none, Darvish continued. "It'll still take us about ten minutes to get to the target area just north of Grand Coulee so we can't wait for the lieutenant. Once you've placed your charges, come up to the switchyards to pick us up and we'll head out. We can't wait around; there's simply too many guards up there. At precisely 4:00 a.m., we'll blow everything."

4:15 a.m., Grand Coulee, WA

"Mokri, it looks like Lieutenant Darvish followed instructions and didn't wait for us. When we come to the Highway 174 junction, let's take that and proceed to the secondary target just north of town. If everything else has gone according to plan, the primary target should be destroyed and the secondary one at least damaged."

"Will do, sir" Mokri replied.

"Lieutenant, it looks like we just missed Lieutenant Darvish. Look up there, off to the left! See that bright orange glow up on the hillside!?!"

"Beautiful, Mokri, just beautiful! I don't see anything up at the secondary target just yet. We'll proceed up there as planned."

"Yes, sir, but, ah . . . how are we going to get back to the ranch?"

"Well, Mokri . . . ."

"Lieutenant! Look! I thought Captain Sassani said there wouldn't be any guards! Where did they come from?" Hossein cried out all of a sudden.

"Sir, we have an unidentified truck approaching the perimeter."

"Another one? We aren't expecting anyone from the BPA yet so don't take any chances; fire a few warning shots to get them to stop. If they don't stop, you are authorized to use all means necessary to stop that truck!"

"They're shooting at us!" Hossein cried out.

"No, those are warning shots, telling us to stop and turn back. Well, Mokri, I don't think we need to worry about how we're getting back to the ranch."

"No, sir; I don't think we do. What do I do?"

"Go ahead and stop. Hossein, grab one of the rifles; on my mark get out on the driver's side and engage as many of the guards on your side as you can; I'll do the same on this side. Mokri, as soon as we begin to fire, try and break through the guards and get to the target. If we can take out all of the guards, we'll run up and join you. Okay, Hossein? Let's go . . . now!"

"Sir, the truck has stopped. Wait, two men are getting out and . . . they're shooting at us!"

"Fire at will! Stop that truck; do not let that truck through!"

No sooner than had Lieutenant Akhtar left the pickup than a hail of gunfire erupted—from up ahead and on both sides of Mokri. He saw a couple of the guards go down, then his lieutenant fell, followed by Hossein. Almost simultaneously, a barrage of bullets hit the truck. Mokri tried to set off the charges . . . but slumped to the floor of the truck before he could hit the detonator.

Mattawa, WA

The Buchanan dairy had been in the family close to seventy years. Doug Buchanan's grandfather had moved to the Mattawa area shortly after WW II and began the dairy with one hundred cows and a full section. Doug's dad had taken over the operation in the mid-70's and began to expand the operation: irrigation rights from the Columbia Basin Irrigation System had yet to become the issue they would for his generation so his dad would expand dairy to about nine hundred head. Ten years ago Doug took over the dairy and built it up to a herd of 4,500 dairy cows. However, the world had become a drastically different place than his father had known: Environmentalists posed a serious problem both for maintaining long established water rights as well as the increasingly restrictive pollution controls they managed to get through the EPA. One of his neighbors actually had been sued by the EPA, costing him over fifty thousand dollars just in attorney's fees—and it was still tied up in court! Doug knew his turn was next and now he had no funds available to defend himself as milk prices had suddenly dropped to half of what they had been only a few years ago. He had already begun to lay off much of his staff as he simply could not afford to keep them on board; some had been replaced with cheaper, less experienced workers. If things kept up, he knew he'd have to downsize his operation, if not completely sell out.

Doug's alarm went off at three thirty these days as he was now taking the place of one of the workers he had to let go. This morning he had seen a pair of headlights go roaring past their place a little before four o'clock in the morning. Immediately after that, he had seen several small, extremely bright flashes out in the distance near the Priest Rapids Dam, followed very quickly by the power going out. He didn't know what had happened—there was no explosion—but there obviously could have been some arcing amongst the power lines; that had happened before but he had never lost power in those instances. His generators hadn't kicked on, either, as he expected they would. Upon checking them out, the fuel tank for the generators was empty—his new farm hand hadn't informed him that they had been refueling the equipment from the generator tank as the main diesel tank had been emptied and no one let him know. He had a real problem—with 4,500 cows, he could not afford for the power to be out for more than an hour. His dairy milked around the clock; if the cows couldn't be milked, he'd really be hurting. If the power didn't come on soon, he'd have to give the Wilco Coop a call as soon as they opened to have them deliver a load of diesel. He had no idea that neither would be coming any time soon.

Wilmington, CA

"Ah, sir," one of Scott's firefighters said, trying to get his attention.

"Yeah, what is it?"

"We seem to have lost water pressure at about half of the fire hydrants."

"What? Did some of the water lines rupture in all of this as well?"

"We don't think so. We still have water in the pipes, just no pressure. It seems that all of the hydrants west of Road 10 have lost water pressure—and this is where the tank farm is located. We don't have any reports of ruptures in the water line anywhere. We've been working with Conoco's staff and they can't figure it out either. We have full pressure for the refinery itself, and we'll get that under control relatively soon, but the fires in the tank farm will be burning unchecked. We're purely defensive anyway and we may simply have to let those fires burn themselves out—but that's a ton of gasoline and diesel left to burn."

"Okay, I'll let Division know and see if they know anything about this."

Ten minutes later, Scott called his battalion officers in to his command post.

"It seems a major power line coming out of Oregon has been severed leaving almost half of LA without power. This includes about a third of the pumping stations for the water district. Folks up at Carson and El Segundo are reporting similar issues with a loss of water pressure. We'll have to make do and string hoses as best we can. Tell your men they are not to take any unnecessary chances. At this point, we are simply looking at property values. I don't want to add the loss of life to this disaster. This isn't over by a long shot, but we will get through it."

By 4:10 a.m., on the morning of the third day since the Israeli attack on his country's nuclear facilities, Rafsanjani's second wave had been delivered. All forty of Captain Sassani's teams had delivered as expected. The thermite charges, properly fixed on two legs—and in a few cases, just one leg—of a power-line tower proved more than capable of cutting through the steel legs of the towers. In addition, in almost every case, as one tower collapsed, the neighboring towers collapsed simply due to the weight of the power lines from the collapsed tower. When Sassani's teams had completed their mission, more than one thousand power-line towers had collapsed along each of the thirteen targeted dams on the Columbia and Snake rivers. Big Eddy and the 500kV switchyard at the Grand Coulee Dam had been destroyed as well. Rafsanjani's one-two punch had been delivered: The west coast of the United States was out of gas and in the dark!

XVI

32,000' Above Newfoundland

"Ah, sir, we have another call for you, Colonel Jackson."

"Okay, patch it through."

"Stonewall, here," Jackson said into the phone, this time on speaker.

"Tom . . . we've got a problem," Jim told him.

Jackson knew this was serious; he'd known Jim Carmichael for years. He never used his first name unless something was seriously wrong. "What's up? This sounds serious."

"It is. A couple hours after the refineries were hit we began to receive reports of power outages throughout the West. Mind you, it's still four thirty in the morning out there so it's still dark on the west coast. However, we're hearing of outages from Seattle, to Denver, clear down to Phoenix and Los Angeles. We're not exactly sure what is happening out there but clearly, we are under attack and we have no idea what else to expect. How many men did you say were thought to be smuggled across the border?"

"We never received a firm number. Our contact in Israel mentioned something on the order of five hundred; we initially thought that to be an exaggeration, and it still might be, but it sounds like the Iranians managed to get in at least two companies of their Quds Force, possibly an understrength battalion. I'll have Dani give Ben a call as soon as we hang up to see if we can't nail down a few more details."

"That's a lot of men. You were in the Special Forces, how much damage could you do with an understrength battalion?"

"Dani and I were just talking about that. At five hundred men, that'd be more than forty Special Forces A teams . . . and we could do a lot of damage," Jackson replied. "Do we know of the extent of the damage to these refineries?"

"We don't have a complete accounting of the damage—it's still very early in the morning on the west coast—but it sounds like eleven large refineries in California and two more in Washington were hit."

"Okay, so if they hit thirteen of the refineries out west, I'd want at least two men per truck—and I doubt these were suicide missions so they'd need someone to pick them up, say half again as many or maybe a few more, . . . say forty people or so involved in the attack plus there'd be a few more back where they came from, so I'd plan on at least fifty men involved in just the refinery attacks. As for the attacks on the electrical grid, I'd really need more information as to what all was hit but I'm sure they used twice that amount in the second attack. I'd still have men left over for another series of attacks—that is if I was planning this."

"That's kind of what I thought," replied Carmichael.

"Well, sir, given the amount of men supposedly smuggled in, and if properly trained, they could do a lot of damage. Have we been able to pick up any one of these guys?"

"No, we haven't. We know some died in the attacks on the refineries. There's been a report of a small firefight up at Grand Coulee: two guards were seriously wounded and three attackers were killed. I believe we have their truck but it's still too early out there to confirm anything at this point. Other than that, my guess is that everyone else in the second series of attacks got clean away. At this point, we believe they've all returned to where they came from but as far as we are concerned, they might as well have evaporated into thin air."

"Well, sir, we are still a few hours out of Andrews. We can stop and then compare notes or we can just simply continue on to Texas; this 'six-fifty' can fly practically halfway around the world without refueling. Once there, we'll begin snooping around."

"No, go straight through to Fort Bliss. Once you get there, head straight to the local FBI office. By the time you get there, I'll have met with the president and the rest of the national security staff in addition to the director of the FBI, Homeland Security, and the attorney general. The director will have briefed the local SAC about your arrival. Right now, you and Dani know more about who, and what, we are up against than anyone. Also, if Dani doesn't have any side arms on that plane, make sure you both pick up a couple from the FBI. Let me know if they give you any grief about this; you and Dani are better trained than any of the FBI agents you'll meet. Let me know if you encounter any resistance of any kind. Don't worry about being subtle; there is no higher priority to this administration right now. The same goes for you, too, Dani. You can offer a unique perspective to this."

"Yes, sir; thank you, but we have a closet full on board. We'll be fine."

"Don't mention it; just get these guys."

"Ah, Jim, are you really thinking that this is a criminal matter?"

"Of course not, we're under attack; that's why I mentioned that if the FBI gives Dani any grief about carrying a side-arm, let me know. It's just that the FBI's the greatest investigative organization in the world—they should be able to give us a good start on this."

"Okay, Dani, let's get Ben on the horn; we need to see where he is at regarding our friend from Beirut. We need a ton of solid information and right now, everything we have is pretty slim. We need the location of that tunnel and any other details he might have for us. Put him on speaker once you have him."

"Ben; Arielle & Stonewall. Have you heard of what's going on in the US?"

"No, we've been a little busy here; we have some more information for you. What's going on in the States?"

"We don't have a lot of details on this but it sounds like Rafsanjani took out several large oil refineries in California; we're not sure of all the damage but it doesn't sound good. Then, a couple hours or so later, several cities out west began reporting widespread power outages. We haven't heard any details on this but it would seem the US is under attack."

"Ho-ly . . ."

"Yeah," replied Dani. "We need as much information from this guy as you can get to us. You said you've learned a few things—what do you have?"

"Well, it sounds like the entrance to the tunnel they've been using is across the street from a large parking lot on the UTEP campus," that is the University of Texas, El Paso. "I don't have a street address but the tunnel supposedly exits in the basement of a house very close to the parking lot located between W. Shuster Avenue & Heisig Avenue. These guys supposedly leave a car or pickup in the UTEP parking lot on a routine basis. If you're looking for someone coming out of the tunnel, I'd check out the parking lot as well and see if there's been a vehicle sitting there for a while."

"Ben, Stonewall here; just how reliable is this information?"

"Our guy is somehow connected to the Sinaloa cartel over there—we're still trying to exactly pin down his connection to them but it seems that someone from Iranian Intelligence has been working with both the Sinaloa and the Medellin Cartels—to what end, our guy doesn't know. He also doesn't know exactly how many men were smuggled into the US via this tunnel system, but he's guessing at least 250. Based on what Arielle is saying, if they've been as busy as it sounds, and if I were running this operation, I'd want at least fifty guys for the refinery portion of this operation alone. Who knows what else they've been up to but it sounds like they've been busy."

"Okay; that information on the tunnel helps a lot. We'll get the Feds to stake out that neighborhood right away; it's not all that big of an area so if they are still using it, we should be able to find it. Give either Dani or me a call should you come up with anything else. Really appreciate this, Ben. Thanks a lot!"

"Dani, let's get Jim back on the line one more time."

"Sure; just a second. Mr. Carmichael, this is Dani. Stonewall's here with me. We appear to have some pretty solid information on where these guys entered the States."

"Jim, we just spoke to Dani's CO. It seems that a tunnel from Juarez exits in the basement of a house in an El Paso neighborhood relatively close to the UTEP campus. A vehicle is often left in a large parking lot on the UTEP campus relatively close to W. Shuster and Heisig Avenues for anyone coming through. We don't have an address but given the reported proximity of the house to this parking lot, it shouldn't be that difficult to find if anyone else comes through here. Since they've already started their operations, we kind of have to figure that they felt they had enough men already over here. However, given the complexities of traveling half way around the world, there had to be some challenges. Maybe we can get lucky and pick up on someone who had some complications with their itinerary. They're not going to want to raise any suspicions anywhere so I would guess they made travel arrangements all over the globe. We need to get some people over there stake out that neighborhood and then I'd alert the UTEP security guys and see if they have any cameras on their parking lot. If so, this could really help us."

"Okay, good job guys. Dani, thanks for getting back to me right away. I'll let Homeland Security know as well as the FBI office in El Paso and relay this to them. I'll let them know you'll be there in a few hours as well. I'm actually heading to the White House as we speak. I should be there in just a few minutes. Oh, and that pickup truck we recovered up at Grand Coulee, my sources are telling me it's registered to a ranch in Eastern Oregon; don't think Bob Harmon wants that out yet but that's the word I'm getting. Do you have anything else I can relay to the NSC staff?"

"Not at this point. If we hear of anything, who should we contact? I assume Felix will be in the same meeting."

"Yeah, Felix will be in this meeting as well. Send anything you have to my assistant—she's cleared for anything you might find and if it's urgent, she knows how to get ahold of either of us."

The White House Situation Room

"Okay, people, talk to me. What's going on?" President Barre demanded.

"*One thousand towers* are down?!? How in the *hell* did they do this?"

"Well, sir," interrupted Carmichael, "since we met yesterday noon, we've learned that the Iranian's attempt to close the Strait of Hormuz was more or less a diversion from their real retaliation plans. We suspected as much at the time, but didn't have anything at all to go on; it was just a hunch. After our meeting yesterday, Colonel Jackson and his Mossad teammates had a chance to debrief Dr. Bagheri to see if he could offer any insight into how the Iranians might retaliate. All he could offer was that something very secret was in the works and at one point, he overheard a conversation between Said Jalili and a Colonel Ashkan Rafsanjani, who is an ambitious—and very capable—Quds Force officer and, from what I understand, the operations officer for their Supreme National Security Council, about using a series of tunnels to gain access somewhere for a very secret operation. Our—that is the Agency's as well as Mossad's—initial belief was that this referred to the complex series of tunnels the Israelis found in Gaza from their latest incursion there. Then, early last evening, we learned from Colonel Jackson's teammates that one of Mossad's operatives in Beirut heard that a couple 'Arab-types' had contacted both the Medellin and the Sinaloa cartels about smuggling some five hundred troops into the United States via a tunnel system from Juarez to El Paso. I let Bob know about this right away but at that point all we really knew we had was an entrance location and a rough estimate as to the number of soldiers who might have infiltrated across the border."

"Wait a minute," demanded Fleming, "you knew we had a situation like this and you didn't tell us?!?"

"Tom, I told Bob; he *is* the secretary for homeland security. I suggested we alert the Customs Border Patrol and the DEA to see if they might have any information on this but I let Bob run with this from here. Realize, we only learned of this about twelve hours ago."

"What all did we tell the Border Patrol and the DEA?" Fleming demanded. "Did we let them know that we might have as many as *five hundred Iranians* that might be running around this country?"

"Tom," Harmon replied, "I told both the Border Patrol and the DEA that we had just learned of a tunnel that the Sinaloa cartel might be using to smuggle illegal immigrants into the country from Juarez to El Paso. I didn't tell them anything about any Iranians or even how many might have been smuggled in here. I thought you might want to keep a tight lid on this."

"Damn right, we do," Fleming added. "The minute this gets out, this administration is over. The Republicans have been screaming for increased border security and the minute they learn that five hundred Iranian soldiers came over the border, there'll be hell to pay."

"Excuse me," interrupted Felix Jones, "but this country just received a blow more serious than what hit us on September 11th, and you're more worried about reelection? I realize we don't have near the fatalities we had then, but this will be a far more serious situation. If you haven't realized it yet, the entire state of California—which boasts the eighth largest economy *in the world!*—is out of gas and in the dark you imbecile! Moreover, the five hundred or so that obviously got through are from their Quds Force, not their Army—these guys are fanatics."

"You don't need to lecture me, *Dr.* Jones," Fleming said acidly. "I know of California's importance, but they'll get through this. We have other refineries and we can ship gasoline to them."

"Tom," Felix continued, "California's refining capacity has been cut by more than seventy-five percent and there are only three pipelines bringing gasoline into the entire state of California—three!! Like I just said, this attack is going to have repercussions far beyond the initial attacks. There will be a ripple effect throughout the economy: there'll be a spike in unemployment, food prices are going to soar immediately and we'll have general inflation for at least a couple of years, not to mention that energy prices are going to sky rocket! We'll be lucky if we only have a serious recession. We've been hit, and hit hard. The question is not how do we seek to preserve this administration—that's over and done with. The questions are: where are these guys, are they going to hit us again, and how are we going to respond to this?"

After a very uncomfortable, pregnant pause, President Barre began, "Okay, now that Felix has ignominiously written the epitaph for my administration, do we know anything else?"

"Mr. President, we managed to stop one of the attackers," Secretary Harmon added. "Up at Grand Coulee, it seems one of the attackers got separated from the rest of his team. By the time this one got to its target, we already had a well-armed contingent guarding the electrical switchyard, presumably the intended target. A short, but intense, firefight erupted leaving two of the guards seriously wounded and killing all three of the attackers—but we have their pickup. I haven't learned if we've been able to find out where—and to who—this vehicle is registered. It is still relatively early out there—not to mention, early in the investigation—but as soon as we know something, I'll pass it along."

"We haven't learned anything yet from this incident?" the President demanded.

"Sir, this happened a little after four this morning. There were three men in this truck and it was loaded with three ANFO barrel/bombs.   Two men got out of the truck and immediately fired upon the guards. They returned fire; with more favorable results. It seems the guards were fortunate enough to kill the driver before he could detonate the bomb; had it detonated, it would have destroyed the entire switchyard and killed all of the guards up there. We've called in a bomb squad from Spokane to defuse this."

"Were we able to find or capture any of these attackers anywhere else?"

"No, sir. They have pretty much evaporated into thin air. As soon as we can track down the registration of this pickup, we'll know a lot more provided it's not stolen or something along those lines."

"Mr. President, Colonel Jackson is on his way to El Paso, along with his Mossad teammate, Danielle Yaniv," Carmichael interjected. "As I said, we believe we know the man responsible for this is Colonel Ashkan Rafsanjani. We believe he is working at the express direction of Said Jalili, the secretary of their Supreme National Security Council.   As I mentioned earlier, Dr. Bagheri stated that he overheard Jalili and Colonel Rafsanjani discussing a plan involving a tunnel operation. Colonel Rafsanjani has been a frequent visitor to Beirut and the Beqaa Valley and we believe he was one of the two 'Arab-types' who met with the Sinaloa cartel in Mexico. Since Jackson knows Rafsanjani the best, I told both him and Miss Yaniv to get to El Paso as fast as they could. I presume the FBI, initially, will be in charge of this so I told them to hook up with the FBI's SAC as soon as they arrive."

"Okay, very good, since the way it sounds, Colonel Jackson is the only one who seems to have any kind of an idea as to what is really going on," replied President Barre.

XVII

The Pentagon

"Axe, are any of the Rangers at home up at Fort Lewis or are they all either deployed or out training somewhere?" Carmichael asked Axelsson.

"I think we have two Companies at home. I believe the rest of the battalion is currently in Afghanistan or on their way home," replied General Kaufman for Axe. "Why, what are you thinking?"

"Back in the Situation Room, Bob just mentioned that we have the pickup truck of that last group of attackers up at Grand Coulee, right? From what I understand—from my own sources, mind you—it sounds like it's registered to a ranch outside of Riverside, OR. We still don't know who exactly owns the ranch but this is not a criminal act; this bears all the hallmarks of a state sponsored attack—this isn't terrorism. I'd at least put one of the Ranger companies on alert for possible action at this ranch. I'd also whistle up a drone out of Creech," referring to Creech Air Force Base out of Las Vegas, "and get it on station just as soon as we can pinpoint the location of this ranch."

"You realize the attorney general is going to go ballistic over this, don't you?" Axelsson added, more of a statement than a question. "You know he's going to

claim you're shredding the Constitution. Since this oc-
curred on American soil, he's going to want the FBI to
take the lead on *all* of this—including raiding the ranch."

"I don't care what he thinks or says. He's another of
the 'useful idiots' of this administration. We are under
attack by a foreign government—not by a bunch of organized criminals. The sooner we can figure out what's
going on, the sooner we can hit back against these guys.
The FBI is the best investigative body in the world, but
we aren't out to arrest these guys. Aerial surveillance
will be a job for the Air Force—the FBI simply cannot
compete with either the Predators or the Global Hawks;
taking them down will be a job for the Rangers."

"Are you sure about this ranch? All Bob had to say
was that it was still too early to learn anything about
this."

"Axe, Bob knows a lot more than he let us all know
in there. I'm not exactly sure just who owns the ranch
but I'd be willing to bet it's owned by some shell corporation or something like that."

"Okay; I'll alert the Rangers and get a drone on station out there." Turning to Kaufman,   "General, how
soon can we get a Predator up there?"

"It'll take a little time and we'll probably base it out
of Mountain Home as this ranch is right at the limit of
the Predator's range."

"How long do you think it'll take to get it on station?"

"Give it four hours or so to get to Mountain Home,
an hour on the ground to refuel and then maybe an hour
to get on station, so we're talking about six hours, maybe
less" replied Kaufman.

"Okay, that'll put it about noon, twelve thirty local
time; mid-afternoon out here. By then, we should know
more about this ranch in Oregon. Stonewall will have
been in El Paso for a few hours as well; hopefully, we'll

have a little more to go on by then. Tell the boys at Creech to step on it."

Robert F. Kennedy Department of Justice Building

"Bob, I've just learned where this pickup out at Grand Coulee is registered." Attorney General Jorge Sanchez said over the phone to Homeland Secretary Harmon. "Turns out it's registered to a corporation named C & D Enterprises. This corporation owns a large ranch outside of Riverside, Oregon, clear in the southeastern part of the state. I've never been out there but it looks pretty remote."

"Do we know anything else about this ranch? The corporate officers, board members, stuff like that?"

"Not much else; C & D Enterprises, Inc., owns the place but the registered agent is listed as Lozano & Ibarra, LLP, out of San Francisco; sounds like a law firm out there. They didn't even list an individual."

"What about the ranch itself?"

"Nothing out of the ordinary, it would seem. It looks like it's composed of twenty-three thousand acres with another forty-five thousand acres under lease in both Oregon and Nevada for cattle grazing—something pretty common out there. They have a rather large number of vehicles registered to the ranch, or so it would seem, but given the extent of its operation, it easily avoided any suspicion. I've spoken with the Special Agent in Charge (SAC) of our Boise FBI field office and ordered him to get a drone out there to do some immediate surveillance but that's going take some time—it's not even 6:00 a.m. out there yet."

"Just how long are we talking?" Harmon demanded. "We need all the information we can get on this ranch immediately!"

"Bob, this is extreme southeastern Oregon; it's a four hour drive from the Boise office and they don't have any large drones that can fly from Boise. I expect it'll be at least five to six hours before we'll know anything more substantial about this ranch."

"That's the best we can do?!?"

"For right now, yes, it is. Whoever set this up knew what they were doing—this place is pretty remote. I've looked at a few satellite images of the general area—and it doesn't look like there's a lot of cover for the FBI field team once they get there either. They'll probably end up working out of Burns, Oregon, to maintain any semblance of normalcy."

"Great; just great!" Harmon reacted sarcastically. "So, we're talking mid-afternoon, *at the earliest*, before we know anything."

"I'm afraid we are. As soon as I hear from them, I'll let you know."

"Okay, I'll schedule a meeting with Tom and the president for four o'clock this afternoon; think that will give them enough time? We'll brief them on what we know at that point."

"That should work. And like I said, if I learn of anything sooner, I'll let you know."

Joint Base Lewis-McChord

"Captain Fairchild, c'mon in," announced Lieutenant Colonel Jacobson, commanding officer of the second Ranger battalion, as he saw his young captain approaching his office. "You and your men getting back into the swing of things?"

"They're getting there. It usually takes a few days to assimilate back into society; Afghanistan is a completely foreign country in more ways than one, sir. We've only been back about forty-eight hours. What's up?"

"Sorry to do this to you, and to drag you into the office at five thirty in the morning, especially when you haven't even been home for two full days yet, but I've got to put your company on alert."

"What?!? Third battalion's still on alert! Alpha and Charlie companies haven't even returned yet and we're going back out? Sir, I heard the news on the way in but we're in no shape to deploy."

"Fairchild, I know that. This is a little different. You're not deploying overseas, though I anticipate that this could very well be a combat jump—in Oregon!"

"What!?!"

"The chairman of the Joint Chiefs called about twenty minutes ago. Not sure what all you've heard about what's going on in California and up here in the Northwest but—someone pretty much lit up the entire west coast. Don't look for a press conference on this anytime soon but this is as crazy as it gets: It sounds like the Iranians have smuggled a couple companies of their Quds Force over the Mexican border. One of the trucks involved in an attack up at Grand Coulee was registered to a ranch outside of Riverside, Oregon. That's all we know at this point. The CIA's got a lead on their suspected entrance point down in El Paso and they have a combined CIA/Mossad team headed there now."

"Mossad's involved in this, too? What the hell's going on?"

"Captain, at this point, you know as much as I do. The Air Force will be getting a Predator up over this ranch in a few hours. Even though they're based out of Vegas, it's still a long way to this ranch. The Predator's going to stop off at Mountain Home and then head out to find this ranch. Worst case scenario, we'll need to be ready for kickoff around eleven thirty; that gives us about six hours. How soon can Bravo company be ready to jump?"

"We'll be ready sir. They won't need much for motivation; not for this. But, ah, sir, with the Air Force flying a Predator over Oregon, my Ranger team prepping for a *combat* jump on an Oregon ranch, and the Agency and Mossad involved in El Paso, what's the FBI doing in all of this? I mean, does Homeland Security know about any of this?"

"That, Captain Fairchild, is a very good question. However, for our sake, we are essentially considering this as an armed invasion of the United States by a hostile country. As such, this is a matter for the US military, and not a criminal one."

"Very well; I'll meet up with you in a few hours, sir. I need to get to work."

Biggs Army Airfield, El Paso, TX

"Colonel Jackson, Special Agent Tom Norris, FBI. I'm the SAC here in El Paso. Nice to meet you."

"Tom, nice to meet you, too. This is Danielle Yaniv. She's with the Israeli government," Jackson added, introducing Dani.

"Tom, call me Dani."

"The Israeli government??" Norris asked rather suspiciously. "The Director indicated you'd both be with the Agency—what do the Israelis have to do with this?"

"Just what all did Youngblood tell you?" Jackson asked.

"He mentioned that the current thinking blames the Iranians for everything on the west coast. He mentioned that we've learned of a tunnel under the border over by the UTEP campus where a few Iranians might have been smuggled into the country. We've had a few tunnels under surveillance but we didn't know of one in this area. I've had several agents scrounging around the neighborhood of this tunnel watching for anyone who doesn't fit in ever since we first got word of this tunnel. That's about it. So, can either of you two tell me just what's going on?"

"We've had the Iranian nuclear program under extremely close scrutiny for some time," Dani began. "A few days ago, we received word that they were within weeks, say a month and a half, of obtaining a nuclear weapon—so our Air Force took out the major components of their program, what, a couple days ago?" She added, looking at Stonewall. "These days are running together now. Anyway, we expected Iran to respond by trying to close the Strait of Hormuz and possibly turn Hezbollah loose on us in northern Israel. They tried closing the strait but your navy beat them back pretty good. Early . . . this morning, I guess it was, we learned that the US is the actual target of the retaliation. Unfortunately, not in time to do anything to stop these attacks."

"So, even though there've been the two attacks, are you thinking there's more to happen?"

"We don't know." Jackson responded. "You see, we don't know how many men they managed to smuggle in through this tunnel. At this point, we know precious little of their operation."

"My CO has a contact who works in Beirut who mentioned that as many as five hundred of their Quds Force members were to be smuggled in. Given the large number and the fact that they traveled literally half way around the world, we're hoping that some of these guys either had some issues getting here or they simply had enough men to initiate their attacks and didn't wait for the rest of their force to arrive."

"Your CO, huh? So much for simply working for the 'Israeli Government'," Norris added sarcastically.

"It works," Dani shrugged. "The pair we believe to be in charge of this are Said Jalili, the Director of Iran's Supreme National Security Council, and Colonel Ashkan Rafsanjani, effectively Jalili's Operations officer. Both of them are experts in asymmetrical warfare. They've been the architects of both Hezbollah's and Hamas' guerrilla attacks on us in both northern and southern Israel. Jalili spent much of the '70s and '80s with the Republican Guards perfecting his tradecraft in Beirut and the Beqaa Valley. After we eradicated the PLO from southern Lebanon, Jalili raised up Hezbollah, practically all by himself. Rafsanjani, seemingly following in his Master's footsteps, has been largely single handedly responsible for the resurgence of both Hezbollah and Hamas and in training them in guerrilla warfare and their various terrorist atrocities. They've learned from the best."

"We now believe, these two have turned their attention to the United States," Jackson continued the narrative. "Several years ago, we believe Rafsanjani and one of his aides met with both the Medellin and the Sinaloa cartels looking for help to smuggle upwards of a battalion of their Quds Force into the country"

"Damn. . . ." was all Norris could say.

*   *   *   *   *

Major Zarin had had a terrible time getting to what was to be his post at Marathon, Texas. His flight to Juarez from Mexico City was just now touching down—after more than thirty-six hours of traveling, Zarin had lost track of what day it was, let alone what time it was. Irritable only began to describe his mood. Given the lengthy process it took him to get to Juarez, he was sure Colonel Rafsanjani had initiated at least the first two stages of their operation. He'd been in the air so long and hadn't been able to check any emails he might have received. He really hoped that he could still be in on the last stage but it wouldn't surprise him if his men had left without him. He knew they were well trained and he, himself, had advised them that if they had received the word to go, they were not supposed to wait for him. Nevertheless, he really wanted to be a part of the final stage that would put a dagger in the heart of the Great Satan.

Zarin had been traveling light with nothing more than a slightly oversized backpack. He and his aid grabbed a taxi at the airport and headed towards their contact with the Sinaloa cartel. He didn't know who he was to meet but he knew the location; a small group of homes and outbuildings on the north side of the Boulevard Ingeniero Bernardo Norzagaray opposite UTEP. From one of the outbuildings on the premises, a tunnel ran to a dwelling in a residential neighborhood directly across the street from a huge parking lot on the UTEP campus. The Marathon ranch routinely kept a car or pickup in the parking lot; the key was in a small magnet box underneath the rear fender.

As Zarin exited the tunnel in the basement of the old house, he couldn't believe his fortune. He had made it into the United States! He couldn't believe he was finally about to embark on the mission to drive a stake into the heart of the Great Satan. Even if his men had left without him, he was extremely proud to have been a part of this. He was more than a little fatigued at traveling for more than thirty-six straight hours, and he still seethed in anger at the situation in Nairobi that left him way behind schedule and whom he blamed for his incredible tardiness in getting to his assigned location. He still believed these mechanics needed to be taken out and shot; such incredible incompetence would not be tolerated in the Quds. Nevertheless, he had made it. Now, he needed to find the pickup truck that had been left for him, travel for another four hours to reach the ranch at Marathon—and he thoroughly detested the thought of that—and he'd be there.

"Well, looky there; we have two guys coming out of that house over there, roughly in the middle of the block, heading over to the UTEP parking lot. They sure don't look like a couple of Latinos; I bet we've got a couple of your Iranian friends, colonel," said Special Agent Tom Norris.

"I bet we do! Your guys getting some pictures of these two?" Jackson asked rhetorically, knowing full well they were. "Have them send the pics to Dani. I'd like her to send them back to her folks and see if one of us can't ID either of these two through facial recognition imagery. If these guys really are Iranian, as everyone suspects, she'll probably be able to get a hit on them before we can."

"Jackson, we can do that, if these guys are terrorists, like Al Qaeda or even the recent Khorasan Group, we'll have them in our database."

"Tom, that's just it," interrupted Dani. "This isn't a terrorist attack. This is a meticulously planned and well organized attack, by a foreign government. If these guys are Quds, you may not have them in your database, but I'd be willing to bet that we do."

"I understand that, but if your two Iranian leaders have farmed out these attacks to another group, we might have them," replied Tom.

Turning to Dani, and virtually ignoring Norris, Jackson asked, "How soon do you think Ben could have something on these guys?"

"He'll get on this as soon as I get it to him; if they're in our system, and we have most of the Quds Force leadership in our system, clear down to their junior officers—if that's who this is, he'll find 'em. He should have them within the hour, probably sooner."

"Great, let's get right on it; let Ben know what to expect."

"What do we have for assets to follow these guys?" Jackson asked Tom, noting that the two individuals had found a club-cab pickup and had started to make their way out of the parking lot.

"We have four cars here and we have a drone in the sky that will follow them if they end up leaving town. We'll have several eyes on them and they won't have a clue. In addition, we have an assault team on standby should we need them. We're covered," responded Norris.

"Okay, Dani and I will stay with you."

"Not a problem; you obviously have some pretty important friends. We'll have the lead on this but you'll have access to whatever, or whoever, you want."

"Tom, I could care less about the turf issues with this; however, you have some legal issues with which you have to comply; I don't. If we need to get some answers, Dani and I will get them, if you can't."

"Well, I hope it doesn't come to that, but . . . given the circumstances, I can't argue with you on that point."

"Not a problem; let's get going."

"Hey, Jim, what's up?" Jackson said answering his phone, noticing Carmichael's name on the screen.

"I'll be meeting with the president in the next few minutes and wanted to see if you've had a chance to learn anything new."

"We found a couple guys exiting the tunnel in El Paso and Dani has already forwarded their pics to Ben; she's thinking he'll be getting back to us within the hour as to who these guys are. Right now, we're following them through El Paso and look to be heading east on I-10. We'll let you know when we learn something new. What's the latest on everything else?"

"Every one of the refineries they hit were seriously damaged; they'll be out of commission for some time, months at the earliest. As for the power outages, it seems that they hit much of the power line network at its source up in Washington and Oregon. None of the dams were damaged, or even targeted, the way it seems. Rather, they hit the power lines as they leave each of the dams along the Columbia and Snake rivers. They also hit two big relay stations: one is the terminus for a 3,100 mega-watt direct current line to Los Angeles and the other is a 500kV switchyard up at Grand Coulee. In addition, they hit several of the lines coming off of the various wind farms up there as well. We should be able to get these towers up relatively quickly but combined with the hit on the refineries, the West has taken a severe hit. The impact on our economy will be monstrous. California refines virtually all of its own gasoline and diesel fuel; in fact, there are only three pipelines from Texas to the entire state of California. The California economy is going to crash; there's simply no escaping it. Even if California relaxes its emission requirements, we simply do not have the capacity to get the fuel out there that the state needs. In the Pacific Northwest, the issue is compounded by the loss of electricity. All of California gets less than ten percent of its electricity from the northwest—but LA gets close to half of it from this DC line.

Oregon and Washington, though, get a huge amount of their electricity from the Columbia Basin; add to this the two refineries that were hit in Washington and the Pacific Northwest's economy, likewise, is going to crash."

"We managed to stop one of the attackers up at Grand Coulee. The guards up there killed all three of them before they could detonate their truck bomb. The pickup is registered to a ranch in Riverside, Oregon—way out in extreme southeastern Oregon—under the name of C & D Enterprises, Inc. We have a Predator monitoring the ranch right now—and it's like a beehive of activity on that ranch. There must be fifty people out there, and a few more have trickled in over the past hour or so. This place is incredibly remote, and it's like an armed camp out there. Axe has placed a company of Rangers up at Fort Lewis on alert. The FBI's going to want the lead on this but these guys are not criminals; this is a job for the Rangers. In the meantime, we're simply watching it to see what else develops. If Dani learns who those two are who you're following, give my assistant a call; she's cleared for most everything and will get word to me."

"Okay, will do; Dani seemed pretty confident that Ben would be able to ID these guys. If we find out who they are, we'll call in right away."

"We just crossed under Joe Battle Boulevard—the last main El Paso exit—any idea as to where these two might be going? It looks like this could be a long drive," Norris asked Jackson.

"Tom, we have no idea. Word is that they have a ranch up in eastern Oregon, so they could be headed to another one out here in west Texas. We simply do not know anything about what these guys are doing or anything about their operation. We need to make sure that drone will be able to follow these guys until they reach their destination, wherever that it is."

"Okay, I'll have our guys peel off here and at Socorro so we don't raise too much suspicion if they've been checking to see if they have a tail. We'll keep going and get off at Fabens and let the drone take over if they don't get off as well. That drone can stay aloft for hours and we've got a FLIR camera on it; they're not going anywhere—we won't lose them even if they drive all night."

XVIII

Whitehouse Situation Room

"Okay, folks, what do we know?" President Barre asked his advisers.

"Mr. President," Bob Harmon began, "the pickup truck we recovered up at Grand Coulee is registered to a cattle ranch outside of Riverside, OR. This place is about four hours southwest of Boise. The ranch is owned by corporation named C & D Enterprises. The actual contact for the corporation seems to be a law firm out of San Francisco. The corporate officers and board of directors remains a mystery."

"Sir," Attorney General Jorge Sanchez interrupted, "C & D Enterprises purchased this ranch through the law firm of Lozano & Ibarra, LLP, in 2009; this is the same law firm Bob just mentioned as contact for the ranch owner. We've been able to subpoena the ranch's tax records for every year since then; they are all signed by a partner of the law firm of Lozano & Ibarra. In addition, we've received copies of the lease agreements for the BLM land the ranch leases in NV; again, it's signed by a partner with Lozano & Ibarra. This is a sizable ranch with several thousand acres in OR and NV. The pickup we've recovered is just one of many that are registered to the ranch. Our FBI office in San Francisco has picked up this partner for questioning but we haven't learned anything from him—attorney client privilege. The Special Agent in Charge of the FBI's Boise field office has set up a temporary headquarters in Burns, OR, and is working on getting a warrant to put a drone up over this ranch to see what all we are up against."

"Mr. President," Jim Carmichael began, "we've already put a Predator up over the ranch; there're three main building sites that currently show quite a bit of activity and there're two others that appear to be vacant at present."

"Wait a minute," Sanchez blurted out. "You've put up a Predator over this place? The CIA has no authority here!"

"Jim didn't put it there, Jorge, I did." Axelsson interjected. "This is not a terrorist attack; it's too sophisticated for a terrorist group, even Al Qaeda or ISIS. We've been attacked by another country—I think that's pretty obvious."

"Mr. President, this is a clear violation of the Constitution and we cannot allow this. This ranch is a legal US corporation and entitled to all the protection of any other US entity. We cannot simply spy on this place without a warrant. Placing a Predator over the ranch to spy on the legal workings of the ranch represents a clear violation of the right to protection of an 'unreasonable search and seizure' clearly expressed in the fourth amendment."

"Mr. President, I've also placed a company of the second battalion, Seventy-fifth Ranger Regiment up at Fort Lewis on alert as well," added Axelsson.

"You what?!?" exclaimed both Sanchez and Bob Harmon in unison.

"Excuse me!?!" Tom Fleming added.

"Mr. President, this is going too far," continued Harmon.

"Sir, I can have 150 Rangers on that ranch in an hour and a half," added General Kaufman, totally ignoring

Secretary Harmon. "Given everything we know so far, this is a job for the military, not law enforcement. We are under attack, and the sooner we can hit back, the better. In addition, we don't know if these guys are going to use this ranch for another attack somewhere else. We need to hit back—and we need to hit back right away. With the Predator in place, we can monitor the place to see if they are preparing for something else; if so, we're ready."

"Mr. President, this is outrageous! We don't know who attacked us and without that knowledge, we cannot simply spy on US citizens without a warrant!" Sanchez again postulated.

"Mr. President, we may not know, 'beyond a reasonable doubt', who is behind these attacks, but this bears all the hallmarks of Said Jalili—the secretary of Iran's Supreme National Security Council; he's the architect of Hezbollah's adventures in Lebanon and northern Israel—he understands asymmetrical warfare as well as anyone."

"Mr. President," Carmichael began, "if I may interrupt, I think we can address some of what the attorney general just mentioned. I've just been advised by one of your Secret Service agents that Colonel Jackson has some vital information for us. We can get him on video if you'd like."

"Absolutely, get him up!"

"Right away, sir. Stonewall? Are you there?"

"Hey, Jim. Dani & I are both here. We pulled off at a Starbucks on the outskirts of El Paso and set up a temporary command post in the parking lot. Get this, Dani got a hit on one of the two guys we've been following."

"So, Miss Yaniv, just who are we dealing with here?" President Barre demanded.

"Mr. President, one of the two men is Major Farrok Zarin—he's Colonel Rafsanjani's executive officer. Mr.

President, you have a known Iranian Republican Guards - Quds Force officer, and presumably his personal assistant, driving through west Texas as we speak."

"Stonewall, are you in a position to pick him up?"

"Negative; we pulled off as Zarin continued out of El Paso. Special Agent Norris has a drone following him. The FBI has a small strike force assembled and we're waiting to see where Zarin ends up. My guess is that he's heading to another ranch they've set up in west Texas, similar to the one they established in Oregon, but that's just a guess."

"Okay, great work you two! Miss Yaniv, thank you very much! This is a game changer!" President Barre exclaimed. "As soon as you know where this major ends up, let us know."

"Will do, sir," Jackson replied.

"General Kaufman, it's now about mid-afternoon in the Pacific Northwest; when would you recommend we drop the Rangers on this ranch?"

"Well sir, if we don't see any additional activity on this ranch—and the Predator can stay up for hours—I'd suggest sometime after midnight, say one - two o'clock in the morning. These are Rangers—we own the night!"

"Very well, go ahead and let them know that kickoff is scheduled for 2:00 a.m.," President Barre added, noting the Ranger tab on General Kaufman's uniform.

"Okay, then; Axe, what do we have in the gulf at our disposal?" President Barre asked Secretary of Defense Axelsson.

"Sir, we have the *George Washington* carrier group in the gulf as well as a battle group centered around the *San Antonio* with seven hundred Marines aboard; in the Arabian Sea, we have the *John Stennis* carrier group— which is also within striking distance of Iran—and the *Theodore Roosevelt* has passed through the Red Sea and

is on the eastern side of the Gulf of Aden, heading towards the gulf at flank speed—she had to leave some of
her escorts behind but they'll catch up as soon as they
can. She's already in striking distance, though she's at
the edge of her range. In addition, we have a squadron
of F-15E's at Al Udeid in Qatar and two squadrons of
drones there as well."

"That's all we have in the region?" asked Pam
McDowell, the president's national security advisor.

"That's it. We didn't leave any troops in Iraq and we
only left a skeleton force in Afghanistan, the nearest
forces would be in Europe."

"What about Incirlik?" McDowell followed up.

"Incirlik, while a US base in southern Turkey, does
not have any US planes stationed there. The nearest
combat aircraft would be in either Germany, England or
Italy. Obviously, we could whistle up some B-2's out of
Whiteman or some B-1's—or even some B-52's—but
we're talking more than twelve hours just for the B-2's
to get on station."

"Okay, Axe, before WW II, the War Department—
as Defense was known then—had a division known as
War Plans. I assume the Pentagon has something similar
to that?"

"We do, sir. We wouldn't be doing our job if we
didn't. We have plans on the books to attack or invade
everything from Argentina to Zimbabwe."

"I thought as much. Get back over there and see what
your folks already have developed for this very situation
we have with Iran. I'm assuming much of that is pretty
current. I want you back here with the Joint Chiefs in
two hours."

"Not a problem, sir. All we really need is your
'Okay' to launch."

Three and a half hours later, Zarin and his aide pulled into the ranch outside of Marathon. He was not surprised to hear that his men had left a day earlier; disappointed, yes; surprised, no. At this point, there was not much for him to do; after spending more than forty hours on the go, he was exhausted—both he and his aide found the nearest bed and fell asleep almost immediately. No one on the ranch noticed a very faint hum coming from several thousand feet above them.

Joint Base Lewis-McChord, Washington

"Gentlemen," Colonel Jacobson began, "the chairman of the Joint Chiefs of Staff called about half an hour ago—we are officially scheduled for an assault on a ranch complex outside of Riverside, OR at 0200—that's less than twelve hours from now. Word is that this ranch is owned, indirectly, *by the Iranian Quds Force.* It was purchased by a shell corporation in 2009. Now, we recovered a pickup truck involved in the attack up at Grand Coulee early this morning and it's registered to this ranch. In addition, we have just received confirmation that a major in the Quds Force just crossed over the Mexican border a couple hours ago and is probably headed to another ranch in Texas. Obviously, he is not our problem. However, this major is the XO of the man who we believe orchestrated all the attacks this morning—and he takes his orders directly from Major General Qassim Suleimani, the head of the Quds Force in Tehran."

Upon hearing this news, every officer in the room sat in stunned disbelief. Finally, Lieutenant Murphy of First Platoon, broke the silence: "You mean, the Iranians have had a clandestine base on a ranch in southern Oregon since 2009?!?"

"That's right, Murph," Jacobson continued. "Okay, now that I have your attention: This ranch in southeastern Oregon has, we believe, as many as fifty-six Quds members, maybe a few more. There are three separate sites we'll need to plan on hitting—all in close proximity to each other, though none is close enough to support another. The overhead photos we are handing out now have been taken by a Predator that is currently circling overhead so they are only an hour old or so. Captain Fairchild will assign who will be assaulting which ranch site. I've tasked three C-17's to load up with three Apaches each and they'll be landing at the airport outside of Burns, OR—that's the closest place to accommodate a C-17. They should be leaving within the hour. In addition, we'll have three C-17's for the whole company so we'll have plenty of room for some extra gear, Humvees, etc.; you know the drill—Captain Fairchild, it'll be up to you to decide how you want these dispersed amongst your men. Again, the plan is to begin the assault at 0200."

"Okay, guys, tell me what you don't see in these photos?" Captain Fairchild asked his platoon leaders.

"Trees, there's no cover here—at any of the ranch sites," noted Lieutenant Jones, who commanded second platoon.

"That's right; that's the main reason we're going in at night—there is simply no cover here. If we showed up in broad daylight, we'd never have the element of surprise—they'd see us coming from miles away. We'll have that now, to some degree, as there is simply no hiding the noise generated by all of the aircraft. As the colonel alluded, we'll have a C-17 for each ranch. The plan is to jump an hour early—hopefully, after they hear the planes—and when nothing happens, they'll relax their guard a bit. However, as soon as we land, we'll need to set up blocking positions at the end of the driveways for each of these locations—if they hear us and get spooked and try to make a run for it, we need to be able to keep them contained. The Predator isn't showing any guards at these spots so we should be able to set up the road blocks without making any noise. It's an hour and a half flight, with an hour on the ground . . . . We'll need to be wheels up by 2245. We'll have nine Apaches for support and, if things go real bad, we'll have a squadron of Eagles on call out of Mountain Home Air Force Base. I don't think we'll need them, but they'll be there just in case. Murph, I'll want first platoon to take the ranch labeled 'A' on the photos—this looks to be the primary location; Jones, second platoon will take 'B', and Fivecoat, you'll have 'C'. I want everyone back here in ninety minutes to coordinate the assault."

"Now remember," Jacobson broke in, "we believe these guys are part of the Iranian Quds Force—they're fanatical, and they are very well trained. They conducted most of their attacks in the dead of night, so they may very well have some type of night vision gear. By dropping an hour early, we'll have time to get organized and let them lower their guard after a while if they hear the planes. Let's get to work."

Tonopah, NV

"Captain Turani, welcome back!" exclaimed Colonel Rafsanjani. "I had almost given up hope that you'd made it. Most of your men have returned safely but we are still missing a few. You are to be congratulated on a job well done!"

"Thank you, sir. It's been an honor and a privilege to have worked with you on this."

"The honor is all mine, Captain. You and your teams performed magnificently. All of the news reports coming out of California indicate that every target has been either seriously damaged or completely destroyed. You and your men succeeded far beyond my wildest expectations. From what we can tell, Captain Sassani's teams did equally well. I'm hearing reports of power outages throughout the West—we've even noticed it here at the ranch. There's just one leg of this operation left and if Major Zarin's teams do as well as yours and Sassani's have done, we will have brought America to its knees. We've already hit them hard, very hard, but Major Zarin's team will deliver the *coup d'grace*. The American people won't know what hit them."

"Well, sir, I don't know of Major Zarin's operation but if it's anything like ours . . . well, I'm just extremely proud to have been a part of it."

"Believe me, Captain, if the major's men succeed in their operation, the entire world will hear of it. Regardless of the major's operation, I don't see an issue which would delay you and your men returning home. We won't be able to get everyone home at once but we should be able to start the return trip in the next day or two. We'll want to get as many out as soon as possible as the Americans will be out for blood. Anything that looks remotely suspicious will likely draw the attention of a swarm of police officers. I'm heading home right away. I'll need to brief Minister Jalili and General Suleimani as soon as I get back."

"That should be a very special meeting for you, sir. Surely they'll make you a general after this!"

"We shall see, Captain, we shall see. In the meantime, go check on your men. You've done extremely well."

"Thank you, sir, and I look forward to seeing you back in Tehran sometime next week."

With that, Colonel Rafsanjani took off with his driver and one of the ranch pickup trucks. He made sure that the spare tank in the bed of the truck had been filled prior to leaving. Rafsanjani knew that he couldn't fly out as he had come in the United States. Even though he had a very good fake passport, after their attacks, he fully believed that the CIA would have captured his, and every other Iranian officers, features on some photo or another and loaded it into some facial recognition software that every airport in the country would be using. No matter how good his passport might be, he did not want to take the chance of flying out of a US airport. As such, he had his driver head north out of Tonopah towards Ely. From here, they would pass through Twin Falls, ID, skirt the Northeast corner of Oregon and travel through east central Washington until they hit the border crossing outside of the small town of Danville, WA. Rafsanjani fully believed that security all along the Mexican border now would be just as tight as it had been porous before. He knew that with his features, he could easily pass for any Mexican or Latin American but he didn't want to chance it. Facial recognition software had nothing to do with whether some border guard believed he could be a Latino. No, he would take his chances at an obscure border crossing in the middle of north central Washington where the most exciting thing up there were how many elk made the crossing each day. Once he crossed the border, they would head straight to Vancouver. He had a four fifteen plane to catch, nonstop to Amsterdam. He'd be in the air when Zarin and his men conducted their part of the operation. Once he landed, he knew he'd hear from news reports on what kind of success Zarin had had. From Amsterdam, getting to Tehran would be easy; he'd be home the day after tomorrow.

Riverside, OR

"Captain Sassani," Lieutenant Darvish began, with a note of concern, "Lieutenant Ahktar has not returned. He should have returned a few hours ago."

"He hasn't checked in at all?" Replied Sassani.

"No, sir. We've been monitoring all communications and there's been nothing from him or his team."

"Lieutenant, after you completed your assignment, did you see or hear anything that could have been from them?"

"Sir, we reached the rally point a little early so we waited as long as we could for them but they never showed up. I assigned another of my men to take Ahktar's assignment as he had ordered, and everything went according to plan. Once we completed the assignment, we did not stick around to look for him."

"Okay, I'm only a two hour drive over to you. I want to get over there and go over this with you in private. I'll be there as soon as I can; we'll see you then."

"Very well, sir, we'll be waiting for you."

El Paso, TX

"Okay, we have them on a ranch outside of Marathon," Norris relayed to Jackson. "What do you guys want to do?"

"Is there any sign of any other activity at this place?" asked Jackson.

"Not at present; actually seems really quiet, almost too quiet for a working ranch," replied Norris.

"I'd get ready to move in on these guys as soon as you can. The drone up top is crucial—if we see any significant activity like that ranch in Oregon, we might need to alert someone from Fort Hood, say a unit from the First Cav. However, the way it looks now, I think your assault force is adequate. This place is so remote, though, that it's going to take the assault team and everyone else a few hours to get organized and get on scene. In the meantime, what do we know about this ranch?"

"Already have people working on that. It appears to be registered to a corporation called 'Cyrus Enterprises, Inc.' We've checked Arizona, California, Nevada, Oregon and Washington for the same name and came up empty."

"Interesting; they named this ranch after the founder of the Persian Empire and the ranch is located at a place with the same name as an ancient Persian battle—Marathon—where they lost to the Greeks. The Oregon ranch is registered to C & D Enterprises—a possible reference to Cyrus & Darius? Okay, check those same states but concentrate on other words related to the ancient Persian Empire, names like Xerxes, Darius, Susa, Persepolis, Salamis, maybe even Thermopylae, etc., anything dealing with the ancient Persian Empire. If they've used something like Cyrus, and specifically chose Marathon as a location from which to operate, in their own minds, they might be trying to bring back the glory of the ancient Persian Empire, however illogical and demented that might seem."

XIX

The offensive firepower of a Navy Carrier Battle Group is truly awesome. The battle group, consisting of an aircraft carrier and its air wing of approximately eighty five aircraft, a cruiser, two or three destroyers, and a submarine, actually has more firepower than most countries. Each of these ships that support the carrier can fire Tomahawk cruise missiles, missiles which can put a one thousand pound warhead in a garbage can over a thousand miles away. Depending on the configuration of each of these ships, this little fleet could easily have well more than two hundred Tomahawks at its disposal in addition to the strike capability of the carrier's air wing of approximately forty-eight F-18 strike aircraft. Each F-18 has a combat radius of over four hundred miles and has eleven different weapons stations giving one squadron (twelve Hornets) the ability to strike over one hundred twenty different targets with precision weapons—and there are at least four squadrons on a carrier—and they can strike over and over and over again. Thus, if the battle group commander really cared about destroying an enemy country, he could do so in an afternoon. Said Jalili and his Iranian colleagues faced two American Carrier Battle Groups; a third was on its way.

Tampa, Headquarters, US CENTCOM

"Gentlemen," Admiral Jack Fischer, commander, US Central Command, announced as he began his video teleconference with Vice Admiral Jeff Ramsey, Fifth Fleet commanding officer, and the commanders of the *USS George Washington,* the *USS John C. Stennis,* and the *USS Theodore Roosevelt* and their support staff. "I'm sure each of you have heard of what's happened on the west coast; refineries in California and Washington have been severely damaged, if not completely destroyed, and the power grid off of the Columbia River Basin has been completely shut down. In essence, the entire west coast is out of gas, and will be for several months, and much of the west, especially the Pacific Northwest, will be experiencing rolling blackouts at the very least. The CIA and the FBI, in a joint operation, have managed to pick up five Quds Force members on a ranch outside of Marathon, Texas. One of these guys is the executive officer to a Colonel Ashkan Rafsanjani who planned and, they believe initiated, the attacks. We still don't know where this Rafsanjani figure is but we have a worldwide manhunt out for him."

"As for us, the president has authorized a full scale aerial assault on Iran for starters. This will be followed, I assume, by a bevy of Special Forces-type of troops— Axe didn't say as much but he indicated that the only forces being alerted for immediate deployment were the SF guys and their Ranger counterparts, and possibly the Eighty-second Airborne and the 173rd out of Vincenza. Anyway, I can't imagine a full scale invasion. The *Washington* and the *Stennis* are simply the tip of the spear; the *Roosevelt* will begin operations as soon as they are within striking distance. The Air Force will begin operations as soon as they can but at present, they only have a single squadron of Strike Eagles at Al Udeid. They'll be able to whistle up some more Eagles out of Ramstein and Lakenheath in a day or two—they're really the closest ones. They'll get a squadron of Lancers in at Diego Garcia but that'll take a couple days at the earliest. Farther out, the SecDef is taking this to NATO to get as much support from them as possible. We're expecting actual military support from most of them, though this could take a while, as well. However, I'd expect the Brits to join the Eagles coming out of Lakenheath but the rest of NATO could take a while longer. Obviously, State will need to get involved as we'll need greater access to Al Udeid as well as several other bases in the region. So, for the moment, we're up."

"Jeff, we need to hit these guys with everything we have, and don't let up. The primary targets include the usual command and control networks, their air defense network, their navy, and every base the Iranians have along, or within range of, the gulf. We also need to hit every one of the Quds Force bases; I don't want a building left standing, and I don't want a ship of theirs left floating. Roberts," Fischer continued, "you've already encountered their Sunburn missile; if you haven't already, get the electronic data on this missile out to the rest of the fleet."

"We've already done that, sir," Roberts offered. "Both the *Roosevelt* and the *Stennis* should already have the data on it."

"Very good. Jeff, we've planned this very situation out a few years back when we were both at the Pentagon: two Carrier Battle Groups vs. Iran, only this time we've already hit them pretty hard along the coast and the strait. Now we need to finish them off. I don't want any targets left for the Air Force, let alone the Brits."

"Don't worry, Jack; everyone here knows what they've done, and besides, we'll have three carriers in just a few hours; the *Roosevelt's* been red-lining it to get here just as fast as she can. In addition, the *Florida* is with the *Washington* and the *Georgia* is with the *Stennis* group. Both of those are SSGNs and have over 150 Tomahawks each—meaning we have over five hundred Tomahawks at our disposal. The first of these will be launching within the hour. We'll time this so that each Quds Force base is hit at exactly the same time; the Hornets will follow. These guys won't know what hit them. By the time the Air Force gets in the game, it'll be all over but the shouting."

Marathon, TX

Admiral Fischer jumped the gun a little bit when he told his officers that the FBI had picked up Major Zarin, but only a little. As Fischer conducted his teleconference with his staff in the Middle East, Jackson, Dani, Norris and the FBI assault team descended in full force upon the ranch outside of Marathon where Zarin and his aid slept.

"What's with all of the helicopters outside? It seems a bit odd for all of this, isn't it?" Zarin asked his aide as he groggily woke up. He'd been asleep for only a few hours.

Before his aide could answer, Norris, Jackson and Dani barged into his room. A look of utter astonishment crossed Zarin's face.

"How? Who are you?" demanded Zarin, suddenly wide awake.

"Major Zarin, I'm Special Agent Tom Norris of the FBI. As for you, Major, your role in Colonel Rafsanjani's expedition is over."

"What??? Where is the colonel?" Zarin was stunned. How could the Americans have found out about their operation so quickly? Only a few hours ago, their attacks had met with unparalleled success—and now the Americans had found him and, apparently, Colonel Rafsanjani. How did they do this? He thought to himself. Had someone sold them out? If so, who? They had organized this so that only a very select few knew the entire plan and no one in the Oregon or Nevada locations knew of his part in the operation. How had they found him?

"I'm not about to tell you where Colonel Rafsanjani is at," replied Norris. "However, I am curious as to your role in the operation now that it would appear the rest of your team has departed without you. It would seem that your presence here serves no purpose whatsoever." Norris, Jackson and Dani had conferred very briefly before they hit the ranch that they would need to be very careful interrogating Zarin as they did not want to tip their hand on just how little they really knew. They all knew that Zarin would quickly pick up on what they knew based on the questions they asked him.

"My purpose here was to lead my men! If it wasn't for some incompetent mechanic in Nairobi who should be shot, I'd be with them!" commented Zarin. All three of them quickly realized that Zarin had just confirmed to them that another attack was imminent—they needed to find out where, and when! Norris already had his staff working with the Texas DMV to find out just how many vehicles were registered to the ranch's location. He had been surprised to learn that in addition to the few pickup trucks in the yard that there were only four other pickups and four fifth-wheel travel trailers that had been registered here that his team could not find on the ranch.

"Aah, yes; leading your men. Well, we have another team in the process of rounding them up as well. Very soon, we'll have your whole team picked up."

"You arrogant pigs; you Americans think you are so smart. I don't believe you even know where my men are at right now. For that matter, I bet you don't even know where the colonel is either. Good luck finding either of them. This is a very big country and my men are very good."

"Well, we found you, didn't we?" Jackson noted icily. "What makes you think we aren't grabbing your men as we speak?"

"Because by your questioning, you've already told me you don't know where to look. You think what we have done so far is bad—the worst is yet to come! And I, for one, will be glad to see you Americans suffer!" Hearing this, Dani grabbed Jackson and pulled him out of the room.

"Stonewall, just how secure are *your* nuclear reactors?" Dani asked him. "So far, they have concentrated on the energy sector of your country. We just took out their nuclear program. What if *your* nuclear power industry is their next target?"

"I think these are fairly secure, especially after 9-11, but why? As far as we know, they only have the four trucks and travel trailers. We don't know what they have for weapons but if all they have is these travel trailers, they are kind of limited in what they can carry for weapons, though it sounds like the next phase of this operation will dwarf the first two. I think the leadership of the country is safe given that Zarin indicated this next attack is intended to make us suffer. If it's not the power industry—and no one says that it has to follow the course of the first two attacks—I mean, what if they only hit four of the largest cities in the country with a biological agent, say hitting conventions in Vegas, New York, Dallas, etc., they could infect thousands and hope that those infected would pass on the infection to others."

"Well, whatever, they have planned, the key is to find those travel trailers. A biological weapon is certainly something that could be transported with them, and hitting a major convention with a travel trailer wouldn't raise any suspicion at all. We need to find them, and right away," interrupted Norris, as he had left Zarin with one of his agents and followed Dani and Jackson out. "We'll put out a nationwide BOLO on these vehicles but that's about the best we can do right now. We don't even know where to look. If they are heading to a major metro area, Dallas, Las Vegas, Denver, and New Orleans would be some of the nearest and most likely targets. If they left last night, they could already be in each of these cities. For now, they had a few laptops and I-phones out that we have but we need to look over this ranch with a fine tooth comb to see what all they were doing here. If they were doing anything like their first two attacks, there should be some evidence of it here."

"How long will it take your tech guys to check out the laptops and cell phones?" asked Dani.

"Depends on the nature of the encryption and security they've installed on their systems. It could take a little while. I don't want to take the time to get this up to Washington with another attack imminent so we'll be working on it here; we've got good people here. We'll crack it. My folks will be working on this all night. These guys helped us in one way—being isolated out on a ranch like this we don't have to worry about any of this leaking to the press. If these guys here are still in contact with their troops, we might be able to learn something should someone decide to call home here."

"Yeah, but if they're following operational security, as I'd have my guys doing, no one's making any calls," added Jackson. "I'm actually kind of surprised they had these. I'd check with our friends at the Puzzle Palace"— the National Security Agency—"and see if they can find any conversations from these phones and just who contacted them, and of course, the conversations of those who contacted them. This could be a huge help; possibly more than these laptops here. On the way in here, I noticed several fighters at Biggs; any chance we could borrow one of these for the night and have either our Air Force or Navy friends fly these cell phones and one of the laptops up to Fort Meade and have their tech guys look them over? I know you want to keep the laptops here, but it wouldn't hurt to have the folks at the NSA work on one of them as well as the phones?"

"That's a good idea; go ahead get that arranged. In the meantime, I'll have one of my guys contact the NSA and give them the info on the phones and let them know to expect a late night delivery."

"Will do; we'll need one of your choppers to get to Bliss."

"Not a problem; it'll be about a three hour round trip flight for you. Hopefully, by the time you get back here, we'll have a little more intel for you."

*   *   *   *   *

"Jim," Jackson said into his cell phone, "we just raided the ranch outside of Marathon. We picked up Major Farrok Zarin and four of his colleagues. We found a couple laptops and cell phones here as well. Norris' team is still looking the place over. Tom wants to keep the laptops here and have his own team pore over these for any information we can learn from these. He's agreed to let one of the laptops loose as well as the phones and get them to Fort Meade. We're on our way to Bigg's Army Airfield. It looks as though the Air Force is conducting some training exercises there right now, at least I saw several F-15's parked on the runway there. Any way you can to talk to your friends at the Pentagon and shake one of the F-15's there loose to get these up to Baltimore? That'll be the fastest way to get them there. It'd probably be a good idea to whistle up some tanker support as well as the pilot will need to refuel. Given the time of the night, they probably won't be able to refuel at any civilian airport. Plus, it'd be a lot quicker if they can refuel in flight rather than even stopping over somewhere along the way."

"Okay, I'll make some calls. How soon before you get to Biggs?" Jim asked.

"We're just leaving now. Tom gave us one his choppers so it'll take us about an hour and a half to get there."

"I'll get on that right away; anything else?"

"Yeah; another attack is imminent. Zarin indicated 'the worst is yet to come.' At present, we don't have much to go on. There are four pickup trucks and four travel trailers registered to the ranch address that are missing. We don't have any idea where these are at; Norris has put out a nationwide BOLO on them but we figure they have at least a twenty four hour head start on us. At that rate, starting from Marathon, they could be practically anywhere in the country by now. Tom's folks are good; if there is anything on these laptops, they'll find it. Hopefully, there's something on them that will help us determine what this last attack is all about. In the meantime, we haven't even been able to crack the cell phones to identify their numbers."

"I'll talk to the folks at Meade and let them know what to expect. You sure about this impending attack?"

"Yeah, Zarin admitted that his men are on the loose and that he'd like to be out with them. My guess . . . they're still together as a group; don't know where but I'd bet they're traveling as a group somewhere, at least for the time being. They might separate later but I'd bet initially they are still together as a group. Also, I'm guessing that the political leadership of the country is safe given that Zarin mentioned that this attack will be worse than the first two and this one is intended to make us really 'suffer'—his term."

"Okay, I'd agree with your assessment. Keep working on this; let me know what assets you need as things develop. I know the FBI has the lead on this but you're the Iranian expert. Also, what are Dani's thoughts on all of this? She's good. Pardo speaks very highly of her."

"Yeah, the first question she asked when she heard Zarin indicate that this pending attack would be worse than the first and intended to make us suffer was about how secure our nuclear reactors are. She reasoned that since the first two attacks hit our energy sector, the third might as well—and hitting the nuclear power industry could cause unimagined damage—and suffering—if in a populated area. However, since 9/11, I believe all of the reactors have been upgraded to withstand a similar attack, haven't they?"

"They have," responded Carmichael. "However, that doesn't mean they won't try, and even though they have been reinforced, there is no guarantee that they could withstand the impact. After all, the Twin Towers were designed to withstand the impact of a 707. Obviously, a 757 is considerably bigger than a 707 but given the extent of the damage the towers sustained, it's doubtful they could have withstood the impact of the 707 as originally designed."

"Okay, then, with that in mind, I'd at least raise the alert level for these," agreed Jackson.

"Stonewall," Dani interrupted, "there are several Quds Force members who have already been trained as pilots—and have combat experience. I think Jim is right; he needs to at least alert the NRC of at least the possibility of a threat, the most likely coming from the air. Increasing the alert will not take any man-power away from Norris's idea of a possible biological or chemical attack. I'd have him at least alert the Air Force as well. Again, this won't impact Norris's investigation a bit but might just make a big difference should we be right."

"I'll let Norris know when we get back about all this. He needs to know and it's the sensible thing to do."

XX

Scranton, PA

Captain Ebrahim Rouhani and his driver pulled into the small RV Park outside of Scranton, Pennsylvania just ahead of their partner rig. They had been on the road for twenty-eight hours straight; time was of the essence, everyone knew that. Zarin had told them that once they received word from the colonel, they were to leave immediately, whether he had reached the ranch or not. And so, once they received Rafsanjani's email, they headed out. Outside of Sweetwater, Texas, Rouhani and his traveling companions in a second travel trailer had split from the two other rigs with whom they were now reunited. At Sweetwater, Rouhani and his partners took a southern route to get to Scranton, traveling I-20, to Fort Worth, where they picked up Interstate 30 and took that to Little Rock. From Little Rock, they traveled up to Knoxville, TN, where they picked up Interstate 81 and followed that up most of the rest of the way. Their other two companions took a more northerly route, traveling through Oklahoma and Missouri where, in St. Louis, they picked up I-70 and took that all the way to Columbus, Ohio. From here they took another interstate up to

Akron where they picked up I-80 and took this most of the rest of the way. Rouhani, at Zarin's urging, had decided to break up into pairs for the four travel trailers as he had picked up on several websites that RV-ers like they presumed to be, often travel in pairs. Two rigs traveling together would not raise any suspicion at all, regardless of where the vehicles were licensed. However, four of them all from the same state traveling together might look a little suspicious, possibly not enough to generate any inquiries but certainly enough that a trained observer might notice and keep note of it. In addition, Rouhani had made sure that the RV Park they stopped at would be large enough that four travelers from Texas would not raise any undue suspicion.

While Rouhani had gone to great measures to keep from arousing any undue suspicion, he made an exception for this night. Each of his men knew that this would be their last night and they were comfortable with that fact. They did not spend the night partying as if this was to be their last night but they simply wanted to be with each other as many soldiers do when they realize their time is up. Moreover, they had volunteered for this mission, every one of them. That was one of Colonel Rafsanjani's stipulations. He had told them the nature of the mission without going into the operational details. However, when each of them had volunteered—and learned of their exact targets—each one had been thoroughly elated at the prospect of hitting out at the Great Satan with the devastating blow the colonel had in mind. Truly, America would suffer from the blow they had in store!

As for tomorrow, well, they had checked on their gear multiple times over; their weapons were ready, they had plenty of ammunition, and their RHIB's (Rigged Hull Inflatable Boats) were ready should they be needed.

They really didn't have anything else for gear. In addition, he made sure that each of his trucks had been completely refueled. The news reports of the first parts of their operation had sent fuel prices skyrocketing—even here on the East coast, which is what they expected. Rouhani, though, did not want to wait in line for fuel tomorrow so he made sure that they had all topped off their fuel tanks. No matter where they were headed, and he was looking to make this decision right away, he wanted to be able to get there on one tank of fuel.

As for his final decision, he and Zarin had planned this part of the operation together with a couple options: they could proceed with four small groups heading to Philadelphia, Boston and two going to New York, or depending on scheduling, all four groups could head to either Boston or New York. Now, after checking the schedules, Rouhani thought it looked as if Boston offered their best option. He was pleased to see this as he really wanted to avoid New York City. He had heard nightmares of the traffic there. The recent closure of several lanes across the George Washington Bridge into New Jersey had caused him countless sleepless nights. He knew his team would not be traveling across this bridge and they would be traveling in the early evening anyway. However, he looked at this as one more example of the unpredictable nature of the Americans. Who would close a bridge simply for political paybacks? Yet, the New Jersey Governor's office had done just that. Tomorrow, of all days, he did not need something like that. However, with the schedules in Boston falling in line, he no longer needed to worry about New York City. With that decision made, he made a quick call to the Hyatt at Logan International Airport to reserve a suite on the top floor of the hotel. He specifically requested a room at the end of the southwest wing which overlooked the inner Boston Harbor. Not surprisingly, a suite was not available but the operator let him know that a two room suite was available on the floor immediately below. Rouhani let the operator know that this would be perfect and made the reservation.

After spending the last twenty-eight hours on the road, he knew his men needed sleep. However, he wanted to brief his men on what tomorrow held for them. Rouhani had picked his spots carefully: they were in a far corner of the Park and the nearest RV to them was well over thirty yards away. He had placed his driver as a guard relatively close to this RV to alert them if anyone ventured into their area.

"Gentlemen, tomorrow is our big day. I've looked over all of the schedules for Boston, New York and Philadelphia and from the schedules I've looked at, Boston seems to offer us the best opportunity. All of us going to the same location also means that we can support each other should that be needed as well. Boston is the farthest away but it is still less than a five hour drive. We'll want to arrive around nine thirty in the evening. Arriving half an hour after closing should allow for as many as possible to leave, making for fewer potential witnesses or obstacles to overcome. Those unfortunate few who remain may need to be killed. We cannot afford to leave any witnesses who could raise the alarm—we have come too far to fail at this point." Rouhani knew this was old news to each of them. They had all reviewed the layout of each target they had selected; the last minute details were the only new items really needing to be discussed.

Fort Bliss, TX

Jackson and Dani arrived at Biggs just as an F-15 flight crew began warming up one of the Eagles on the flight line.

"You must be Stonewall. I assume you, then, are Dani? Hi, I'm 'Vapor', Major Lori Washington."

"Vapor?" asked Jackson.

"Yeah, I had one mission that was pretty top secret and they waived the minimum fuel requirements for me. By the time I landed . . . , I had less than one hundred pounds of fuel; hence 'Vapor' for my call sign."

"Well, this could be another repeat of that mission for you, Major."

"That's what I understand. My CO tells me this little package I'm delivering is tied to the guys who hit California pretty hard. We should have everything arranged. I'll be meeting up with a couple tankers out of McConnell refilling with the first one somewhere over the Oklahoma - Arkansas border and then the other over Kentucky. By then, I'll have enough to get to Andrews. The FAA has rules about supersonic flight but my CO told me not to worry about those," Vapor added with a sly grin. "I'll get to Andrews before you get back to Marathon."

"Great; the laptop and these cell phones need to get to Fort Meade just as fast as possible. Everything is encrypted on these so the sooner they can get working on them, the sooner we can crack who did this and, possibly, find out if they have anything else in store for us."

"Sir, if that is the case, why don't I just land at Tipton instead of Andrews, or even BWI, for that matter?"

"Tipton? What's that?"

"Tipton's an old Army Airfield that was BRAC-ed back in the late 80's. It's a civilian airport now but it's located literally right across the highway from Fort

Meade. By the time I land and hand over this little package, the whiz kids at Fort Meade will have this in five minutes. It'll be closed this time of night but for the delivery I have, I'm sure you'd be able to have someone open it up for me to land there."

"You wouldn't have any trouble getting your Eagle in and out of there?"

"Nah, Tipton's runway's three thousand feet long; I only need a third of that."

"Vapor, just how do you know about Tipton?" Dani asked.

"I'm from the Baltimore area and I have my own private airplane hangared there. I've got a WACO YMF 5D Super—it's a biplane, and is she fun to fly. I've often wondered what it would be like to fly my other plane—this Eagle here—into Tipton! Now, sounds like I might get the chance," she added with a wondrous sense of fun in her eyes.

"Okay, Vapor; I'll make some phone calls. Go ahead and plan on landing at Tipton. Once you've made the delivery, do you want to hop on over to Andrews to refuel and spend the night there or, since you're from Baltimore, have you already made your own arrangements?"

"No, sir; I'll go ahead and hop over to Andrews. I'll spend the night there and then boogey on back here tomorrow. They need the bird here to continue training. Of course, I won't be getting back here as fast as I left, but I still need to get back here tomorrow."

"Okay, then, Major. Thanks for stepping up and making this flight. I know it's not very glamorous but it's extremely urgent."

"Don't mention it, sir." And with that, Vapor climbed up into the cockpit, dropped her canopy and began her way out to the runway.

As Vapor lit-off her afterburners on the takeoff, Jackson turned to Dani and said "I never tire of hearing the thunder of those engines! Let's get something to eat; it's been a long day and I'm starving."

"What, you're not going to cook dinner for me?" Dani asked with a huge grin on her face. "That breakfast was awesome!"

"Some other time," Jackson replied, smiling back at her. "Right now, I'm famished."

"Yeah, me too. I saw a Buffalo Wild Wings on the way in that looked pretty close. That work for you?"

In addition to breaking one of the F-15's loose for the flight to Fort Meade, Jim Carmichael had made sure that Jackson had access to a vehicle while he was at Biggs. He didn't know if he would need it or not but thought it might come in handy.

Taking their seat at a corner booth at the restaurant, Jackson got back to business with Dani. "So, just what is your take on all of this?" he asked her.

"Well, to begin with, we're up against someone who understands asymmetrical warfare to a very high degree. We know that another attack is imminent. Early this morning they hit more than a dozen of the largest refineries on the west coast. Right on the heels of this, they hit the power network coming off of the Columbia River dams in the Pacific Northwest. So, obviously, they are targeting your energy sector and infrastructure. Every president that has been elected since Nixon has campaigned on developing some type of national energy policy but not a single president has really done anything about it. Now, it would seem, we are up against someone who understands the vulnerabilities of not having one."

"So, you think the next attack is going to hit the energy sector again?"

"I do," replied Dani. "It's the most obvious part of their operation, short of their attack in the Gulf. Think about it: the first two attacks were not designed to kill or injure anyone in particular—they were designed to hit the country; to punish the country. By taking out the refineries, what is that going to do to the price of gas for those in California? California has what, the eighth largest economy in the world? After this morning, that economy doesn't have a gallon of gas or diesel fuel—an exaggeration, I know, but none of these petroleum companies stockpile fuel—they all refine as much as they need to deliver the next day. As such, no one will be going to work as every car will be sitting in the garage; every semi-tractor/trailer rig will be parked; not a single farmer will be able to work his fields due to a lack of diesel—essentially anything that requires any transportation will come to a screeching halt. Food prices are going to skyrocket as truckers won't be able to get produce, milk, cattle, etc., to market. Construction will come to a halt as building materials won't be able to get to construction sites. The list goes on. As to the power grid, the impact won't be as significant as the refineries but it will be significant in its own right. You can't take out over twenty-one thousand megawatts of electricity and not have a serious impact. The Pacific Northwest will be impacted by this the most, but other states will be impacted, probably more than most people realize. In short, your economy has just taken a huge hit that will have a direct impact on at least fifty million people and an indirect impact on millions of others. If you can keep your economy in a recession, you'll have done a remarkable job."

"You sure know how to paint a rosy picture. So, if this next attack is supposed to be worse than the first two, what do you think they have in store? I mean, they've already put the US economy in a major depression with just the first two attacks; why do you think this next one will be another strike at our energy sector? They've already hammered us pretty good on that note."

"Yes they have, but everything's been on the west coast. I think the next one is going to hit the East coast, and I think they will be going after your nuclear power industry. After all, we just took out theirs."

"Yeah, but theirs wasn't for power generation; it was strictly a weapons program."

"You know that, and I know that, but the rest of the world still has to choose what to believe. By hitting your nuclear power industry, it lends credence to their claim that their nuclear program was for power generation as well. Look, if this attack is going to be worse than the first two, several things become apparent: first, agent Norris seems like a good man but I really don't think we are looking at either a chemical or biological event for the next attack. To my knowledge, Mossad has no information on the Iranians having either type of weapons program; nuclear, definitely, but not chemical or biological. Secondly, they have already attacked two segments of your energy sector; why not a third. Third, have you looked at a map of where your nuclear power plants are located? There are roughly six of them in the Chicago area, there's another eight of them concentrated from North Carolina to Georgia but in the Mid-Atlantic to New England states, right long the seaboard from Norfolk to Boston, there're fourteen plants! If they hit just four of these—and they'd have to hit the right four, mind you—and caused a melt-down at each, you would literally have to *evacuate* over thirty-five million people! The loss of power from these four reactors would be a very minor issue here, but nothing like the necessity of having to evacuate all of these people. Remember the problems caused by the evacuation of New Orleans for Hurricane Katrina—and you had, what, two or three days warning?   That's child's play compared to what this would be—and you will have no warning whatsoever!"

"If they were going to do this, just how would they hit these reactors? They are guarded quite well and you heard Jim mention that they have been reinforced to withstand another suicide attack from the air, ala 9-11 all over again."

"Yes, I know your reactors have been reinforced, and you know that, but do the Iranians? Moreover, just because they have been reinforced to some mathematical formula developed by some engineer, doesn't mean they can actually withstand the impact of a major jet plane like a 757 or a 767, even a 737 for that matter. Engineers will do their best but there really is no way to actually test out their theories. Trust me, I've done a little work with nuclear engineering; I wouldn't want to even think about someone flying a 757 into a nuclear reactor. I don't care how well it's been reinforced; unless it's built into the side of a mountain, it would be a disaster of unimaginable proportions."

"Okay, let's sit back and think about this: what else could it be? I mean, if the intent is to make the country suffer, that kind of rules out a lot of things and if you're correct the lack of either a chemical or biological weapons program, that doesn't leave much. However, Saddam Hussein and the Syrians reportedly have manufactured Sarin. Is there a chance they could have gotten some of this when we deposed Saddam? Would Assad of Syria have worked out a trade with the Iranians: Sarin, in exchange for assistance fighting ISIS? Can you imagine what would happen if these guys dumped some Sarin gas into the water supply in LA, Dallas, Chicago, or any other major city? Talk about making a city suffer? Then again, is there a chance the Iranians could have gotten their hands on an old Soviet 'suit-case' type of nuclear bomb? Nothing says 'mass destruction' like a nuke going off?"

"I've thought about these. We, Mossad, don't have any reports of the Iranians receiving any chemical weapons from either Saddam or Assad. If they had, we should have picked up on this by now."

"Wait a minute, though," interrupted Jackson. "The Iranians managed to pull this little stunt off this morning and we all thought we should have been able to pick up on this as well—and we blew it. I think it's safe to say Mossad didn't have any intel on this either, right?"

"You're right, there; we had no knowledge of this coming down either. And, as big as this is, you'd think at least one of our agencies would have picked up on it. However, that being said, I still discount the possibility of the Iranians picking up any chemical or biological agents from either Saddam or Assad. As to the suit-case nukes, that's more of a Congressional scare tactic than a reality. Your Defense Department actually had engineers over in the old Soviet republics dismantling most of these things. If any got away, your Pentagon would know of this. In all of my research on this, I haven't heard of a single warhead that went missing. Which brings me back to the possibility of an air attack on your nuclear reactors on the east coast, ala the 9/11 attacks. Only this time, I'd look for them to either avoid a civilian jetliner, or be armed to the teeth to prevent the passengers from trying to overpower the hijackers. However if they do that, they'd lose the element of surprise—not so much with the passengers as with the authorities as in the wake of this morning's attack, I don't see anyone in the chain of command taking any chances with these guys: If there is a reported hijacking in the next few days, they won't hesitate to shoot down an airliner with 150 passengers, they're going to do it."

"Okay, so when we get back to Marathon, we need to let Norris know that the Air Force has been put on alert by Carmichael and that we think the most likely scenario for the next attack is to originate at an airport probably east of the Mississippi with the likely target being a nuclear power plant along the eastern seaboard from Virginia to Boston."

"That's the way I see it," replied Dani. "Nothing else adds up."

XXI

0100, Riverside, OR

"Captain," Sergeant Abedini called to Sassani, waking him out of a sound slumber. "The guards are reporting low flying aircraft. They've heard what they think are three different planes in the area; one pretty close to us."

"What?!? Did they see anything at all? Any paratroops? Have they heard anything?"

"Nothing else, sir, just the sound of the air planes."

"Where's Lieutenant Darvish? I need to see him right away."

"Right here, Captain. Sir, something's going on. I've been here for a few years now and have never even seen a plane fly anywhere near the ranch—and now, three of them at one o'clock in the morning; something's going on."

"Lieutenant, let's not take any chances. Get everybody up; we're evacuating within the hour—all three sites. Make sure that all computers and laptops are destroyed. Squad and platoon leaders are the only ones who should have a cell phone; destroy all the others. As we leave, set the charges for every building—I don't want a single thing left for the Americans to find."

"Yes, sir. I've already alerted the men, here and at the other two sites. They've already started the process; we can be ready to leave in ten minutes."

"Very good. Split your men in half; I'll take half of them with me to the Princeton ranch right away. Let the others know we're evacuating immediately and then take everyone else to the Fields ranch once you have finished the destruction."

"Captain, I think they are on to us," Lieutenant Murphy called to Fairchild. "There's a lot of activity for one o'clock in the morning."

"Same here," added Fivecoat.

"Okay, are all blocking positions set up?" Fairchild asked.

"All set," replied Lieutenant Jones. "We're good to go; nothing's getting passed us!"

"Captain," Fivecoat suddenly broadcast, "they are definitely aware of us. I've got two large building fires at my location. We're moving in."

"All units, attack—fire at will! The Apaches are going to be a little late to the party; road blocks, get ready for a mass exodus—they're going to be coming fast and hard."

"Cap'n, they're already hitting us—I've got two men down," replied Murphy. "How soon before the Apaches get here?"

"Half an hour out—we're way ahead of schedule. I'll send a squad over to you; five minutes."

"Roger that."

"Lieutenant," Captain Sassani radioed Darvish, who acted as the rear-guard, "we're a little late. They have roadblocks set up; we're going to have to fight our way out."

"They're starting to press in on us, sir; we're way out-numbered and out-gunned here. I'll break loose as many men as I can but we're not all going to make it out. Good luck, Captain!"

"I think we'll out-number them at the roadblock so some of us should get out. Good luck, Lieutenant."

"Cap'n, we've got more vehicles headed our way," Murphy calmly radioed Fairchild.

"No one gets through, Murph. No one."

"Roger that, sir. They've concentrated their forces . . . ."

"Murph! Murphy! Murphy, are you there?" Fairchild yelled into his radio.

"Ahh, . . . Sorry about that, sir. Three additional vehicles just came around a berm in the driveway and we traded fire: they hit us with machine gun fire; we hit them with three Javelins—I took a round in the shoulder and dropped the radio. Looks like everything is secure here. No additional activity."

"Jones?"

"We're good, sir. Still exchanging fire but we've got 'em. I don't think we'll be able to take any of them alive."

"Fivecoat?"

"Mission accomplished; we have the building site—no casualties, no prisoners either. We got here before all of their charges could be detonated. We found a couple laptops and cell phones they destroyed; I'm no techie but I think we might be able to salvage something from the hard drives on these things. We're rummaging through the place now."

"Okay, nice work guys; I'll let the colonel know we have the ranch, though no joy on any prisoners."

* * * * *

"Jim," Stonewall said into his cell phone, "we're on our way back to Marathon. Dani and I've been talking about a few things. For starters, you can expect delivery of our little package at Tipton Airfield, right across the highway from Fort Meade. The pilot, Major Lori Washington, is from the Baltimore area and knew of Tipton. She suggested landing there and simply having someone drive across the highway to meet her. Figured this would be the quickest way so I told her to plan on this. Next, Dani & I've been thinking about this next attack. We both think we're up against another 9/11 type of attack, with these guys taking some more planes and flying them into some of the nuclear reactors along the Eastern Seaboard from Virginia to Boston. We obviously don't know which ones but we believe this to be the most likely scenario. Neither of us at the CIA or Mossad believe the Iranians have a biological or chemical weapons program and neither of us have heard of them acquiring any of Saddam's or even Assad's weapons so we're thinking an air attack is the most likely scenario. Plus, the Israelis just took out their nuclear program; I can certainly see them going after ours in a big way. Looking at where our nuclear power plants are located, I'd suggest putting up an actual CAP (combat air patrol) over the eastern seaboard from Virginia to Boston; I'd have another up over the Chicago area and then a third over the Carolinas. The last two are just for good measure; we really think the Mid-Atlantic region from DC up to Boston should be the main focus."

"Okay, I'll be talking to Bob Harmon at homeland and let him know of this and to the FAA as well; they're going to have the lead on anything regarding air traffic. How sure of this are you two?"

"Sure of this? Not a bit, but we've discussed this quite extensively. As far as we are concerned it's the most plausible scenario. Plus, an attack from the air like this has been done before; I'd be willing to bet they'll try it again but with some variations. I wouldn't expect a hijacking like Al Qaeda did but I would expect them to grab some planes that might be sitting over night or something on that sort and fly them into a reactor or two."

"I'll take this right to the Director and the FAA as well as the head of the FBI. Give me a call when you get back to Marathon. I'd like to set up a conference call with both of you, Agent Norris, the Director, and the heads of the FAA and the FBI. Oh, one more thing: The army just raided that ranch in Oregon. They put up a stiff fight, but no match for the Rangers. We managed to find a few more laptops and cell phones, though most of these were seriously damaged, if not completely destroyed. There were no survivors."

"Any idea as to how many there were?"

"General Kaufman said they found fifty-seven bodies; all Iranians."

"Wow! And that's just one location that we know about; wonder how many more they have?" Jackson asked rhetorically. "We've just taken off from Biggs so it'll be at least an hour and a half before we get back to Marathon. Vapor should be at Tipton in about half an hour. Talk to you in a couple hours."

XXII

Beirut

Lieutenant Colonel Sayyid Bukhari had been to Lebanon several times. Often enough, that the Israelis had established a not too insignificant dossier on him. Bukhari himself had helped reorganize much of the Hezbollah military arm, their "Jihad Council", to make it far more functional, and effective, as a military force. Many of his trips had been to the Beqaa Valley to oversee Iran's rocket shipments and to ensure that they were housed in secure and bomb-proof shelters underground. His trips to Beirut had all been to meet with the Hezbollah commanders and advise them of Iran's overall purpose for supplying them with their weapons—and at times enforcing that purpose as well. Keeping a tight rein on some of these commanders had not been easy over the years but, for the most part, he had been able to keep them under control. Israel's attack on Iran's nuclear program had caused a firestorm within Hezbollah, especially on the more radical element within this already radical organization. Bukhari looked forward to this latest trip though. He'd finally be able to unleash the full fury of Hezbollah upon Israel. They had provided them with literally thousands of rockets over the years and now was the time to unleash this radical element within Hezbollah. They all knew of Israel's Iron Dome missile defense system, but their plan was to simply overwhelm the vaunted system with thousands of rockets launched just as quickly as possible.

"Muhammed," Bukhari exclaimed as he walked into the underground conference room, "it is good to see you once again."

Muhammed abu Abbas commanded Hezbollah's military arm, the "Jihad Council." Hezbollah is largely a military/terrorist organization but having a separate "military wing" allowed for some countries to accept the fiction that the "Jihad Council" was a separate military wing of Hezbollah and thereby supposedly supporting the one without supporting the other.

"It is good to see you as well, my friend," replied Muhammed. "What news have you brought us today? I trust you will let us take part in retaliating against these apostate Jews for what they have done to you and your country."

"Yes, we have plans to retaliate against the Jewish scum and you will play a part at the proper time. You have no doubt heard about the attacks in the United States; the attacks on their refineries in California and the attack on their power grid in their northwest. There is one more attack to come and it will happen very soon. When the attack on their government is completed and we have taken out their Congress, their Supreme Court and their President they will be in chaos, only then are you to attack. Once you begin the attack, you are to launch all of the rockets with which we have provided you—and launch them in a swarm. We want to completely overwhelm Israel's vaunted 'Iron Dome' defenses so that we are assured that most of the rockets find their targets in Israel."

Kiryat Shmona

"Did you hear that?!?" David asked his lieutenant. "Those guys aren't done yet. There's another attack coming and they're going directly after the US government!"

"Where's Ben? We need to get this to him right away. Also, make sure the general gets a copy of this. The IDF is going to need this info as well."

"Already calling him. Ben, David here. Say, we've got something extremely hot up here. The Iranians have another attack coming on the United States. It sounds like this one is intended to be worse than the first two and this one is aimed directly at their government."

"Are you sure of this? Where'd you get this information?" Ben asked his friend.

"We've really beefed up our intel in Beirut since we hit the Iranians. We kind of figured they'd retaliate so we've called in every resource we have to see if we can get ahead of whatever they have planned. One of our sources told us of a Quds Force colonel that was arriving in Beirut to meet with Mohammed abu Abbas and a few of his Hezbollah cronies. We had him followed and eavesdropped on his meeting. Ben, we've got it on tape; Lieutenant Colonel Sayyid Bukhari is a promising young officer in their Quds Force. This sounds very legit. I'm sure he had no idea we had the place bugged; the chances of this being a plant are slim to none. He specifically mentions attacking the US Congress, their Supreme Court and the President."

"Okay, send me the recording right away. I want to listen to it before I call Langley."

Tel Aviv

"Arielle, is Stonewall around?" Ben said into his satellite phone.

"Yeah, he's right here. What's up?"

"We just got wind that it looks like there might be a third leg to this Iranian attack."

"Yeah, we know. We're working on that now."

"Do you know that they are trying to take out the US government? I haven't seen or heard from anyone that they're increasing security anywhere in Washington."

"What?!? Are you sure of that? We've picked up Major Farrok Zarin, Rafsanjani's XO, and he indicated that the next attack is intended to punish the United States, to make them 'suffer'—his term. We figured that there next attack would be a repeat of the 9-11 style of attack, only on their nuclear power facilities. Just a second Ben; I'm going to put you on speaker."

"Stonewall, you there?" Ben asked.

"Right here with Dani," Jackson responded.

"The nuclear option Arielle just mentioned is perfectly logical, but we've got Lieutenant Colonel Sayyid Bukhari, another Quds Force officer, on tape talking to the Hezbollah leadership in Beirut—literally, just a few minutes ago—that the next attack will be targeted at the US Congress, Supreme Court and the President. He did not indicate just how the attack would take place but he indicated that 'when we've taken out their Congress, Supreme Court and the President,' Hezbollah is to launch their attack. We're pretty sure that this is legit. I just sent the recording to your phone; you should have it any time."

"Ben, are you sure this isn't some major disinformation drop?" Dani asked. "I mean, it just doesn't add up. We are in the midst of a major attack on the US and it has been far more successful than I would bet even Said Jalili could have imagined. Moreover, these guys have nothing but contempt for the American government—they see them as very weak. Remember, this government has allowed them to pursue a nuclear weapon, not us. We were the ones who attacked them, not the United States. I wouldn't even be surprised if members of the president's own cabinet don't fully understand how seriously they've been hit. I don't see them taking out a government like this—it just doesn't make sense. The Iranians couldn't have a better administration in Washington."

"Arielle, I hear you; however, there is no way they could have known we'd be able to pick up this information this quickly. I'm sure they'd think we would pick up on this at some point, but not this quickly."

"Ben, thanks for the head's up on this. We've been thinking that the next attack would be from the air—and they'd only need two planes to take out the Congress and the Supreme Court; the president could be done a number of ways as they'd only need to take out one man. But, I tend to agree with Dani—are you sure this isn't a case of disinformation? I mean, Hezbollah could care less about the nature of the next attack; it doesn't seem like he needed to give them the specifics. Are you sure this wasn't meant for you to hear?"

"Sure about it? No, but like I said, I really doubt that Bukhari knew we were listening in on this conversation."

"I agree Bukhari probably didn't know you were eavesdropping, but he isn't new to either Beirut or Hezbollah. Is it possible he could have released this information with the intent that it might get leaked back to you?"

"Yeah, that could be the case," Ben agreed, "but if this next attack is in any way imminent, and I believe it is, he couldn't guarantee how soon we'd get this information if it is intended to draw your resources away from somewhere else."

"Good point. I'll get this to the Director right way. Thanks a lot! We owe you one."

Tehran

"General, come on in," Said Jalili said as he welcomed General Suleimani. "How are you faring with this onslaught?"

"It is about as expected: Every one of our Quds bases have been hit, and hit hard. We've lost a lot of men. They've hit as far inland as Bidganeh, just outside of the city. They must have hit Bidganeh with a couple dozen of their Tomahawk missiles as the devastation is complete; nothing has been left standing. Similar reports are arriving from the garrisons at Ahwaz, Kermanshah, Marivan, and Naqadeh—every one of them decimated; nothing has been left standing."

"General, did you think that the Americans would not respond. While we have been hurt, and it will probably get worse, reports out of the United States indicate that they have probably suffered the worst attack in their history. However, look at it this way: they have hit us, and hit us hard, but it is nothing we cannot surmount as our economy has not been touched. On the other hand, the American military might remain strong but their economy—and their country as a whole, has been decimated! General, there really is more to power than simply military might. We'll withstand this present onslaught and when it is over, we'll rebuild—and Moscow will resupply us. The Americans, on the other hand, obviously, will rebuild—but it will take them years to recover from what we have done so far. If Major Zarin's

attack tonight succeeds as well, it will be years more before they recover. As for us, by this time next year, not
only will the Russia's have resupplied us, but everything
will have been upgraded."

"Have we received any word from Colonel Rafsanjani?" Jalili continued.

"No, we have not," Suleimani replied, "and I really
do not expect to hear from him until he at least reaches
Amsterdam tomorrow morning. By that time, we should
have an idea as to how Zarin's unit made out. If they
succeed to the extent that the first attacks did, you can
expect more of the same from the Americans."

"Yes, I am sure of that. Do we have any means left
to defend ourselves? I'm sure they have hit the coastal
areas along the gulf extremely hard. Do we have anything we can transfer from the Eastern Frontier borders
with Afghanistan and Pakistan? If so, now would be the
time to move them."

"Our navy in the gulf is gone; every ship and small
boat was sunk in the first half hour of this onslaught. The
air force planes we initially sent up were all shot down
as well, with no victories on our part. Our Air Defense
Network has been neutralized; huge holes—air corridors
for their pilots to fly through—have been blown in our
Network but it's also been neutralized. They seem to
have figured out some way to counteract our radar systems so that even though we can see them on radar, our
missiles miss their targets by several kilometers. They
are not jamming our signals so much as it seems sending
false returns to our systems."

"Is there anything we can do to counteract this?"

"No, there isn't," replied Suleimani. "We use the
same ADN that both Libya and Syria have used—it's the
old Russian S-200 system. The Americans and their
NATO partners flew over Libya with impunity and you
saw how easily the Israelis defeated Syria's system when

they raided Dayr az-Zawr and took out their lone nuclear reactor. They are doing the same to us. We really needed the upgraded Russian S-300 system. Without that, there is simply nothing we can really do. Is there any chance we can get our ADN up graded from the Russians?"

"Not at this point. I am sure there is nothing more that the Russians would like to do than to stick it to the Americans but I don't see this as being the right time. Once this is over, though, you can plan on it."

"I kind of thought so; with that being the case, then, there is very little we can do to deny the Americans complete aerial supremacy over the country. We still have several of our point defense systems, like the Shalamcheh which is essentially a clone of the American HAWK system, some man-pads and of course small arms and some other AAA, but aside from that, it's pretty bleak."

"Are there any signs of their Special Forces or SEAL Teams within our boarders?"

"Not at present—and there wouldn't be. If we happened to locate any of them, they'd have their fighter bombers all over us. You remember how quickly they took down the Taliban in Afghanistan. The same will not happen here but that is an example—not to be forgotten—of just how effective their Special Forces can be."

"So, for the time being, there is very little we can do to stop the American onslaught. We'll have to hope that Major Zarin's force will meet with the same success as Colonel Rafsanjani's initial attacks had."

"That is correct, Said, but hope is not a strategy."

Somewhere in the air over West Texas

"Tom, Dani just received a very hot call from her team leader back in Tel Aviv; hold on while we get Jim on the line as well."

"Jim, Stonewall and Dani here," Dani said over the phone. "Sorry for the late night call. We have Tom Norris on another line here as well. I just received a phone call from Benjamin Givon, my team leader back home. Turns out one of our northern teams very recently received a tip that a Quds Force officer named Lieutenant Colonel Sayyid Bukhari was going to brief the Hezbollah leadership on their plans for Hezbollah to attack Israel so they listened in—don't ask how. Colonel Bukhari is one of Suleimani's top assistants. In his briefing to Hezbollah, Bukhari claimed that the impending attack would be targeting the US government, specifically the US Congress, Supreme Court and the President. They didn't say just how this attack was to unfold, only the targets."

"That could explain a few things," Tom chimed in. "It looks as though we have about twelve men on the loose. We found a couple bunk houses with 6 beds in each. Each bed appeared to have had someone sleeping in it until quite recently as none of them were made. We found quite a few partially burned receipts in their burn pile for a lot of ammunition, 9mm, .223, and .300 Win-Mag. I could understand the nine mil and the .223 but the Winchester's a sniper round. Now it kind of makes sense. These guys are armed to the teeth. How much damage could a dozen men do with fully automatic weapons plus a possible sniper? If they broke up into a few assault teams with ten men assaulting the Capital and two men attacking the Supreme Court, they could almost literally capture the entire House and/or the Senate."

"Dani, Stonewall, what are your thoughts on this?" Jim asked them.

"Sir, the information from Ben just doesn't make sense." Dani blurted out. "The Iranians have nothing but contempt for the US government and President Barre and his administration. They see this administration as weak and thoroughly incompetent. Personally, I wouldn't be surprised if there were people in the Cabinet who don't fully understand just how badly the United States has been hit; pardon my frankness, sir, but Tom Fleming's an idiot and secretary of state Andrea Johnson has no concept of international politics. However, this administration has allowed them to pursue a nuclear bomb; we were the ones who attacked them. Jalili thoroughly understands the concept of asymmetrical warfare. He knows he can't defeat the US—he isn't trying to. He has hit you—hard, probably harder than the US has ever been hit—and exposed your vulnerabilities for all the world to see. He knows you will retaliate and he fully expects their military to be decimated, but he fully expects their government to survive as he knows President Barre just doesn't get it. He knows you will not invade so if he can weather the aerial onslaught, everything will be back to normal in a few days. It simply doesn't make sense to take out this administration—the Iranians couldn't ask for a better situation in Washington. That being said it's a theory, but it's just that. We don't have any intelligence at all to support it—unless Tom's team has been able to find anything on those two laptops."

"Jim, Dani's right, in so far as we don't believe the government is at risk. Said Jalili is the architect of this attack: the attack in the gulf was in response to the political leadership in Tehran; the attacks in the states are all Jalili. If the politicians in Tehran are calling the shots, the political leadership in DC is definitely at risk, but I don't think they are; this is all Jalili. He fully understands that he can't go toe to toe with us militarily, and he has just demonstrated that. Furthermore, I think he fully understands that this administration allowed them to pursue the Bomb; as such, these attacks are designed to punish the US for its support of Israel. The best way to do that is to continue the attacks in the same manner he started."

"Okay, Tom, where's your team at with the laptops?" Jim asked.

"We haven't been able to break through the encryption yet, but it's still early. We've only been on this for a couple hours. We've also found several receipts for diesel fuel so it obviously appears that they were stockpiling this anticipating that it might be hard to find at the very least. Based on the amounts listed—and these are very recent purchases—they have enough fuel to travel to either coast, Seattle or Boston. They don't have any fuel barrels here on the ranch, so they had to have taken it all with them. As to their intent, aside from what you just learned, we don't know much more than we did a couple hours ago. Right now, all of our intel is more on the side of their capabilities—and they would appear to be very capable."

"Okay guys, I'll let the Director and the Secret Service know about the threat to the Congress, the Supreme Court and the President. In the meantime, Dani, I'm not ruling out your idea of an attack on the nuclear power industry out here. I'm keeping the alert on for the Air Force, the FAA and the NRC, though I think we'll focus the air threat on the New York to Washington corridor. Go ahead and fill Tom in on your idea once you get back to Marathon. I think it's very plausible."

"Will do, sir. We'll be there in about half an hour."

* * * * *

Norris met them as soon as the helicopter landed at the Marathon ranch.

"So, Dani, just what is this little theory of yours?" he asked.

"Stonewall and I have been discussing their intent— and capabilities—for the past few hours. We were thinking that we're in for another 9/11 type of attack, only this time directed at your nuclear power industry—at least that is until Ben called."

"What makes you think that?" Norris asked.

"Here's the way I see it:" Dani responded. "First, Zarin indicated that this attack is intended to make you suffer as a country and that it will be worse than the other two. To me this rules out any attack on your political establishment. I'm not going to rehash our phone conversation. That idea's preposterous. Secondly, to our combined knowledge—and by that I mean the CIA and Mossad—the Iranians do not have either a biological or chemical weapons program. Nor do we believe that they have picked up either of these from either Saddam's crumbled fiefdom or from Assad in Syria. The question of an old 'suit-case' nuke from the old Soviet Union has arisen but your own Defense Department handled that in the old Soviet republics and in my own research—I have a PhD in Nuclear Engineering—I have never come across anything that would indicate any of these ever got loose. Finally, we are dealing with the Quds Force here: they are fanatics, they are very well trained, and they have their own 'air force'—if you want to call it that— within the Quds and many of them have air combat experience."

"She convinced you of all this?" Norris said, looking at Jackson.

"Oh, yeah. And there's more."

"You see, Tom," Dani continued, "your nuclear power plants are really concentrated in three main areas: you have six reactors around the Chicago area, eight more in the Carolinas, but there are fourteen concentrated along the eastern seaboard from Washington to Boston. If just four of the reactors along the eastern seaboard are hit and suffer a melt down—and we are talking the right four—you would have to evacuate more than *thirty-five million* people! I don't think I need to remind you of the evacuation problems associated with Hurricane Katrina, and you had two to three days warning on that one."

"We had already discussed this with Jim Carmichael; that's what he meant by keeping the alert on for the FAA, the Air Force and the NRC."

"That all sounds real good, but as you yourself alluded, we simply do not have any intelligence to support this idea, whereas it would seem your team leader just gave us the most current intel, that of an attack on the government."

No sooner had Dani finished discussing her idea than Jackson's phone rang.

"Yeah, Jim, what's up?" he asked.

"Stonewall, is Dani there as well?" Carmichael asked.

"I'm here, Jim," she responded as Jackson placed his phone on speaker.

"Agent Norris seems to have things pretty well under control down there so I really don't think you are needed there right now. I want you two to head up to the airport at Fort Stockton; it looks like it's probably a forty-five minute drive for you; considerably less if Norris will give you a lift in his chopper. I'll have a G650 waiting for you; your first stop will be Fort Campbell—I believe you are familiar with this place."

"Absolutely; what's the plan?"

"You're still a colonel with the Fifth Group, Special Forces. I've spoken with the SecDef; you are being temporarily reassigned back to the Army and picking up an ODA team at Campbell; you will be in command. From there, you'll head back to Israel and meet up again with Dani's team. Ben, Dani and the rest of their team will lead you back into Tehran. We'd like you to get there just as soon as possible. The Fifth Group's already been alerted; they'll have a team waiting for you. We want you in Israel . . . , I guess at this point it would be later this evening and in Tehran by tomorrow."

"What's the plan once we get there?"

"We're still working on that but we want you in theater as soon as possible. From what I understand, Dani's team has the gear for pretty much whatever we decide from a sniper mission to lasers for a pin point bombing campaign."

"That they do, sir; it's a pretty impressive armory."

"Jim, we have pretty much whatever you might need, regardless of the nature of the mission. We've set it up to be completely self-contained for any event imaginable," Dani chimed in.

"How soon before the plane's at Fort Stockton?" Stonewall asked.

"The plane's already in the air. Took off from Randolph Air Force Base in San Antonio so I'd bet it'll be landing in about half an hour."

"We're on our way. Give us a call when you have the mission details."

XXIII

Bahrain, U.S. Fifth Fleet Headquarters

Vice Admiral Jeff Ramsey would have preferred having a fourth carrier. He had had three carriers operating on continuous air ops since the initial Iranian attack and he knew needed to give his crews a rest. He started with the *Washington* as she remained in the gulf and had already had to dodge the initial onslaught of Sunburn missiles. The *Stennis* and the *Roosevelt,* both in the Arabian Sea, would continue for several hours, especially the *Roosevelt* as she had been the last on scene. Oh, but for a fourth carrier. He could only imagine having the six carriers at his disposal that both General Norman Schwarzkopf and General Tommy Franks had in their respective operations in their wars in this region. He knew that with the advances made in munitions since Tommy Franks, and especially "Stormin' Norman", that his three carriers more than equaled the might of their six carriers but just the same, to have the might and power at his disposal of a fourth carrier, he could have two carriers conducting round the clock air ops indefinitely! Having commanded the *Lincoln* several years ago, he knew the powerful capabilities of a single carrier, let alone the three that he currently had but with a fourth, Admiral Fischer at Centcom wouldn't even need the Air Force working out of Al Udeid—the Navy could handle this little operation all by themselves. In fact, by the time the Air Force got their act together, their vaunted B-1 Lancers or F-15E Strike Eagles wouldn't have much to do but bore holes in the sky. That is, unless the Pentagon had more in mind than simply an aerial assault on these mad mullahs. He hadn't heard of any special missions coming down for the SEALS or the Army's Special Forces but even if plans for this type of action were in the works, his carriers could work with them as well as the Air Force. In the initial stages of the Afghan war, the Navy's carriers played a huge role for the Special Forces on the ground. If the Navy could work there, they surely could work here where the distances were far closer than having to get into Afghanistan. He wondered if Fischer didn't have this in mind. Sure, the US could invade Iran, but what would be the point; after Afghanistan and Iraq, a third invasion seemed counterproductive. A Special Forces mission on the other hand seemed the perfect situation here. Discontent with the Mullahs in Iran seemed to be growing and an outright invasion by the Great Satan would only play into the hands of the Mullahs. However, inserting a few ODA's into the country could wreak havoc for the mullahs, which, is what we really wanted, wasn't it?

"Jeff," as Admiral Fischer welcomed him on the video conference, "how's the operation going over there?"

"Well, sir, we've pretty much eliminated all of the primary targets we had. Every one of the Quds bases has been leveled—there isn't a building standing on any of their bases. We've eliminated the threat from their navy and every base where they could possibly have stored their Sunburn missiles has been hammered. We've taken out the last of their air force, their Air Defense Network has been neutralized and anything resembling a Command and Control network has been eliminated. I'm guessing that they still have a few of the old HAWK air defense systems remaining but we've taken out the ones that they activated. Aside from a few man-pads we know they have, we have complete aerial supremacy over the entire country. At this point, I have the *Washington* standing down while the *Stennis* and the *Roosevelt* are just finishing up. What's next on the agenda? We've hit them really hard."

"The Republican Guards are next. We want the Quds and the IRGC completely eliminated. Essentially we are trying to take out the radical element of the Iranian defense forces. We are deliberately leaving their army bases alone to the extent that they do not pose a threat to us. In addition, we will be inserting at least one combined Special Forces ODA and Sayeret Matkal team; they should be on the ground in Tehran by tomorrow."

"Tehran? Are we going for 'regime change' here?" Ramsey asked.

"That hasn't been decided yet. However, at the very least, we want to do what we can to eliminate the radical element within the country, and the Republican Guards command is based in Tehran, which is where General Qassim Suleimani, their commanding officer, is located. Remember, in addition to the havoc they've wreaked across California and the Pacific Northwest, these guys have continued to use Terrorism as an instrument of their foreign policy. We want to take this opportunity to shut that down once and for all. By inserting an ODA team, with more probably following, we'll at least be prepared for a wide range of options the president may want to pursue."

"I'll get the *Washington* turned around then. They headed for the small 'bay' in the gulf between Qatar and Abu Dhabi when the Iranians launched their first attacks in an effort to close the strait."

"Sounds like a good idea. In the meantime, you'll be getting some help out there. The Air Force is moving a couple squadrons of Eagles and a tanker squadron to Al Udeid. They're also putting some B-1's out of Diego Garcia. The Brits will be getting a couple squadrons of Tornados over to Al Udeid as well. Most of these should be arriving either today or tomorrow. In addition, with NATO getting involved, the Turks have agreed to let us use Incirlik for strike operations as well. Both the Brits and the Germans will have a squadron of Tornados there."

"Well, let the Air Force, Brits and anyone else know that we've done the heavy lifting for them. We have a few of our Tomahawks left so we'll use the rest of these on the Republican Guards bases. By the time everyone else gets in the game, virtually all of the 'hard' targets will have been eliminated but a lot of the soft targets, armor, etc., will remain."

"Very good, Jeff. I'll keep you in the loop regarding the Special Forces teams as things develop."

Barnes Municipal Air Port

Major Eric "Thor" Esbjornson's Air Force career had been fairly distinguished—his Scandinavian heritage and his chiseled 6'4" frame made his call sign pretty obvious. In the past five years he had served a tour in Afghanistan and three tours in Iraq in his relatively short career. The truth of the matter was that he'd been young and single for each of these tours and just loved flying the F-15—it really was a remarkable fighter that, in one instance of a mid-air collision, an F-15 had lost an entire wing yet the pilot managed to bring the plane back to base with a relatively perfect landing! However, Thor had recently married and he assured his young bride that at the first chance, he'd transition to the Air National Guard. He had requested duty at one of NORAD's alert duty stations on the east coast if possible as both he and his wife were Vermont natives. When an opening at the Barnes Air National Guard Base in Westfield, Massachusetts arose, he jumped at it. His wife couldn't believe the news—they'd essentially be stationed less than a couple hours from both of their home towns—quite the contrast from Mountain Home, Idaho!

Thor's first day on the job as an alert pilot started out as expected—he met with his new crew chief and the rest of the maintenance personnel and then met up with Captain Jason "Blackjack" Brady, the SOF, or Supervisor of Flying. The Alert shack, itself, was just that—a shack, Thor thought to himself. This thing had to be a relic left over from WW II—it had all of the requirements of an alert shack but that was it. There was a bunk room for each of the pilots, an office for the SOF, and a lounge/kitchen area for them—and that was it. He couldn't believe the Spartan nature of the place; he made a mental note to bring in much of the accouterments he had when he'd been stationed at Kandahar—if he could liven that place up, he could certainly do the same here."

"Thor, good to see you again, man!" Snowman bellowed out as he entered the alert shack. The F-15 community is rather small and Thor had flown with Captain Chris "Snowman" Whiting in Afghanistan when he'd had been on a TDY tour.

"Hey, Snowman! Good to see you, too. Heard a rumor you were an Alert pilot up here; glad there was more to that rumor than most," Thor added. "But, ahh . . . , what have you done to this place. I mean, this shack rivals Kandahar—and that's sayin' something!"

"Yeah, well, I haven't been here on Alert status all that long myself; we'll get this place fixed up!"

"Damn right, we will," Thor agreed as they walked past the lounge where the maintenance crew had Fox News on—quite loudly—as a Fox News Alert interrupted the morning scheduling.   Martha MacCallum broke into the Fox and Friends program with the startling news that several of the refineries in the Los Angeles area had reported a series of explosions and that fires had been raging out of control for a couple hours, compounded by a loss of water pressure at some of the fire locations. They were also getting word of widespread power outages throughout the Pacific Northwest. Details on both were sparse—it was still dark on the west coast—and attempts to connect to an on-scene reporter failed each time the attempt was made, leaving Mac-Callum to ad lib for much of the News Alert. Finally, after repeated failures, Elizabeth Hasselbeck asked Martha if she could get back to them once they established communications with their LA branch, to which she readily agreed.

"What do you think of that?" Snowman asked Thor.

"That's going to hurt! The west coast, and California in particular, is unique to themselves when it comes to their gasoline supply; I remember a time while I was out at Mountain Home, BP, Shell or some other gas company had one of their refineries down for routine maintenance up at Bellingham, WA, and then a fire erupted at one of the large refineries in California—gas prices spiked to more than $4.25 a gallon out west. Early news reports are always spotty and short on accuracy but if there is even a hint of truth to this, the West—at the very least—is in for a world of hurt!"

Like most days at the Alert shack, nothing much happened, but on this day, the crews pretty much stayed glued to the round-the-clock news coverage on Fox. By late afternoon, a pretty clear picture had developed of what had happened out west, and horrific did not even begin to describe the situation. Live footage from Los Angeles to San Francisco echoed much the same on every news station. The fires were out but the damage remained incalculable. Around nine thirty that evening, Captain "Blackjack" Brady came barging into the lounge.

"Hey Snowman, I just heard from 'Huntress'!" referring to the Eastern Air Defense Sector (EADS), "they're putting up a Combat Air Patrol up over Washington, D.C., and New York City!"

"What?!?" Snowman & Thor cried out in unison.

"What the hell's going on?" Snowman added.

"They've never done that before," Thor continued. "Back on September 11th, Huntress put up a CAP later in the morning but by then, everything was over and it was too late to do anything about what had happened. Do we have any idea as to what this is all about?"

"Huntress didn't say, other than that they are using the Alert planes from both Langley and Atlantic City, NJ. Has there been anything on the news regarding anything here on the east coast? Huntress was very short on details, probably because we weren't scrambled."

"Nothing's been said, much less even speculated, and you know how news channels really excel at that!" replied Snowman.

"Well, we're already on an alert status," added Thor. "If they call our number, we'll be ready."

"Roger that!" replied Blackjack.

XXIV

G650 over the South Central US

Dani and Jackson arrived at Fort Stockton just as the Air Force G650 touched down at the municipal airport. Both of them had long since lost track of their duffle bags so as soon as their plane came to a stop, they boarded the craft, secured the cabin door, and prepared for takeoff. The US Air Force version of this craft had many of the same amenities as the Israeli version had, though the configuration of this one anticipated several more passengers. This one had to accommodate another twelve people they'd be picking up at Fort Campbell so the main cabin had a row of leather covered seats on each side of the craft with four berths in the rear with a double bunk in each. The galley in this craft, similarly stocked as the prior Israeli craft, was situated between the berths and the cabin seats. A small shower and rest room occupied the very tail end of the cabin.

"We've got about a three hour flight to Fort Campbell so choose the berth you want and I'll take another one. We're going to need some sleep," Jackson said to Dani.

"That's for sure, I'm exhausted. Do you have any idea as to who we'll be picking up in Kentucky? For that matter, any idea as to what we'll be doing?"

"No, you know as much as I do. I still know quite a few guys in the group but no idea as to what team we'll be picking up. The Special Forces are a pretty small fraternity so I'm sure I'll know someone on the team but aside from that, no ideas. Since we're going to Campbell, though, I'm sure we'll be picking up an A team and not a Delta detachment; they're usually located at Bragg in North Carolina. Not that that matters all that much—an A team is still a very versatile—and very capable—unit. My guess is, we'll be the first of many, if indeed we don't have any other teams already over there."

"We've heard of a lot of dissension within the Iranian military; I'm sure you've heard the same thing. Think they're tasking us to link up with some of the dissidents?"

"That's the mission we train for, though there is usually some chatter with the brass about an operation like that. I haven't heard a thing. Guess we'll just have to wait and see."

"Is there a shower on board this thing? We have them in ours; I forgot how hot and muggy Texas can be. Oh . . . wait, we left our bags at Fort Bliss! Great!! Well, I'm going to hit the rack. Give me a half hour notice before we land at Fort Campbell. I'll wash up then."

"Will do."

Two hours later, Jackson heard a knock on the cabin door.

"We're about half an hour out of Campbell, Colonel," the copilot added as he knocked on the door.

"Gotcha," replied Jackson.

Pulling his cargo pants back on he got up, knocked on Dani's cabin door and said "C'mon sunshine, we're about half an hour outside of Campbell."

"Sunshine?!? Stonewall, can't you read a clock?" Dani hollered through the door. "It's still the middle of the night. The sun's not due up for hours!"

"It has nothing to do with the sun; it's about your attitude," Jackson said, standing in the door way as she opened the door.

"Ah!!!" Dani shrieked as she took one look at Jackson.

"Stonewall!! What's with your eye?"

"Like it? I've got a spare eyeball; this one's all black and I've had the Special Forces insignia engraved in gold on it—pretty cool, huh?"

"Stonewall, you are so maddening!" Dani exclaimed as she charged at him hitting him in the shoulder and arm as he fended off her little attack.

"You still wearing that filthy sports bra?" He asked her, noticing she wore the same sports bra as on the flight over. "You know, you could take that thing off."

"Yeah, you'd like that wouldn't you? Sorry, Cowboy, but that's not gonna happen; not yet anyway," she added.

Marathon, TX

Special Agent Tom Norris had kept his team working through the night in an effort to crack the encryption on each of the laptops they had recovered. By noon, they had managed to get into each of the computers but each one appeared to have a multilayered encryption setup: they had gotten into the computer and had found several files of interest but each one had its own security features. He had heard from Fort Meade and they were about as far along on the cellphones as his team was on the laptops. His lead techie had told him that the hard part had been done. Now that they were in, he was advised it was only a matter of time before they cracked the encryption for each file. What Norris obviously did not know, was just how much time he had—or didn't have.

Scranton, PA

Captain Rouhani had let his men rest about as long as he thought he dared. His men had now rested for about eighteen hours and he anxiously wanted to get on with their mission. They only had about a five hour drive ahead of them and then the final act of this operation would really begin. Rouhani told his men that they would be leaving one of the trucks behind; three vehicles would be enough for them and their equipment. At this point, all they really needed were their arms and ammunition. Each one carried an M-4 carbine and a Glock 19 9mm pistol, plus spare magazines for each weapon. They weren't planning, much less hoping, to get into any kind of a firefight, but again, Rouhani wanted to be prepared should they have to fight their way in to their target. A little after two that afternoon, then, Rouhani and his men gathered up all of their gear, loaded up and headed out on I-84 towards Boston.

Fort Campbell, Kentucky

"Stonewall!" Sergeant Nick Rossi announced, "Good to see you."

"Hey Rossi, didn't know you'd be here," Jackson announced as he saw his former weapons sergeant board the plane with two large duffle bags. "Good to see you, too. Dani, this is Sergeant Nick Rossi, who I believe, is now . . . the operations sergeant for the team? Rossi was the senior weapons sergeant on my last team."

"Nice to meet you Sergeant Rossi," Dani responded.

"Likewise. Hey Ferro, c'mon up and look who's here," Rossi yelled back to Sergeant Marcus Taliaferro.

Jogging up the boarding stairs of the plane to meet them, Ferro yelled out "Hey, Colonel, good to see you again. Heard you've been a little busy lately."

"Yeah, you could say that. Ferro, this is Dani. Dani, this is Sergeant Marcus Taliaferro. Ferro was the senior medic on my last team with Rossi."

"Nice to meet you, Ferro," Dani said.

"You, too, Dani. If you'll excuse me, I still have a few things to pack up. I'll be right back, Colonel."

"Ah, Colonel," Rossi called out, "when I heard we'd be picking you up, I made some discreet phone calls. It sounded like you've been on the go for a little while and probably didn't have your bags. I took the liberty of grabbing a couple uniforms for both of you. Danielle, your CO-"

"Sergeant Rossi, its Dani," she cut him off. "A friend of Stonewall's is a friend of mine. Please, call me Dani."

"Very well, call me Rossi. Dani, your CO made it sound like you two were an item, so I put everything in one bag. . . . Ah . . . hope I didn't overstep anything." Rossi added, noting that Dani had immediately blushed and stole a rather quick and surprised glance at Jackson.

"Thanks, Rossi, really appreciate that. I think we've both lost track of where we ditched our bags, probably back at Fort Bliss somewhere," Jackson added.

"Ah, Dani, from the way your CO described you, it sounded like you were about the same size as my wife; she stopped at the PX and grabbed some undergarments, couple sports bras, stuff like that. I didn't get your rank but I understand you're third on your team, so made you a major. The Captain didn't appreciate that but that's too bad. Hope you don't mind the American uniform."

"Sergeant Rossi, thank you very much," Dani replied, clearly more than a little embarrassed. "You're very thoughtful; the American uniform is fine; so is the rank, though I'm going have to have a little talk with Ben, my CO."

"Thanks again, Rossi," Jackson added with a huge grin on his face, "really appreciate this. Let's get the rest of the team on board and get the rest of the introductions out of the way."

"You bet, sir. Captain," Rossi yelled out the cabin door, "let's get everyone on board. We've got a schedule to keep."

"Roger that, sergeant. Okay, boys, you heard the man," Captain Robert Sanchez, the commanding officer of ODA 5114, announced.

One by one, the introductions were made with the men of ODA 5114 as each one boarded. Once everyone found a seat, Jackson finished up the introductions by letting the team know the little he knew of their mission. "I'm not sure what all Captain Sanchez has relayed to you but our first stop will be Tel Aviv where we will be picking up Dani's team. From there, our next stop will be Baku where we'll infiltrate into Iran. By this time tomorrow, we should be in Tehran. Just an FYI, don't let Dani's charm deceive you; she is a full member of the Israeli Special Forces, Sayeret Matkal, she has a PhD in Nuclear Engineering and she's a concert pianist."

Hearing Dani's resume, more than a couple of the team members let out a long slow whistle. "I think I'd rather meet up with a battalion of Taliban than face a girl like that," exclaimed one of the guys.

"I didn't think women served in the Sayeret Matkal" interrupted another one of the sergeants.

"There's actually two of us. You'll meet Zivah later today; she's also on the team," Dani replied. "And Stonewall exaggerated a little bit, I'm not really a concert pianist—that's my sister."

"Dani is a full member of the team; she's actually third on her team," Stonewall added. "We don't really know what our mission is at this point so we'll need to be ready for anything, which I know is pretty much par for the course for you guys. I anticipate we'll be laying up at the team's safe house in Tehran—where you'll be suitably impressed. If there aren't any questions, let's get on with it." And with that, the team buckled up and the plane headed out to the runway.

Though Stonewall and Dani had only had a couple hours' sleep in about the past twenty four hours, they both spent the next few hours mingling with the men of ODA 5114. Jackson had some catching up to do with both Rossi and Ferro while Dani simply listened in to their conversation. Half an hour into the flight, Rossi decided to check out the galley. Dani immediately followed him.

"So, Rossi," Dani began rather quietly as they reached the galley, "just how long have you known Stonewall?"

"Well, like he said, I was one of his weapons sergeants. We've served together for several years and I was the senior weapons sergeant on his last team and that would have been back in, what, 2006."

"Did you serve with him on his first team in Afghanistan?"

"*He* didn't tell you about that, did he?"

"No, Tamir told me about it a few days ago."

"Take a seat; I'll fill in a few of the gaps for you about him while Ferro has him occupied up front."

"Thanks, I'd appreciate anything you can tell me about him. He's always asking about me and I've never talked so much about myself with anyone but he's pretty quiet about himself."

"I've been with the Special Forces for seventeen years now—and that is still the boldest, craziest thing, I've ever done. He told you about the idea of marching down to the valley floor with the lanterns, right? Bet he didn't tell you that's where we gave him his call sign, did he?"

"Ah, no; what's that about?"

"Stonewall picked out about the narrowest place on the valley floor for us to set up our position. If the Taliban chose to make a serious attack, we didn't want them to have too much room to maneuver or to use their numbers to full effect. So there we were, Stonewall, myself, our comms sergeant, and nine of the Afghanis. We set up as many claymores as we could in the short time we had and then we each had a SAW (Squad Automatic Weapon) with at least five 100-round belts. Of course, we had a ton of grenades as well, anything that was loud and disorienting. Well, we had this parade coming down the hill and it looked impressive as hell but then, the Taliban figure they better attack right away before too many guys come over the hill. Mind you, it's still pitch dark but we can see extremely well with our gear; we were so outnumbered I didn't think we had a chance. Stonewall walks up to each of us and lets us know to let all hell break loose on his command. He waits until the second tier of Taliban get to the claymores before he trips these—their first element are all within twenty feet of us or so when we unload on them. I don't think he realized how many he actually let pass in that first element as some of them got to knife fighting range. Anyway, we had eleven guys hammering away with the SAWs and Stonewall's all over the place, running up and down the line, letting go with grenades, his M-4, his own SAW, even his pistol—all designed to make them think there were far more of us than a mere dozen guys. It was so chaotic that when we had finally routed them, I looked at Stonewall and said 'you know, I hear there's a Marine Corps general with the call sign "Chaos"; if it's good enough for him, it's certainly good enough for you, sir.' He took one look at me, and simply said, 'I like it!' Ever since then, that's been his call sign. I've never seen anyone like him; he literally thrives on chaos—the more chaotic the situation, the better he is."

"So, just how did the name 'Stonewall' come about? I get the notion that it follows the Civil War general of the same name but just what happened?"

"He hasn't told, you, huh? Yeah, that figures. He doesn't talk too much about some of the things he's done. Yeah, that's Stonewall. Well, suffice it to say that we had been dropped into Northern Iraq back in '06. We had several Humvees dropped along with us and that was as heavy of anything we had. Our initial assignment had us holding a major intersection of two major highways and a couple other minor roads. We had the place occupied and established some good defensive positions. A short time later, we noticed this Iraqi company coming up the highway a few miles away as they emerged from a bend in the road behind a small little ridge that obscured their column. We were seriously outnumbered, I don't know seven or eight to one, or something like that; remember, we're just a single "reinforced" A team— Stonewall picked up an additional weapons sergeant and another medic. The infantry trucks came first and we were pretty confident that we could hold against them even though we were that outnumbered. Then came the tanks—five of them, along with several armored personnel carriers. Remember, the heaviest thing we had was a Humvee with a .50 mounted on it. We had a pretty good supply of the new Javelin anti-tank missiles, but its effective range is something like 2,500 yards—and at this point, we were still more than 1,500 yards beyond that! By this time, heavy machine gun fire is ripping the ground up all around us and their mortars have us bracketed. Anyway, Stonewall grabs a Humvee by himself with six of these Javelins and proceeds down the crossroad at this intersection *towards the Iraqis*. He immediately draws some fire but the rest of us are holding the highway junction so we continue to receive most of their fire—by this time, their mortars have found the range and most of us have an injury of one sort or another. About five hundred yards in front of us, Jackson stops, pulls out one of the Javelins and fires at the closest tank, now getting a pretty good bead on us with their main guns. Anyway, from about three thousand yards, his first shot hits the lead tank. At this, all the Iraqis turn their full attention on him. In the next two, two and a half minutes, he took out the other four tanks and one of the APC's. Of course by then, we figure they might even be within range of us and, sure enough, we took out the rest of the APC's and all their trucks. However, for that two minute span or so, Stonewall bore the brunt of every gun and mortar in that Iraqi company; it's amazing he survived, though he got shot up pretty good. Ferro saw the mortar round that hit him and grabbed a Humvee and charged right up to him. There was blood all over the place by the time Ferro got there: his left shoulder and part of his arm had just been shredded; the left side of his face was covered in blood and his eye was gone. Ferro got him bandaged up and brought him back to the junction just as the Eighty-second arrived. In spite of his injuries, he was up and around making sure the rest of us received the aid we needed—he had to be running on pure adrenalin at that point. He literally saved the entire team—and that's no exaggeration. Neither Ferro nor I

would be here if it wasn't for Stonewall. Those tanks
had us bracketed with their main guns and the mortars
were really raining down on us. Their next few rounds
would have taken us out. Personally, I think he deserves
the Medal of Honor. He was put in for the DSC but that
got down-graded to a Silver Star—gotta love Army politics. The Theater Commander was a 'Big Army' guy
and thought those of us in the Special Forces were nothing more than a bunch of renegades. Anyway, the colonel in command of the regiment from the Eighty-second
that relieved us saw what he did and commented that that
was just like the Stonewall Jackson of old. The name
obviously stuck."

"I was wondering; I asked him about the scars on his
chest and shoulder and he played it pretty low key,
though he quickly changed the subject."

"That sounds like him. He's really a pretty humble
guy. He's been in more hairy situations than most of us,
and that's saying something. There's something else you
need to know about him."

"What's that?" Dani asked somewhat concerned.

"His iron will—and he's demonstrated that time and
time again. By the time of our little battle in Iraq, Stonewall knew he'd made major but wouldn't be pinning on
the oak leaves for a few months, so he knew he had commanded his last A team. Nevertheless, he wanted to stay
in the Special Forces, and he really wanted to lead a CIF
(Commander's In-extremis Force) team. To do this,
though, he needed to go before the Medical Review
Board to re-qualify and demonstrate that he was still
among the best of the best. As a major, he qualified to
lead the team but he had a monumental battle ahead of
him given the extent of his injuries. It took him a few
months but he cleared the Review Board and he got his
team, though it went all the up the Special Operations
chain of command. There's never been anyone like him,

even in this rarified community. I know I can speak for everyone that's ever served with him—we'd follow him anywhere. There isn't a single one of us who wouldn't do anything for him. He's pretty special that way. Now that he's a colonel, I'm sure his serious combat days are behind him, but he still has that unbelievably fierce determination that is just incredible."

"I haven't seen that part of him yet, but I'm sure I will at some point."

"Look, I didn't mean to embarrass you earlier. It was kind of obvious when I mentioned what your CO told me."

"Oh, don't worry about that. I think we both got a laugh out of that. And the change of clothes is really appreciated!"

"Yeah, well, knowing Stonewall the way I do, and from what you're telling me, he really digs you. I've never seen anyone more determined and absolutely driven at anything than he is—and everyone in the Special Forces has a pretty gritty determination, but Stonewall's in a class by himself. If he wants something, he's going to get it. If you're in his sights, you might as well give up as you'll be his. On the other hand, if that's what you want, he'll also be yours."

Dani had to admit, she liked the sound of that. Seeing her eyes immediately light up and her broad smile told Rossi that he had instantly hit home with her.

"Thanks, Rossi. I'm going to hit the shower!" and with that, Dani turned and walked away with a noticeable glow about her.

XXV

Marathon, TX

By four o'clock that afternoon, Norris' team had cracked several of the files. He now had the complete attack plans for the California and Pacific Northwest portions of their attack. He knew where the attacks had originated, the particular ranches in both Oregon and Nevada, as well as how many had been involved in each of the attacks. Norris realized right away he had a big intelligence coup with this information—and he knew he needed to get this up the chain right away.   Though he had Rafsanjani's plans right he front of him, he still couldn't believe the complexity of this—the Air Force would need to put up *six more* drones and the Army would need *two entire battalions* of either Rangers or the Eighty-second Airborne division to hit the six remaining sights in both states. He knew the Army keep a unit on alert around the clock, but he suspected this might surpass what they kept on alert. After all, with six locations to hit—at the same time—they'd need an infantry Company for each location—if the Riverside, OR ranch served as an example—which meant probably at least two C-17's per location for an even dozen of the massive transport planes. Would this many be available for immediate duty? Probably he thought, though possibly not all from the same base, which would delay any possible assault. Fortunately, he knew, this was not his problem.

More importantly, though, his IT staff was now finding references to the JFK airport in New York—something which really got his attention. At this, he began to wonder if Dani's idea of an airborne attack on some of the nation's nuclear power plants might just be their objective. However, he knew he needed more than just references to JFK—he needed solid intel on what these guys had planned, and he didn't have that as yet. He knew that alerts had already gone out to the FAA, the Air Force and the NRC. However, if he could get more specific information out to these agencies, he just might actually be able to prevent the last portion of this attack.

Finally, about six that evening, one of his staff members gained access to one of Major Zarin's files in which there was a detailed plan with all twelve of Zarin's men hitting the JFK airport from the water. The attack called for three RHIBs to land after dark at the perimeter of JFK from Bergen Basin. Once they made their landing they would proceed to a nearby cargo terminal and hangar and take over at least four planes. As Dani had predicted, all of these men were trained pilots. Zarin appeared to have scouted out the airport quite well: the cargo terminal was located at the immediate end of one of the runways; a couple hangars were immediately adjacent to the cargo terminal. Once they had the plane, or planes, they could take off in very short order. Nothing in this plan, at least nothing they had as yet discovered, alluded to any targets once they had the planes airborne. However, Norris now had the specifics he needed. His first call was to the New York Port Authority. His second call was to Homeland Security.

Tel Aviv

"Good to see you, Arielle," Ben greeted Dani as she got off the plane. "That uniform looks pretty good on you."

"Arielle, I thought you might have hit it off with Stonewall here, but I really didn't think you'd be wearing his uniform already," Tamir added in, chuckling to himself.

"Thanks, guys, you're all heart!" Dani replied. "We left our bags clear back at Fort Bliss, so yeah, Rossi picked up a new uniform for me. Ben, just what did you tell him?!? It's been a while since I've been that embarrassed. I swear, I'm going to get even with you!"

"Yeah, he called up yesterday when they got word of their deployment. I just tried to fill in a few blanks for him," Ben added.

"Ah huh," Dani said. "Just remember, I'll get you for this."

"Tamir, good to see you once again," Jackson interrupted.

"It is good to see you as well, my friend. I see Arielle has met a few of your friends here."

"That she did. Turns out a couple of these guys were on my last A team; we've got a good team here. Any word on the mission for us just yet?"

"Nothing yet, though, I understand you and your friends here need to get to Tehran rather quickly."

"Yeah, the sooner the better. We'd really like to be there by this afternoon if possible."

"We shall do what we can to get you there. Ben and his team have been waiting for you. Your plane is all fueled and ready to go. We'll simply need to transfer what gear you have into our plane; you can be wheels-up in ten minutes. We'll have you in Baku in less than two hours. From there, you should be able to make the border crossing around seven this morning putting you in Tehran right around the noon hour if all goes well."

"Perfect. Will we be staying at the same safe house?"

"Yes, you will. There will be plenty of room there for all of you. If I remember correctly, Dani gave you a brief tour of the place. All of the gear and equipment you could possibly want should be there. My team has orders to assist you and your men with anything they might need from weapons to communications."

"Thanks, Tamir; I really appreciate that. I'm not exactly sure of what our orders will be but we're prepared for anything."

"Quite right. I do believe that is why they are sending you and your team. Good luck; and I hope to see you back here in a few days."

And with that, Jackson boarded the plane as Ben shut the door behind him. Jackson was pleased to see that they were back in a six fifty. Once again, introductions were made amongst the combined teams. Even with nineteen passengers, the plane seemed quite spacious. With the introductions completed, Ben began a brief summary of how the infiltration would work.

"We'll be landing in Baku around 0230. Once we land, my team will convoy to the border in five vehicles—it's about a three hour drive. Captain Sanchez, you and your team will be conducting a HAHO jump and drifting over the boarder for about fifteen to twenty kilometers. Once we land in Baku, your team can begin the pre-breathing and prep-work for the jump. You'll be jumping from about twenty-five thousand to twenty-eight thousand feet. The jump master on-board will give you the landing zone coordinates; we've used the place several times before. One of my guys will be there by

0500 to mark the drop zone for you in case we're delayed. His code name is Levi. Jackson's code name, if he hasn't told you by now, is 'Chaos'—go figure, right? You won't need much in the way of extra gear for the jump; feel free to take a weapon or two, pistol, carbine, or so; we'll have all the gear you'll need once we get to Tehran. Our highway to Tehran runs right along the coast of the Caspian Sea and a mountain range. There is roughly a two mile wide stretch between the sea and the mountains. About fifteen kilometers or so down the highway, there is a fairly large grove of trees on this plain that will shield you as you land behind them."

"Sounds like a pretty straightforward jump," replied Sanchez.

"Yeah, this will probably be the easiest combat jump you'll ever have. Like I said, we've done this before. The way your navy is keeping them busy in the gulf, we shouldn't have any problems at all up here."

Marathon, TX

"Director," Norris said into his phone, "we have some potentially conflicting information. We've been able to crack part of Major Zarin's laptop. We know how they conducted the first two attacks, and from where. We've also uncovered a detailed plan on a proposed attack on the JFK airport in New York City. I've already called the New York Port Authority to put them on alert and gave them the specifics of what was on Zarin's laptop. Sir, if this is indeed their plan, we need to be prepared for another 9/11 type attack. We don't have a timeline but I'm sure this could happen at any time."

"Tom," Director Stevens replied, "do we know if this is definitely what they have in mind? I mean, the Israelis seemed to have solid intel on what would be happening?"

"No, sir, we don't. What we know for sure is that we have a detailed plan of theirs that spells out precisely how they would attack JFK. We do not have a timeline, or anything else. For that matter, there are still several files that we have yet to crack so this could be just one option that they have proposed. However, while we have yet to crack all of the files here, nothing that we have found lends credence to, or contradicts, the intel we received from Mossad."

"Okay, Tom; keep digging. I don't think we'll find a direct link to exactly what this last group is going to do, especially if their commander has any freedom to pursue options that have been proposed by Zarin and Colonel Rafsanjani. We're simply going to need to be prepared for just about anything. We'll have alerts out to every law enforcement agency in the country raising the alert level to our highest level."

Tel Aviv

"Dr. Bagheri," Tamir Pardo addressed his surprised visitor. "I trust your accommodations meet with your approval? I apologize for not getting back to you sooner but we've had a few items that needed my attention of late."

"I can only imagine," replied Dr. Bagheri. "From what I hear, my countrymen have been rather busy in the United States. I wish I could have been more useful to both of your countries."

"That's what brings me here, as well as my guest. Dr. Bagheri, this is Ambassador Bill Richards from the United States. I don't know the intentions of the US Government, and I don't believe Ambassador Richards here does either, but most of the assets are in place should the United States decide to try and remove the current Iranian government. What assets that are not currently in place soon will be. My question to you is, if the Americans decide to take out the government of the Islamic Republic, would you be willing to return and establish a new government. No one knows that you are here. We could smuggle you back into the country just as we got you out. We would assist you in letting it out that you were not home when we destroyed your home and you went into hiding immediately after your home was destroyed. Again, I do not know what the Americans have in mind but should the opportunity arise to do something like this, would you be interested?"

"That is a lot to think about General Pardo. I was just getting used to my new home here in exile. I would of course, love to return to my home, but if word ever got out of the role that I played in all of this, I would be convicted by any court in my country with an immediate execution."

"Dr. Bagheri," Ambassador Richards began, "we would see to it that you would have all of the resources you would need to establish a new government. We would work to normalize relations with our two countries just as soon as possible. I know our country is not all that popular with your countryman but we would be more than willing to work with or through several other governments like the Pakistanis, the Uzbeks, or even the Indians. In short, we could funnel a lot of support your way very quickly if you would be so inclined."

"You make it sound so simple, Mr. Ambassador. Surely, some of the leadership of the Republican Guards would remain. They will certainly play a role in whatever government survives this onslaught."

"Dr. Bagheri, we are doing everything we can to take out as much of the Republican Guards leadership as we can. We are trying to eliminate as much of the radical element of the existing government as we can. No matter what remains for a government in Tehran, we want this element completely removed from the scene. You taking over, would really help us."

"Well, if we can completely guarantee that my involvement with all of this will not get out, I would love to return to my country."

"Thank you for that, Dr. Bagheri," Ambassador Richards replied. "But as I indicated, right now we are just exploring our options. Absolutely nothing has been decided as yet."

XXVI

Boston

Captain Rouhani's team arrived at the Hyatt at Logan International about seven thirty in the evening. As Rouhani had hoped, their room provided an excellent vantage point from which he could survey both the harbor as well as the entire airport and the cargo terminals. He and three of his men had taken up positions to scout out the airport terminals as well as the Inner Harbor. They were very confident that their mission had not been discovered but Rouhani had taken up their over watch position to survey the area just in case. He would have the next couple hours to watch over everything just to make sure. The rest of his men had broken up into three different groups and stopped in at the Hyatt's restaurant for dinner. They all had very official looking fake ID's and credit cards to match so Rouhani remained confident that their cover would hold, and it only needed to hold for two more hours.

By nine fifteen, Rouhani called all of his men up to the room; it was time to go. Each of his men changed into the uniform of a Fed Ex pilot or copilot's uniform; over that, they each wore the overalls worn by the cargo handlers. By nine thirty, Rouhani and ten of his men left for the Fed Ex cargo terminal. He left his lieutenant at the hotel in an over watch position. Each man had a radio, a Glock 19 with suppressor, and a K-bar knife; they left their M-4 carbines in the trucks.

Rouhani knew he had a real tactical problem and he'd need more than a little bit of luck to pull this off: He needed to steal four 757 cargo jets without anyone alerting the authorities. The first plane was scheduled to leave at 10:14 and the second one, seven minutes later with all four airborne by 10:43. Rouhani and his men arrived to find all four aircraft parked side by side at the terminal with the push carts attached to all four jets ready to push them back on to the taxiway. Rouhani and his men blended in perfectly with their cargo uniforms, and with four cargo planes in various stages of being loaded, all the grounds crewmen remained preoccupied with their own duties so that no one noticed the additional men. At precisely 9:50, three of his men grabbed the cargo manifests for each of the first three planes from another of the grounds crewmen. With the cargo manifests in hand, the raiders broke up into three parties of three men each and nonchalantly proceeded up the stair carts that led to the cockpits of each of the first three Fed Ex cargo jets. Once inside the plane, the pilots were killed by two of the hijackers while the third member of the raiding party stood in the entranceway of the plane blocking the view of anyone who might either try to see what was going on or try and climb up to the cockpit. Rouhani and one of his sergeants remained on the tarmac keenly watching to see if any alert had been given. His lieutenant remained keeping an over watch on the entire area from the Hyatt, ready to alert them all if he noticed any threat to their little operation.

By 9:55, Rouhani was pleasantly surprised that the first three jets had been taken and no one had noticed a thing.

"Lieutenant Najafi," Rouhani radioed to his executive officer, "we have the first three. Have you seen anything that would indicate we've been discovered? This was way too easy; these Americans are way too complacent."

"I haven't seen anything that would indicate we've been compromised. Everything looks like it is going to plan, sir," replied Najafi.

"Very well; the first plane is backing out as we speak. The second one is hooked up and ready to go. Get over here as soon as you can. The last one is scheduled to leave at 10:43 so we'll need you over here in a few minutes. We just might pull this off yet."

"Be right there, sir," replied Najafi.

At precisely 10:14, Fed Ex 820 took off; seven minutes later, the second one followed. The third one was being pushed back away from the terminal and onto the taxiway. Rouhani now needed to grab the fourth plane if he was going to succeed.

As the third plane backed out onto the tarmac, Rouhani, Najafi and their last remaining soldier climbed the steps to enter the cockpit of Fed Ex 1003. As with the first three, the initial deception went very well: they had the cargo manifest and no one challenged them as they proceeded up to the cockpit. However, the pilot of this plane had been an Air Force pilot who had seen service in Operation Enduring Freedom and had been stationed at Bagram for a couple tours. He immediately recognized Najafi's accent and, upon looking at the three men coming up towards the cockpit, realized something was amiss. He keyed his mic and asked them what they wanted—he had never had three men approach his cockpit like this before.

"Just wanted to go over the manifest with you, Captain," Rouhani replied.

"It doesn't take three of you to do that. Tell the other two to head back down or I'll be calling security."

"That's fine. These guys are new and aren't familiar with all of the procedures we have," Rouhani pointed out, trying to reassure the pilot.

"Yeah, well, I still don't want them up here. Have them get down or I'm calling security; I won't tell you again."

Air Traffic Control had been listening in on this and immediately asked if everything was okay with the plane. The copilot replied that everything seemed to be in order at present but to hang on for a bit.

"Okay, okay; I'm sending them down," Rouhani claimed. At this, he turned towards his compatriots as if to tell them to get down. However, as soon as he had turned towards them, he pulled out his Glock, which was now hidden from view from the pilot, and suddenly turned back towards the pilot and fired two rounds into both the pilot and co-pilot, killing both of them instantly. However, the pilot had kept the radio mic on the entire time. The Controllers in the tower immediately heard the four suppressed gunshots.

"Fed Ex, Ten-Oh-Three, is everything okay over there? I thought I heard some gunshots."

As soon as Rouhani heard the tower calling, he grabbed the headset from the pilot.

"Tower, everything is fine. We had a mix-up with the cargo manifest but we've straightened that out."

"Are you sure?" the controller responded. "I thought we heard some gunfire."

"Gunfire?" Rouhani replied. "Must have been static over the radio, control. We didn't hear anything over hear."

"Okay, as long as you're sure everything is okay," Control replied. However, to be on the safe side, the tower alerted the airport police to check out the plane and the terminal without warning the Fed Ex terminal. The controller was sure he had heard four separate shots; they had been muffled, but he thought they were gunshots just the same.

"Lieutenant, let the ground crew know that we are ready to depart and running behind schedule. We need to get this plane out of here before the police show up."

Before Najafi took his seat, he took his overalls off, stuffed them in the restroom with the bodies of the pilot and copilot and stood out the doorway yelling at the ground crew to get them pushed onto the taxiway. With that, he stepped back in the plane with his two compatriots and shut the door. For now, anyway, no one on the ground was the wiser.

With the door shut, the ground crew began pushing Fed Ex 1003 onto the taxiway.

"Well, at least we've made it this far," Najafi proclaimed. "You were right, Captain. We might just pull this off."

"We have a long way to go before we can call this a success, Lieutenant. The police are on their way. We need to get on the runway before they get here and, as big as this airport is, it will not take them long to get here—especially since the controller indicated he heard gunshots over the radio. I'm surprised they aren't here already," Rouhani exclaimed as he hit the throttles on the plane to head towards the flight line. As they approached the runway, Rouhani noticed that they had an empty runway—not a single plane was waiting to take off.

"Tower, this is Fed Ex Ten-Oh-Three," Rouhani spoke over the radio, "requesting take off."

"Ten-Oh-Three, just hold on a second. We've had a report of a disturbance over there and the police are en route to check it out. We don't have anyone else in the pattern right now so hold tight for a minute while we sort this out."

"Tower, what was the disturbance? We were just over there and didn't notice anything out of the ordinary."

"Ten-Oh-Three, hold on. We'll get back to you."

"Lieutenant, let's get ready to go, just in case they tell us to return to the terminal. If they tell us to return, we're taking off but not until we hear from the tower."

"Understood, sir."

Waiting is one of the hardest things anyone can be asked to do and for Captain Rouhani, this was no exception. He was absolutely certain that no one had seen anything with any of the four planes his men had taken. The ground crews had all been very busy and, while the facility had been fully lighted, shadows remained and his men had made the most of these in gaining access to the terminal. The only thing that worried him were the four gunshots that were transmitted over the radio when the pilot had keyed the mic; they were suppressed and, he hoped, could be attributed to static over the radio but he was not sure of that. Forty five seconds later, he had his answer.

"Ten-Oh-Three, can you head back to the terminal? Looks like there's something that needs to be checked out. Once we get that cleared up, you'll be on your way."

"Tower, what's going on? I have a deadline to meet," Rouhani replied. While responding to the tower, he motioned to his lieutenant to take off immediately. In unison, they fire-walled the throttles and headed down the runway.

"Ten-Oh-Three, you are directed to abort your take off and return to the terminal. Is that clear?"

"Ten-Oh-Three, do you copy?"

"Ten-Oh-Three?"

In the tower, the manager on duty, who was already monitoring the situation, picked up his phone and hit the speed dial for EADS.

"Huntress, Sergeant Forrest," answered the tech at the Eastern Air Defense Sector.

"Huntress, this is Boston Center, TMU. We have a suspected Fed Ex cargo jet that has been hijacked."

"Excuse me, sir; did you say *Boston Center TMU?*"

"Yes, that's correct. Why? We just had Fed Ex Ten-Oh-Three take off without authorization. We initially had a report of gunfire over the cockpit radio. The police were dispatched but the plane managed to make it to the runway before they got there. The pilot was told to return to the terminal but took off instead."

"Boston, we have an active alert notice that JFK could have been a target for a hijacking but not you. Confirm, this is a Fed Ex cargo plane?"

"Huntress, that is correct; Fed Ex Ten-Oh-Three is presumed to be hijacked."

"Boston, is this the only suspect plane? We have an alert out for possibly three more."

"Huntress, we launched four Fed Ex planes within a thirty minute span; this was the last one and the only suspicious one of which we know. The police are still at the terminal. I'll let them know to do some snooping. If they were going to take four planes, something must have been left behind."

"Tower, this is Sergeant O'Rourke of the Airport police. We've done some looking around here and found three pickup trucks in the Fed Ex parking lot. All three are licensed in Texas; found a dozen M-4 automatic rifles in them. We just ran the plates for these; turns out the FBI has a nationwide APB on them. Are you sure we only have the one hijacked airplane?"

"Huntress, did you hear that? You better watch all four of those Fed Ex planes."

"Roger that, Boston. We're on it."

131st Fighter Wing, Barnes MAP, Westfield, MA

"This is Huntress scrambling Yankee Five-Six and Yankee Five-Seven, I repeat Huntress is scrambling Yankee Five-Six and Yankee Five-Seven. Time is 0245 Zulu. All parties acknowledge."

"Yankee Five-Six, Yankee Five-Seven, scrambling," came the response from SOF Captain "Blackjack" Brady.

In the lounge, the klaxon announcing the scramble alert pierced the relative calm of the evening to such an extent that Thor thought his wife could hear it at their new home clear out in rural Huntington. When Thor received word of the CAP that Huntress had put up, he told the flight crews to add a large centerline fuel tank to both of the alert Eagles just in case they received orders to scramble. He figured that since they were already in uncharted territory with the CAP, he might as well make sure the Eagles had as much fuel as possible for any extended action they might see. He also put his flight suit on so that he'd be ready himself should the klaxon go off. A minute after receiving the scramble order, both pilots were in their F-15's practically ready to head out— as an Alert pilot, they are to be airborne within five minutes of the alert, and Thor knew they were going to beat that!

"Huntress, Yankee Five-Six, what is the mission?" Thor asked, identifying himself as the lead pilot.

"Yankee Five-Six, we have a hijacked Fed Ex cargo plane out of Boston, initial flight to Memphis. Be advised, we could have up to four hijacked Fed Ex flights all out of Boston en route to Memphis. Storm Two-Two and Two-Three are on CAP out of Langley currently over Baltimore and will be heading north to intercept."

"Huntress, do we have any call signs for these flights?" Storm two-two asked.

"Storm Two-Two, the call signs are Fed Ex Eight-Two-Zero, Six-Eight-Three, Twelve-Sixteen, and Ten-Oh-Three. Ten-Oh-Three is the flight of immediate concern as he took off from Boston without authorization."

"Do we have a fix on any of these planes?" Yankee Five-Six asked.

"Eight-Two-Zero is currently located at 41.980868/-72.943726; Six-Eight-Three is currently at 42.074718/-72.449341; and Twelve-Sixteen is currently at 42.262002/-71.757202. Ten-Oh-Three is just leaving Boston airspace at 42.43657/-71.169434. All planes are currently on course. Storm Two-Two and Two-Three, proceed with intercept of Fed Ex Eight-Two-Zero and Six-Eight-Three; Yankee Five-Six and Five-Seven take Fed Ex Twelve-Sixteen and Ten-Oh-Three."

"Roger that; Storm Two-Two and Two-Three taking Fed Ex Eight-Two-Zero and Six-Eight-Three; ETA to intercept fifteen minutes."

"Roger; Yankee Five-Six and Five-Seven taking Fed Ex Twelve-Sixteen and Ten-Oh-Three; ETA to intercept two minutes."

FAA Headquarters, Washington D.C.

"Jim, we have a report of at least one hijacked Fed Ex plane out of Boston; destination unknown, though EADS is watching it, as well as three other Fed Ex planes—all of which took off, on schedule, within half an hour. They have directed two of the fighters from the CAP we had over Washington and scrambled two more out of Barnes. Local police at Logan have also found three of the pickups we were looking for at the Fed Ex terminal parking lot. Looks like this was one stop on their target list."

"Boston?" interrupted Director Steve Youngblood. "Tom told us that the information he had so far only referenced JFK."

"Yeah, but he also told us that they still had several files to decrypt. Plus, we don't know what the Quds commander had for operational flexibility. He could have had several airports scouted out and selected Logan at the last minute," Carmichael added. "Let's get Tom on the phone and see what all they have by now."

"Tom, this is Director Youngblood. We've got some developments out here. Have you learned anything new?"

"Yes, we have, sir. We have decrypted everything on Major Zarin's laptop and are looking through everything; trouble is, he has a lot there. There's a lot of good intel but we haven't come across anything yet regarding an attack on Washington. Other than the initial threat on JFK, we haven't found anything more on that, either."

"Have your staff search the files for anything dealing with Boston or Logan International. We have a report that a Fed Ex cargo plane has been hijacked out of Logan; EADS is monitoring this. Local police also found three of the pickup trucks on your APB so it looks as Boston plays a key role in their next attack."

"Okay, that'll help narrow our focus. I'll let you know as soon as we find anything."

28,000' above New England

"Omar, this is Captain Rouhani. Where are you?"

"We're on course, approaching the Connecticut-New York border."

"Our flight has been discovered. We had a problem taking off. I would expect that we will have an American fighter on our tail in a couple minutes. Since you are already at the New York border, I want you to proceed to Indian Point. If we can bluff our way past the American fighters, we'll take Peach Bottom. If you are already at the border, you should be able to hit Indian Point in less than five minutes."

"That's correct, sir. We're about thirty miles out so we could hit Indian Point in about four minutes. We'll start our descent now. . . . It's been an honor to serve with you, sir."

"The honor is all mine. Good luck, Omar."

XXVII

"Huntress" EADS, Rome, New York

"Colonel, Fed Ex Eight-Two-Zero just changed course and altitude; she's losing altitude fast," exclaimed Sgt. Forrest.

"What's the new course and altitude?"

"Ma'am, they were on a course of two-six-zero degrees at 28,000'; they are now located at 41.831168 x -73.374939 on course two-one-eight and descending very rapidly, Ma'am. Let's see, that new route puts them on course for . . . . *Ma'am, where is Storm Two-Two?!?"*

"Storm Two-Two; how soon before you can intercept Eight-Two-Zero?"

"Huntress, I'm about fifteen minutes out."

"Yankee Five-Six, how soon can you intercept Eight-Two-Zero?"

"Huntress, ah, let's see, at the last coordinates, I'm five minutes out."

"Yankee flight, Storm flight, change of orders! Yankee Five-Six, take Eight-Two-Zero; Storm Two-Two, continue with Storm Two-Three on flight Fed Ex Six-Eight-Three. Yankee Five-Seven, continue with Fed Ex Ten-Oh-Three; we'll keep an eye on Fed Ex Twelve-Sixteen."

"Roger that, Yankee Five-Six taking Fed Ex Eight-Two-Zero."

"Yankee Five-Six, what is your load out?" Huntress inquired.

"Huntress, say again?"

"Yankee Five-Six, what is your load out?"

"Huntress, I'm carrying four Sidewinders, four AM-RAAMs, and a full load of 20mm."

"Very good, Yankee Five-Six, your target is Fed Ex Eight-Two-Zero, currently located at 41.831168 x -73.374939 on course two-one-eight and descending *very* rapidly. Supersonic is authorized."

"Huntress, say again."

"Yankee Five-Six, this is Huntress Actual. Eight-Two-Zero is off course and appears to be on a direct path to the Indian Point Nuclear Power plant. Firewall it Five-Six! I don't care how many windows you break. If Eight-Two-Zero is targeting Indian Point, they could crash into the place in approximately three minutes. Weapons are free. I repeat weapons are free. Give them two warnings; if they do not respond or change course, a shoot down is authorized."

"Huntress, this is Yankee Five-Six. Going to full AB; will be within range in ninety seconds. Weapons hot. Repeat, weapons hot."

"Roger, that Five-Six."

"Fed Ex Eight-Two-Zero, this is Yankee Five-Six. You are off course and descending very rapidly. Is everything all right?"

"Fed Ex Eight-Two-Zero, please respond. You are off course and descending too rapidly."

"Fed Ex Eight-Two-Zero, respond. What are your intentions?"

"Fed Ex Eight-Two-Zero, what are your intentions? If you do not return to your original course, you will be shot down."

"Omar, we are about five miles out. Answer them; it might buy us the time to reach the target."

"Yankee Five-Six, this is Fed Ex Eight-Two-Zero, we are having major hydraulic problems and have lost steering."

"Eight-Two-Zero, you must change course or you will be shot down."

"Three miles, Omar. I see the target."

"Yankee Five-Six. We are having problems with our hydraulics and have lost steering. There is a river directly ahead of us. I will try to make a water landing."

"Two miles."

"Negative, Eight-Two-Zero; turn or I will be forced to shoot. This is your last warning."

"Fox three, Fox three," exclaimed Yankee Five-Six as Thor fired two of his AMRAAMS.

Indian Point Energy Center is located directly on the east bank of the Hudson River, thirty eight miles north of New York City. Its two nuclear reactors generate more than two thousand megawatts of electricity that feeds thirty percent of the City's electrical needs. More importantly, though, upwards of 17. 6 million people live within a fifty mile radius of its two reactors. If even one of these reactors suffered a meltdown, every one of these people would need to be evacuated. A plane the size of a 757 crashing into the right spot here could cause a disaster unimaginable in scale and unprecedented in the history of the United States. The 9/11 attacks on the Twin Towers, as horrific as that was, would pale in significance should a couple reactors on the Eastern Seaboard suffer a meltdown.

Captain Rouhani knew he was so close to achieving his mission. He knew his plane had been discovered. He could see the strobe light of the American fighter behind his plane. However, he still had three planes out there which the Americans did not know. He knew that in the wake of 9-11, the Americans had dramatically improved their response time to stray aircraft so he realized he would never make it—to Peach Bottom or anywhere else for that matter—the Americans were already calling for him to return to Logan. However, Limerick, Salem, and especially Indian Point, were still distinct possibilities for his men.

"Yankee Five-Six, this is Huntress. Do you copy?"

"Yankee Five-Six."

"Yankee Five-Six, this is Huntress Actual. Our spotters on the ground indicate that a large aircraft crashed into a wooded area roughly a quarter mile north of the Indian Point Nuclear facility. Well done, Five-Six. Yankee Five-Six, reverse course and pick up Fed Ex Twelve-Sixteen, now located at 42.129548, -72.206268."

"Roger that; Yankee Five-Six heading to 42.129548, -72.206268 to pick up Fed Ex Twelve-Sixteen."

"Fed Ex Six-Eight-Three and Fed Ex Twelve-Sixteen, this is Huntress, you are directed to land at the nearest airport. Do you copy?"

"Fed Ex Six-Eight-Three, do you copy?"

"Fed Ex Twelve-Sixteen, do you copy?"

"Colonel, both Fed Ex Six-Eight-Three and Twelve-Sixteen just turned off their transponders. Looks like we have two more."

"Storm Two-Two; this is Huntress. Fed Ex Six-Eight-Three is refusing to answer and has turned off its transponder. Be advised Yankee Five-Six shot down Fed Ex Eight-Two-Zero as it intended to crash into the Indian Point Nuclear reactor."

"Yankee Five-Six; Huntress. Fed Ex Twelve-Sixteen is not responding and has turned off their transponder. Looks like we have a second one for you tonight."

"Roger that, Huntress."

"Yankee Five-Seven, this is Huntress. Continue to stay with Fed Ex, Ten-Oh-Three. Be advised Yankee Five-Six shot down Fed Ex Eight-Two-Zero as it intended to crash into the Indian Point Nuclear reactor."

The Pentagon, Washington DC

"Jim, I just received a call from the FAA," Secretary Axelsson said over the phone. "The Air Force just shot down a Fed Ex cargo plane that intended to crash into the Indian Point Nuclear facility; it actually impacted less than a quarter mile from the plant. They are tracking, with fighter escort, three other Fed Ex cargo planes—one of which the Air Traffic Controller said he heard four gunshots over the radio. All three have turned off their transponders and I'm guessing that they will try and hit three other nuclear plants—their route brings them very close to three more reactors; the Air Force won't let them get near any reactor, even if it is along their route. They'll most likely be shot down as well."

"So, it looks like Miss Yaniv was right; they were trying to take out four of our nuclear power facilities. The intel the Israelis received from their source in Beirut had to have been intended for us to discover. I think the only real question, now, is how far will our retaliation go?"

"From what we have received from Tom in Marathon, this would appear to have been the last of their attacks. We'll now focus on rounding up these guys out west. We've scrambled every available drone out of

Creech. Fortunately, a few of these ranches are relatively close by so we've had them under aerial surveillance for the last few hours; there's a few more in Oregon—we're still working on getting the surveillance up for those. However, now that we know what we're up against, it's all hands on deck. We'll start moving our forces to surround all of these ranches by tomorrow morning. We should have most of them rounded up by tomorrow afternoon at the latest."

"Well, it would seem your sailing force has been hammering them pretty hard in the gulf. This last attack will most likely be the *coup d'grace* for the Iranian government. Our final pieces for doing just that should be getting into place right about now."

White House Press Room

"Thank you all for coming in this late at night; I know it's been a long day," Christine Thompson, the president's press secretary announced. "I have just a brief statement and then I'll answer a few questions for you as I'm sure you all have more than a few of them. Okay, you all know what happened this morning. As a direct result of that, elements of the US Navy have been conducting round the clock airstrikes throughout Iran. This evening, I'm sure you've all heard reports that several aircraft reportedly crashed tonight in the New York/New England area. I can confirm that four aircraft did, indeed, crash: one in New York, two in Connecticut, and one in Massachusetts. I can also report that no passengers were either killed or injured in any of these aircraft. We have yet to hear of any damage on the ground or whether any of these planes crashed in any populated areas. Are there any questions?"

"Chris, that's it?" Several members of the press corps hollered out.

"Since no one was injured, do we know the types of aircraft involved?" Another reporter yelled out.

"Yes, I believe we do; all four were cargo planes."

"What about the flight crews?"

"I'm sorry, but I have no information on them."

"Does this have anything to do with the reports we've received of several sonic booms heard over Connecticut this evening?" One of the reporters yelled out.

"I don't know what you're talking about," Thompson replied.

"Chris, we've all heard the reports of sonic booms over the Northeast and now you are confirming that four planes have crashed—did the Air Force shoot these planes down? And if so, why?" Another reporter asked.

"No comment."

"Did the downing of these planes have anything to do with what happened this morning?"

"I said nothing about 'the downing' of any planes. All I can confirm is that four planes did indeed crash tonight."

"Chris, it's very suspicious: the only planes in the region capable of generating a sonic boom are Air Force fighters and the sonic booms were heard in the same area where these planes supposedly crashed."

"Good point, that is suspicious. No comment."

Chris Thompson had no idea that her press conference served to initiate yet another round of violence; the only real question was who would pull the trigger first?

Beirut, Lebanon

"Did you hear that?" Lieutenant Colonel Bukhari almost demanded of Muhammad Abu Abbas. "Major Zarin's force completely failed; the US Air Force shot all of his planes down. Are your troops ready to launch their rockets?"

"Colonel, we can launch within minutes of the order."

"Are all of the rockets positioned and targeted as I've indicated? We need to overwhelm their Iron Dome defenses and concentrate on specific targets rather than simply launching everything and hoping for the best."

"Everything has been done as you have directed."

"Very well; how long will it take for you to notify everyone to launch their rockets?"

"We can get the word out in fifteen minutes," Abbas replied.

"Okay, it is now twenty minutes past the hour. I want everything to be launched at forty minutes past the hour—that gives you twenty minutes to spread the word, and make sure—no electronic communications, absolutely none—we do not want those Israeli pigs eavesdropping on this. We need the element of surprise."

"Absolutely; we have swept this room for bugs and will be spreading the word person to person. We have a well-established network and we can get the word out to every launch site in a matter of minutes. We are ready."

"Very well; get the word out immediately. At precisely 0640, we launch with everything we have."

Tel Aviv, Israel

General Pardo knew the directorship of Mossad came with immense prestige; after all, there had only been eleven others in his position, and many of them had legendary reputations amongst the intelligence community. He also knew that its prestige often took a back seat to the real world of long hours and very little time with his family. This Iranian mess had really kept him busy: he usually arrived at the office well before six in the morning and didn't leave the building until well past ten in the evening—on a good day. His latest routine—as he very often changed "routines"—had him starting the coffee first and turning on Fox News, second. He had a general disdain for all things media but he kept Fox News on whenever he was in the office. He didn't trust the media but he tended to trust Fox a little more, especially as the current presidential administration seemingly did not. He had access to the network's Israeli version but chose to listen to Fox's broadcast real-time so he could remain up to date on all of the happenings in Washington—something extremely crucial over the past week. He could usually catch at least the last half of Sean Hannity before O'Reilly came on. This morning, though, proved a little different—no sooner than had O'Reilly started than Fox switched to a White House press conference—this got his attention. Who held a presser at eleven o'clock at night?—he thought to himself. About twenty minutes into the press conference, one of the correspondents asked Press Secretary Thompson if the four planes had been shot down. Alarm bells immediately went off in Tamir's head as he grabbed his phone.

"General Malka, get your planes in the air NOW!!!" Pardo barked into his phone to the Air Force chief of staff. "Hezbollah will be launching an attack within the hour."

"What's going on?" Came the immediate reply.

"We received word . . . , yesterday, I believe, that Hezbollah would be launching an attack of their own as soon as the Iranians carried out their third attack in the US. The downing of the four planes in the New York area would seem to figure into that. Word is that this will be a massive missile attack coming from Lebanon, seeking to overwhelm Iron Dome; other than that, we don't know too much. We know Iran has supplied tens of thousands of missiles to Hezbollah, many of them capable of hitting clear down to Ashqelon, maybe even Beersheba. The sooner we can get your planes in the air, the better off we'll be, but we need to be able to hit clear up into the Beqaa Valley as this is where most of their longer range missiles are located."

"Very good; we've known of their missile sites for some time. Scrambling the alert force now; the entire squadron will be airborne in twenty minutes."

"Excellent. I'll contact Bibi to let him know of the impending strike and see if he'll authorize a preemptive strike."

Israel's Iron Dome missile shield is widely regarded as the preeminent missile defense system in the world—to date, intercept rates as high as eighty-five percent have been reported. A common misconception with Iron Dome, though, is that it is designed to take out every missile fired into Israel. Rather, Iron Dome uses a highly sophisticated radar to determine the estimated impact area of an incoming missile—a missile bearing towards a rural agricultural setting or heading out to sea will in all likelihood, simply be ignored; a missile heading towards downtown Tel Aviv will receive immediate action. The only limiting factor with Iron Dome is the number of missiles within its batteries: Iron Dome has five thousand missiles within its batteries; Hezbollah had literally over one hundred thousand missiles stockpiled, though the number of launchers remained a mystery.

Colonel Bukhari now experienced the same anxious frustration Rafsanjani experienced a couple days earlier: the order had been given, all he could do was wait. He had seven thousand medium range missiles scattered throughout the Beqaa Valley at over three thousand launch sites and vehicles, many of these with twin launchers.   Of course, he had many other short range missiles and artillery pieces located along the heavily defended Israeli-Lebanese border.   However, the primary focus of the initial volley would consist of the medium range Tishreen missiles, each capable of reaching clear into central Israel—and all targeted at Tel Aviv. However, he fully believed he had a golden opportunity to finally do some damage: He knew Iron Dome would intercept many, maybe even most, of these missiles but even if just ten percent of the Tishreen force got through—that would mean seven hundred missiles would be striking in and around Tel Aviv. Moreover the Tishreen missile carried a 450 Kg warhead—the punishment he, *HE*, could inflict on the Zionist pigs, he thought to himself, would surely bring retribution to his enemies and glory for himself!

The pilots of the Israeli First Fighter Squadron served General Malka well: All twenty four of the squadron's F-16's were airborne in eighteen minutes. General Pardo had forwarded Bibi's authorization for a preemptive strike and every pilot raced to previously known missile sites in the Beqaa Valley. At precisely 0640 hours, each one of the pilots noticed the initial exhaust plumes of smoke coming from literally thousands of missiles as each pilot released all six of their own Maverick air-to-ground missiles. At 0641, the Iron Dome radar picked up the Tishreen missiles.

"General Malka, is David's Sling ready to go?" Tamir asked over the phone, referencing Israel's latest missile defense system.

"We're tracking seven thousand incoming medium range missiles as we speak—and some are going to get through. Even if a third of these veer off target, our missile magazines simply aren't large enough between both Iron Dome and David's Sling—David's Sling is still so new we don't have a full complement of missiles yet. I can hear the air raid siren in the background where you're at; they're also going off in Haifa. You heading to a shelter?"

"No, there's simply no time with these things. I know they've improved the guidance of these things but with only a two to three minute warning, we don't have time to evacuate the building."

"Understood. I've scrambled every attack squadron we have and put every Fighter squadron on alert. It'll take us a few sorties but we'll take out every static launch site we know about; the mobile ones will be tougher but we aren't fooling around—we are going to take out everything they have. The Army is already unleashing a massive artillery barrage on known sites across the border; I expect they'll be moving in very soon. We've had a plan on the books for cleaning up Southern Lebanon for several years: the army's going all the way to Beirut and rooting everything out on the way up there. Once things settle down, we'll pull back and occupy everything south of Tyre. With the US in the midst of completely destroying Iran—they won't be a threat to the region for at least a decade—and Syria tied down with its own civil war—there's no regional power to stop us so now is the time to clean this place up once and for all."

"Muhammad," Colonel Bukhari said into his phone, "did we get everything away? I'm hearing several fighters overhead."

"The first volley's away. No sooner than did we get the first volley off than we got hit by several airstrikes. We're reloading now before we get hit again. It's a race against time; it seems the Israeli's know of many of our sites. We're hearing of reports along the border where the Israeli army is hitting us hard but most of the longer range rockets are all up in Beqaa outside of the army's range."

"Have you been able to locate the frequency of Abbas or this Colonel Bukhari?" David Eitan asked his lieutenant.

"I just found it! Seems like the good colonel just called up Abbas."

"Do we know his location?"

"Got 'em! Sending to the Air Force . . . Now!"

"Colonel, I really think we should get off the phone. The Israelis routinely monitor our communications."

"I'm sure they do, but I think they're a little busy trying to take out all of your missiles right now," Bukhari answered smartly.

"Do not underestimate them, Colonel. I'm in a pretty deep bunker but even I don't think this might be deep enough."

"Relax, Muhammad, I really don't think there's anything to worry about. We have missile sites to keep them . . . ."

"Colonel?"

"Colonel . . . ?"

"Colonel Bukhari, are you there?" Abbas asked, knowing the futility of the question even as he asked it as the line had gone dead.

"Tamir, how'd you make out?" Jim Carmichael called.

"The last missile came in about ten minutes ago. It's bad; it's too soon to determine how many got through but Tel Aviv looks like London during the 'blitz. Our complex took a couple hits, I can see a couple skyscrapers that got hit . . . This is going to be bad. I would expect casualties to be in the hundreds, if not thousands."

"Let us know of anything we can do to help. The *Wasp* is currently in the Med and had been headed your way—we could tell her to step on it and have her there in roughly twelve hours; she boasts a six hundred bed hospital on board, if that would help. We can get more over there, but she's the closest."

"That would probably be a good idea. I think we're going to need that as I'm just now getting a report that both the Sourasky and the Edith Wolfson Medical Centers have been hit."

"I'll let Axe know to get them over there as soon as possible. I'm calling Stonewall next and I'll let them of your situation. I know they don't need the distraction but they're going to find out anyway."

"Go ahead and do that; I'm a little busy here."

"Okay, then. Let me know of anything else we can do, my friend."

"I'll do that. Thanks, Jim."

XXVIII

Tehran

"Stonewall, how are things going?" Jim Carmichael asked over the satellite phone.

"Going fine, sir. We picked up our package a few hours ago and are almost back at the house. How are things with you?"

"Just to bring you up to speed; Dani was right all along. Four Fed Ex cargo jets out of Boston were hijacked and they attempted to crash them into four different nuclear power plants in the northeast. We shot the first one down about a quarter mile from the Indian Point nuclear plant roughly twenty five miles north of New York City. The other three were shot down as well. With events of the past two days, the president will be going before Congress later today looking for a full blown declaration of war. He's going to get it."

"We aren't talking a full blown invasion, are we?"

"No, as you know, there's a growing movement of discontent throughout the country. We'll simply give that movement a big shot in the arm by taking out the top echelon of the government: their Supreme Leader, the Assembly of Experts, the Council of Guardians, etc. You know the leadership of this country better than most.

In addition, we have received word from some friends of ours that Colonel Rafsanjani was sighted in Amsterdam catching a flight to Tehran. He should be arriving their later tonight. We are expecting that he will have a meeting with their Supreme National Security Council first thing in the morning. We have a special assignment for you and your team; this is something Ben and his team have been working on for some time and we finally have the opportunity to implement it. You'll have the complete cooperation of the Air Force and the Navy to coordinate any close air support you might need. Once the mission is completed, you are to make your way to an abandoned airfield about one hundred miles southwest of Tehran right off of Highway 71 on the way to Cheshmeh Palang. A C-130 will be waiting for you, along with a company of Rangers for security."

"Roger that, sir. As soon as we're back at the house, I'll talk this over with Ben and Dani—she's actually Operations—and see what he has in store for us."

"Very good; Ben and his team know the city very well. Like I said, they've been working on this operation for quite a while but haven't had the resources or the opportunity—now we have both. We'll be holding off on any bombing in Tehran until you give us the word. Once you've given the word, again, the Air Force and Navy will give you all the close air support you need to cover your withdrawal; you'll have everything from A-10's and F-16's to B-1's stacked up to cover you."

"Okay; I'll brief the team, and have Ben brief us on the plan. This could be the most excitement I've had since my 'CIF' team. Anything else?"

"Stonewall, there's one more thing . . . . Tel Aviv's just been hit. Hezbollah apparently launched a massive missile attack with the Tishreen missiles they received from Iran. Both Iron Dome and David's Sling performed admirably but they were simply overwhelmed. Tamir's fine but told me to pass on what we know; their building got hit, two of the hospitals in Tel Aviv got hit; casualties are probably going to be in the thousands the way Tamir talked but it's way too soon for any specifics. I've spoken with Axe; the *Wasp* is in the Med and she has a decent sized hospital on board to help with casualties. She had already been headed towards Israel but will now be there in about twelve hours."

"Damn! It figured that they'd let the Israelis off too easily. I'm sure they knew it was coming, just not when. Do me a favor, let me know if you can find out anything regarding Dani's family; her parents and sister all live in Tel Aviv."

"Yeah, I can do that. Give me a call when you're on the Herc on the way out."

"Will do, sir."

Arriving back at the safe house, Zivah greeted Dani as she walked in the front door.

"Hey, Arielle, where'd you get the new uniform? Looks pretty sharp on you; anything going on that I should know about?" she added light heartedly.

"Zivah, shut up! We've been on the go since we left Tel Aviv, what a couple days ago? We left our bags clear back at Fort Bliss and Sergeant Rossi, here, was kind enough to grab a couple extra for us."

"You don't have to explain to me. You've got my support, whatever you're up to," she replied with the biggest grin on her face.

Before Dani could respond, Stonewall corralled her.

"Ah, Dani, we need to talk."

"What's up?" she asked rather suspiciously.

Grabbing her by the arm, Stonewall led her to the first unoccupied room he could find—which happened to be a bedroom—and shut the door.

"Ah, what's going on?" she asked, taking note of Stonewall's directing her into the bedroom.

Noticing the slightly awkward location, he let out a sheepish grin.

"Oh, sorry; I was simply looking for a room out of earshot from everyone else; this room looked available—didn't realize it was a bedroom."

"I see," Dani replied, with a bit of an impish grin on her face.

"I got off the phone with Jim a little while ago. A couple things: Hezbollah just hit Tel Aviv and it sounds bad. Jim didn't have specifics as it had literally just happened but said casualties appeared to be pretty high. He said that Tamir mentioned Mossad headquarters got hit, a couple hospitals got hit as well and so they expect casualties to be high. The *Wasp* is en route so you can figure that's likely the case—she has quite a hospital on board. I'm sorry," Jackson continued, as he noticed Dani's horror-stricken face, "but he didn't have any specifics on anyone; it's just way too soon, though I asked Jim to check on your family."

"We'll get by; we always do," Dani added, obviously stressed by the news. "Thank you."

"Secondly, you were right—Zarin's team hijacked four Fed Ex cargo planes out of Boston with the intent of crashing them into four different nuclear power plants. The Air Force shot all four of them down, the closest crashed a quarter mile from the Indian Point nuclear facility twenty five miles north of New York City. Ah, he also mentioned that we'll be launching an operation you guys have had on the books for a little while. He mentioned something about having the entire inventory of Air Force and Naval Aviation at our disposal to cover our withdrawal—and that we'll meet up with a team of

Rangers and a C-130 about a couple hours south of Tehran to get us out of the country. Any idea what he's talking about, since you are Ops for the team?"

With the brief description of this operation, Dani's countenance took a much more serious turn.

"So, we're going to do it, huh? I haven't had a chance to speak with Ben about this yet."

"So it would seem, but just what are we doing?"

"Well, you know Mossad and Sayeret Matkal have conducted some pretty bold operations in the past, like the raid on Entebbe, right?"

"Dani, everyone knows that."

"Yeah, well, if we pull this off, it'll make Entebbe look like a cake walk."

"Okay, you've got my attention; what's up?" Stonewall said has he sat down on the side of the bed.

And with that, Dani proceeded to spend the next ten minutes, pacing back and forth across the bedroom, outlining the operation.

"We've never had all of the pieces in place to do something this ambitious," she concluded. "Now . . . , it would seem we do. Remember, I haven't discussed this with Ben, but if this is what you're talking about, and I assume it is, this will be the gold standard by which all other Special Ops missions are measured!"

"Wow, you aren't kidding!" Stonewall admitted, letting out a slow whistle and crossing his hands behind his head as he fell back on the bed, still blown away by how ambitious this operation was.

"No, I'm not kidding. And, who knows, if we both get through this, maybe we'll get a chance to meet up back here in this room!" She added with very mischievous grin, as she leaned over and gave him a rather passionate kiss. "Let's go Cowboy, we need to discuss this with Ben."

At that, Stonewall was dumbfounded, first by the audacity of the operation, and then by Dani's kiss.

"Rossi, Captain Sanchez," Jackson yelled out from the kitchen of the safe house. "I need you and your men to gather in the basement. Ben's got a mission for us."

"Yes, sir. Okay guys, you heard the man. Let's go," Rossi yelled out.

Several long, slow and quiet whistles emerged as each one reached the basement. The array of weapons and equipment that lay before them thoroughly impressed each one. This truly, was the most complete safe house they had ever seen—and they had seen a great deal.

"Okay, guys," Jackson announced. "You'll get your tour in a bit. For now, we have a mission to prepare for. Not sure if you've all heard the news but there have been a couple attacks while we were en route over here. Tel Aviv has just been hit by Hezbollah; casualties are reported as high. This literally happened within the hour so that's all I know. The other one seems to have involved the hijacking of four Fed Ex cargo planes out of Boston with the intent of crashing them into four nuclear power plants encircling New York City. All four were shot down, the closest one landed less than a quarter mile from its target."

"Holy Mother of God," whispered Ferro. "Those bastards. Someone's gotta pay, sir."

"Yeah, well Ferro, I think that's what Ben, here, has in mind," replied Jackson. "Ben, it's all yours," Jackson said as he turned to Ben.

"Okay, gentlemen; I understand your reaction. We've had an operation on the books that we've been exploring for a couple years—but never had the opportunity. Colonel Rafsanjani, the architect of the attacks in the States, will be landing at Mehrabad this evening. First thing tomorrow morning, there will be meeting of the Supreme National Security Council—where we expect Rafsanjani will give a briefing as to the success of his operation. The meeting will be held at the Ministry of Intelligence and Security in the northern part of Tehran. Spread out before you is a three dimensional model of the complex. As you can see, there are only a few entrances to this complex; we'll be focusing on the northeast entrance. Across the street from this entrance is a six story office building. We'll have two snipers, initially, up on the sixth floor in an over-watch position to see who all enters the place. Once the word is given, the sniper team will take to the roof and take out the IRGC sniper/over-watch force—one of you will be up there with Jonah. Zivah will be on the street below ready to provide your escape. At the southern end of this complex, Ayal will team up with two from 5114 to create as large of a diversion as you can—it needs to look credible enough without being too large to seem like we are bombing the city." And so began Ben's briefing.

Three hours later, with the briefing completed and all questions answered, the teams paired up to go over the operation and their particular parts in the raid. The two weapons sergeants in the team got a tour of the safe house's arsenal and selected the weapons their teammates would be using: HK MP5N submachine guns, HK Mk 23 pistols with suppressors, and a couple McMillan TAC 338 sniper rifles. The comms sergeants checked out the communications gear and made sure everyone was on the same frequency, as well as reviewing the various assets they would have available from the Navy and Air Force. In addition to their communications duties, they would also be functioning as the JTAC—Joint Terminal Attack Coordinators—for the team. A few others checked out uniforms, all reviewed the escape routes needed . . . there wasn't much time available for sleep, though, after having been on the go since they left Fort Campbell, everyone knew they needed to get a few hours. By 5:00 a.m., the two snipers were in their over-watch position with Zivah in the coffee shop on the first floor of the same building.

XXIX

"How was your trip, sir?" Amir, Rafsanjani's driver, asked him.

"It was . . . eventful." Rafsanjani replied after thinking of the proper adjective. "But it's good to be back home again, Amir."

"I assume today we are heading to the Ministry, sir?"

"That's correct. I have an early meeting with Jalili and General Suleimani. I've heard the Americans have been bombing us quite heavily. Have they hit Tehran very hard yet? From what I've seen, the city seems to be pretty normal."

"They haven't hit us as yet, sir. All of the roads and buildings in the city are completely untouched. They have really hit the Guards and the Quds bases, and our Air Force, but everything else has been left untouched. In fact, I don't think we've even seen any American airplanes this far north. It seems odd, sir. I'm not complaining, but I would have thought they would have hit us a lot harder."

"Well, this isn't over by a long shot. We need to be ready when they do, and rest assured, they will be coming up here as well."

"What time is your meeting, sir?"

"Seven thirty, but I wanted to get there a little early to go over everything that has arisen in my brief absence."

"Not a problem sir. I'll have you there a little after seven."

A few minutes later, Amir noticed something indeed was amiss. "Colonel, just who all is going to be at this meeting of yours? The Expressway is normally packed. It looks as though something has completely shut down the highway."

"I see that. I haven't heard anything as yet and no one has told me anything out of the ordinary. One more thing to worry about this morning, Amir."

"Well, at this rate, sir, I'll have you at the Ministry in just a few minutes."

"Chaos, Hawkeye," the sniper team lead called to Jackson, "we have a vehicle entering the compound. Looks like we have a staff car coming in. Based on the security setup, they aren't letting too many vehicles into the place."

"Roger that, Hawkeye," Jackson replied.

About ten minutes later, a small motorcade approached the compound entrance and passed through the secure entrance site without even stopping.

"Chaos, Hawkeye. We have a small motorcade entering the compound. This looks like what we're here for, Chaos."

"Roger that. Let's give them a few minutes so everyone's in their place. We don't need any surprises at this point."

Five minutes later, another staff car pulled up to the entrance. The driver gave the guard his pass and before the guard could object that the pass didn't meet the day's security clearance, Benjamin Givon put two 9mm slugs into the guard's forehead. Sergeant Rossi, in the passenger seat, jumped out and stormed the guard house. Before anyone knew it, the four guards at the entrance had been eliminated.

"General, why are we not meeting in the bunker? Surely the Americans have this building targeted," Rafsanjani asked his boss, General Qassim Suleimani.

"Colonel, the Americans have been bombing us nonstop for the past two days," General Suleimani explained. "The military, especially Quds and the IRGC, have borne the brunt of this, as has the Air Force. However, they have not hit a single governmental building or office yet, and they have had ample opportunity. More specifically, they have not even dropped a single bomb here in Tehran. Director Jalili is right, the American president is clueless and does not understand a thing."

"General, it is very dangerous to underestimate the Americans," Rafsanjani replied a little louder than was probably necessary. "The American president may be an idiot but do not forget what they initially did in Afghanistan—many of their current military leaders were there and have not forgotten this."

"Colonel, relax. The Americans will not be bombing us," Said Jalili added as he walked in. "They will continue to target our military but we can replace everything we lose. Yes, we will lose some men, and that is unfortunate, but we have the money and our infrastructure remains undamaged, unlike that in the United States, which you properly addressed. Besides, we have a special guest today . . . ."

Before Jalili could tell Rafsanjani about their guest, and almost on cue, Supreme Leader Grand Ayatollah Khameini entered the conference room.

As soon as Jonah saw the staff car approach the entrance, he and Sergeant John Luna grabbed their gear and headed towards the roof. In addition to their sniper rifles, they each carried a silenced MP5. As the two approached the stairway leading to the roof, an IRGC guard challenged them, though he was not as prepared as Jonah and immediately fell from a double tap of 9mm slugs to the upper chest. Jonah and Luna emerged from the stairs on the roof to find two guards perched at the edge of the roof thoroughly engrossed in the assault on the Guard House across the street directly below them. Before they could get a warning out to the unit commander both guards collapsed in a pool of their own blood from a series of slugs stitched across their back and head.

"Chaos, Hawkeye; over-watch secured," Luna reported to Jackson.

"Roger that; primary team has passed the entrance."

No sooner than Ben and Rossi had eliminated the threat posed by the entrance guards than a large fireball erupted from the parking lot immediately adjacent to the southeast office building of the complex. Rossi could just see the top of the fireball behind the main building in the complex but a plume of thick black smoke made its presence clear to all around. As Ben pulled up to the main entrance of the Ministry, the guards, clearly preoccupied by the source of the unknown eruption in the parking lot behind them, did not immediately challenge him, Rossi or their two passengers in the back seat. Rossi rushed up to the first guard at the entrance asking, actually, almost yelling, about what was going on? The guard never had a chance; Rossi put two slugs into the man's face before he could respond. Ben and the other two members of the primary team fanned out and took out the remaining guards outside of the entrance as Rossi entered the building.

"Chaos, Jericho." Rossi called to Jackson. "We're in the building."

"Jericho, we're right behind you," replied Jackson as he saw Ben enter the building as they pulled up to entrance. Within seconds, the entire assault team entered the building. The remaining guards outside of the three other buildings had no idea an assault on their complex had just begun. The confusion caused by the fireball in the southeast parking lot temporarily caused enough confusion that the sudden appearance of additional "security personnel" did not arouse any suspicion. On the contrary, a few of the guards from the adjacent building actually rushed in to join Jackson and the rest of the assault team.

Four main buildings form the heart of Iran's Ministry of Intelligence and Security. Each of these is a perfect square with either an open-air veranda or a highly secure conference room, similar to a "situation room", in the middle of the square not unlike the middle of the Pentagon in Washington D.C. The middle of main building of the complex contained a situation room, actually what amounted to a separate building, though the average onlooker would have had to look closely to notice that. This "situation room" had been designed with lead walls encased in a concrete casement: the room was not only fire proof, but, at the time it was built, completely bomb-proof as precision munitions had not been developed. As a consequence, the room was also sound-proof to an extent that all but the loudest of noises could not penetrate the secure environment. Even the blast Ayal set off in the parking lot to distract the guards had gone unnoticed by the present occupants. It did not go unnoticed by their guards.

Not only had the guards outside of the conference room heard the explosion, they were a little better prepared than their brethren, but only a little. Ben and Rossi remained on point and as they rounded the last corner in the hallway to approach the entrance to the conference room the guards saw them approach and began to raise their AK-74's to fire—too late—as Ben hit the first guard with a three round burst and Rossi hit the second guard with another three round burst. However, the guards had managed to get off several rounds of their own before they fell to the floor: Up until now, all of the gunfire had come from the silenced MP5's of the commandos. The little noise that these made had been covered in the confusion caused by Ayal's explosion in the parking lot. However, there is nothing like the sound of a series of 7.62 rounds from an AK-74 in a concrete walled hallway: the automatic fire was deafening—and now everyone was on alert. Jackson, Dani and Captain Sanchez followed Ben and Rossi into the conference room—to the astonishment of all the occupants.

"What is the meaning of this? How did you get in here?" demanded General Suleimani.

"General Suleimani, I presume?" asked Jackson. "Colonel Thomas Jackson, United States Special Forces. You, Dr. Said Jalili, and Colonel Ashkan Rafsanjani need to come with me. Dani, will you see to Supreme Leader Grand Ayatollah Khameini?"

One of the staff officers immediately jumped in front of Dani and tried to grab her MP5 as she moved towards Khameini. Dani didn't hesitate; a quick six round burst sent four rounds into the staff officer's chest and, as the Supreme Leader remained seated, two rounds into his head, killing both instantly.

"Rossi, get the pics of Tecumseh," Jackson ordered, referring to the lifeless body of the Supreme Leader.

"You'll never get out of here alive," yelled Colonel Rafsanjani.

"Frankly, Colonel, I never thought we'd get *in* here" replied Jackson. "Let's go," Jackson continued as Rossi and Dani placed the three of them in flexi cuffs; Ben was busy with something else.

As they headed towards the door to leave, Jackson placed one last radio call.

"Archangel, Chaos Actual. Geronimo, Cochise, and Crazy Horse are in custody," referring to his three captives. "Beginning extraction now."

"Roger that, Chaos. What's the status of Tecumseh?" 'Archangel' Admiral Jack Fischer asked.

"Enjoying his seventy-two virgins," replied Jackson. "Two rounds through the melon; pics forthcoming."

"Roger that," Archangel replied. Fischer still thought a SEAL team would have been better for this mission but he had to admit, the ODA team was able to get their first and had already secured their target; now he knew the fun would begin. "Chaos, be advised Greyhound is in en route and will be at the Bat Cave waiting for you. Good luck, son."

Jackson smiled at that; only the Navy would refer to their Air Force extraction flight as a bus ride. In the meantime, he still had to get there, and it looked—and sounded—as though they'd have to fight their way out. Sanchez and his team had the hallway secured to the entrance of the building but getting to their vehicles would not be easy. The entire operation—from taking out the guards at the entrance to the capture—had taken less than five minutes so far and they all knew that every second's delay dramatically increased the hazard of this mission.

"Archangel, we'll be there waiting for that bus ride," Jackson replied.

Ben made sure he was the last to leave the room as the small party exited. He made sure that the doors were shut and locked so that no one could get out. A few seconds later, a large explosion rocked the building; the large, heavy doors of the conference room completely flew off their hinges, crashing through the walls on the opposite side of the hallway. Clearly, no one could be left alive in the room. Tamir had told him to make sure that none of the present Security Council personnel escaped to either form a new government or to succeed the Supreme Leader within the present government.

"Just a bit of overkill, don't ya think, Ben?" Jackson asked him.

"Just wanted to make sure the job was done," he replied.

"I kind of think you succeeded with that," Dani chimed in.

"Okay, folks, let's get out of here while we still can. Sanchez, your team ready to mount up?"

"Roger that, sir. Let's get out of here."

XXX

Ministry of Intelligence, Tehran

Ayal and his two teammates had joined the half of the team that had been left to commandeer the motorcade limousines and form somewhat of a perimeter so that the assault force could make it back to the limos relatively easily. However, things had really heated up after the initial gunfire from the conference room guards; that short AK-74 burst alerted the entire complex. Though less than a minute had elapsed from that time, dozens of IRGC forces descended upon the complex and, while Sanchez's perimeter team had been able to keep the IRGC at bay without injury, that couldn't last.

Sergeant Rossi was the first to go down. No sooner had he exited the building than he took a round to the lower abdomen, just below his Kevlar vest. Ferro rushed to him and dragged him the short distance to one of the limo's and quickly began the triage to treat the wound. The one nice thing about these presidential limousines, Ferro thought, was that they had plenty of space in which to work; he needed that now.

Ben, Dani, and Stonewall had each grabbed one of their captives and ran the gauntlet to the parked motorcade together. All three found the enemy fire relatively light until they reached the motorcade, whereupon as soon as each captive entered their respective sedan, the incoming fire increased exponentially. As soon as Ben threw General Suleimani into his sedan, he took two rounds to his right upper chest, each stopped by his vest, and a third to the right shoulder just where the vest ended. The impact of the three successive rounds to his right spun him around and actually dropped him into the sedan where upon Ayal pulled him clear of the door and slammed it shut behind him.

Dani and Stonewall each headed to the same sedan, with Jackson and Rafsanjani about ten feet behind her and Jalili. As Dani threw Jalili into the car, she took two near simultaneous rounds, one just above her right breast, the other just below her right shoulder blade. Her vest stopped both rounds, though the impact felt like a sledgehammer hitting her from the front and back at the same time. Just before she collapsed under the impact of these two bullets, a third round found her thigh, completely taking her down. Stonewall, following immediately behind her, threw Rafsanjani into the car, picked Dani up and threw her in and then he himself took four rounds to the back, literally propelling him into the car on top of Dani.

"I told you, you'd never get out of here alive," Rafsanjani hissed.

Stonewall took one look at him and followed that up with a powerful blow to Rafsanjani's jaw. "You just watch, Colonel. You'll be on a plane out of here before you know it."

"Ah . . ." Dani moaned in pain. "I wish you'd have let me do that!"

"Sorry, wasn't up for discussion. How's that leg of yours?" Jackson asked.

"Hurts like hell; think I've got a broken rib or two, as well; it really hurts to breathe. How's it look?" She asked.

Jackson had already ripped open her pants leg and began examining the wound. "There isn't a lot of blood; looks to be through and through. Looks like the Kevlar stopped the other two. Can you take a deep breath?"

"No, I can't. It really hurts," Dani exclaimed, obviously short of breath.

"Hey, Ferro," Jackson called to his senior medic up ahead. "Dani took two rounds on either side of the chest and I think she's got a collapsed lung. I think . . . ."

"Chaos, I'm a little busy here. You know what to do—you've done it before; just let me know if any blood comes out once you stab her."

"Okay, will do."

"Jericho Six; Chaos." Jackson called to Captain Sanchez as he quickly rummaged through the limo's first aid kit. Being a presidential limo, the first aid "kit" rivaled that of a small clinic. "How'd we make out? Is everybody on board and ready to roll?"

"All present and accounted for, Chaos. Let's get out of here."

"Hawkeye, we're on our way out. We're all in the presidential motorcade limos—there should be five vehicles. Take out anyone following us. We'll meet you at the junction of the Shahid Hemmat Expressway and the Emam Ali Highway; we'll be waiting for you. Don't take too long."

"Roger that; see you in a couple minutes."

"We need to get that vest off of you," Stonewall said to Dani as he began to remove her vest. "I think you've got a collapsed lung in addition to a couple broken ribs. This is going to hurt but I need to insert a needle into your chest to get that lung re-inflated."

"Jericho Six; Chaos. What's are status?" Jackson called out as he continued working with Dani.

"Chaos, looks like all four of you got hit. Rossi took a round to the gut just below his vest. Ferro's working on him now. Ben took three rounds to the shoulder—his vest stopped two of them. I think we've got the bleeding under control but he's hurt bad. How'd you two make out?"

"Arielle took two to the vest, one to the thigh, though it doesn't look too bad. I think she also has a collapsed lung from the two hits she took," Jackson replied as he finished cutting away Dani's shirt.

"You know," Dani remarked, grimacing in obvious pain, "this isn't exactly how I planned on you getting my top off."

This brought a wry smile from Stonewall. "Don't worry, I left your Under Armour on. Okay, you ready for this?" He asked her as he felt around looking for the gap between her second and third ribs.

"Ready when you are," came her reply.

"Ah!!!! Oh, that hurt!" Dani cried out, as Jackson inserted the needle from the large syringe. As he pulled back on the syringe it quickly filled with air and a small amount of fluid.

"Archangel, Chaos; we're on our way out and will be meeting up with Hawkeye in a couple minutes. You can tell the boys in blue to 'cry havoc and let slip the dogs of war'; just don't cut our escape route!"

"Roger that, Chaos," Archangel replied. And with that, Admiral Fischer gave the order for a full squadron of B-1's and half a dozen B-2's orbiting Tehran to commence their operations. Virtually every remaining IRGC member, and every governmental official and office who in anyway supported the radical theocracy came under the awesome destructive firepower of either a Lancer or a Spirit.

"Archangel, are we going to have a doc on that Hercy-bird? We have three Whiskey India Alpha, two severe."

"That's a negative, Chaos. Get to the Bat Cave and we'll have medics standing by when you land."

"Roger that."

"Jonah, looks like we have couple tails on our friends," Sgt. Luna said to his compatriot. "I'll take the first car; you can take the second one."

"Will do," replied Jonah.

With that, Sergeant Luna took a bead on the first car that began to chase after his team. The perch that Ben had picked out for them provided them a perfect over-watch for any vehicle exiting the complex: every single vehicle exiting the complex had to drive straight towards them for the last couple hundred yards before it left the parking lot. As the first vehicle rounded the corner for the last two hundred yards, Luna centered the reticle of his high-powered scope right on the driver. When the vehicle was roughly fifty yards from the exit, Luna pulled the trigger. The .338 Lapua round leapt from the rifle with an enormous report. The driver of the vehicle heard the loud report, and instinctively knew there was trouble, but never had the opportunity to do anything about it: the .338 slug entered the driver's body just above center mass where the breast bone ends and the neck begins, virtually decapitating the driver. The vehi-cle, now driverless, careened out of control crashing into the guard shack and coming to rest there, blocking the entrance lane into the complex.

Jonah took the second vehicle and timed his shot about the same as did Luna, with very similar results. Jonah's shot actually came just a few seconds after Luna's with the result that the second vehicle crashed into the back end of the first vehicle. The parking lot exit wasn't completely blocked but anyone trying to get out of the lot would now have a serious obstacle to overcome.

"Nice shooting, Luna," exclaimed Jonah.

"Not so bad yourself," replied Luna. "Let's get out of here while we still can."

"Roger that. Zivah, we're on our way down."

"Ready to rock n' roll whenever you get down here," Zivah exclaimed.

"Jericho Zero-Three, if you haven't already, let's get that CAS going." Jackson said to the senior Special Forces communications sergeant, referring to the close air support they were supposed to have. "We're supposed to have virtually everything in the arsenal at our disposal."

"Roger that, Chaos. Eagle Control advises that we have a complete squadron of Warthogs at our immediate disposal. We also have Vipers and Super Hornets standing by but the Warthogs are immediately available. We might get lucky and get some Apache Longbows; they're on their way but had to refuel and re-orient their payload at the Bat Cave."

"Jericho Zero-Three, Eagle Control knows our escape route?" Jackson replied, referring to an orbiting E-2D Hawkeye from the *George Washington*. Jericho Zero-Three and Zero-Eight, the two Special Forces communications sergeants for the team, would be the JTAC's—Joint Terminal Attack Controller—for the little convoy while Eagle Control in the orbiting Hawkeye would control the air assets available to the Jericho team.

"That's affirmative, Chaos. Eagle Control has our planned route and has been advised that we are in the supreme leader's motorcade."

"Okay; let's make sure they are aware of the one trailer we have with our Hawkeye team."

"Already done, sir. As soon as they show up we can head out. The Hawgs are standing by."

"Hawkeye, Chaos. What's your position?"

"We have you in sight, sir; be there in a few seconds."

"Roger that. Jericho Zero-Three, let the airedales know we are on the move. Let's move out."

"Eagle Control, Jericho Zero-Three. Who do we have for the Hawgs?"

"Jericho Zero-Three, their call sign is Sun Devil. Sun Devil Zero-Six is their lead and they are on this frequency."

"Jericho Zero-Three, what is your position?" asked Sun Devil Zero-Six.

"Sun Devil Zero-Six, we are at the intersection of Shahid Hemmat Expressway and Emam Ali Parkway in a five vehicle presidential motorcade, all black limos."

"Roger that, Zero-Three; I have you in sight. I have a Humvee-type vehicle heading your way at a high rate of speed on the Shahid Hemmat Expressway."

"Zero-Six, that could be our sniper team."

"Roger that; have them flash their head lights Zero-Three."

"Hawkeye, Jericho Zero-Three; flash your headlights."

"I see them. Okay Zero-Three, we have your route to the Bat Cave; we'll escort you along the way. I'll be your FAC(A);"—Forward Air Controller (Airborne)—"my whole squadron's here with you Jericho Zero-Three. We'll get you home."

"Roger that, Zero-Six. Appreciate the escort; be advised I'm in the second vehicle; Jericho 08 is in the last vehicle operating as the rear JTAC."

"Chaos, Jericho Zero-Three; not sure if you heard, we have a squadron of Hawgs with us; call sign Sun Devil. They are on station and have us in sight. Sun Devil Zero-Six will be working as our FAC(A)."

"Roger that, Zero-Three. Hawkeye just showed up so let's get going."

"Sun Devil Zero-Six, Jericho Zero-Three; we're heading out. Let us know how the traffic looks along the way. Tehran is notorious for traffic—the last thing we need is to get stuck in a traffic jam. We are in the Supreme Leader's motorcade so that will help clear the way to some extent but nothing was done to clear the way ahead of time. We are at the tail end of their rush hour so I'm expecting we could get some congestion somewhere—even without the IRGC giving chase."

"Jericho Zero-Three, always wanted to be a traffic reporter once I leave the Air Force—we'll give you an up to the minute report on any traffic accidents we happen to see."

"Copy that, Zero-Six. And, if we happen to see any missile batteries or man-pads, we'll be sure and let you know," replied Zero-Three.

"You do that, Zero-Three. A simple man-pad could really ruin our day out here. You are aware that your route is taking us directly past the Doshan Tappeh Air Base, right? We've eliminated their Fighter threat but the AAA threat remains."

"Wasn't responsible for putting this route together Zero-Six, but if we see anything, we'll be on it and let you know."

"Sun Devil Zero-Six, Jericho Zero-Eight; we have several vehicles coming up behind us very fast. We're going to need them taken out right away. They are way too close for missiles; I sure hope you guys have a full load of thirty mike-mike."

"Roger that, Zero-Eight; we're fully loaded. We'll be coming from directly ahead of you; keep your heads down, guys."

Not ten seconds later, a sound similar to a very loud zipper erupted over the small motorcade followed by four IRGC cars, which had been chasing the motor cade, being completely shredded by the impact of a couple hundred rounds of 30mm shells. The one unique feature of the A-10 Warthog—Hawg, for short—is its 30mm Gatling gun. The A-10 had been designed specifically for close air support: the pilot actually sits in what amounts to a bullet-proof titanium bathtub while the entire aircraft has been built around the Gatling gun. The aircraft also has a dozen fixed hard-points under its wings to carry all sorts of CAS munitions. Its original intent had been to take out Soviet tanks rumbling through the Fulda Gap in Germany, and its gun could literally rip a Soviet tank to shreds. The demise of the old Soviet Union did nothing to eliminate the effectiveness of the Warthog: it remains the preeminent fixed wing close air support aircraft—and Jackson and his Jericho team had a dozen of these planes escorting them through Tehran and out to the Bat Cave.

"Nice work on those IRGC guys, Zero-Six; they're completely shredded."

"Chaos, Jericho Zero-Eight; I think word has gotten out that we either don't have their Supreme Leader with us or that we've taken him out. The intensity has really picked up. We're starting to get direct fire of all types— the RPG's are as thick as hail—and they don't seem to be too worried about our passengers."

"Zero-Eight, Chaos; yeah, I noticed that, too. The RPG fire hasn't been too accurate but it's only going to take one hit to ruin this parade. Keep that CAS coming; that's about the only way we're going to get out of here."

"Roger that, Chaos."

"Sun Devil Zero-Six, Jericho Zero-Three; we are approaching an overpass at Masil-e-Bakhtr and it looks as though the IRGC has a welcoming party there for us; going to need some help here."

"Roger that, Zero-Three; we're on it. Approaching from directly behind you; keep your heads down."

Once again, a loud zipper-like noise erupted directly over the motorcade; this was followed by another Hawg flying perpendicular to the motorcade and directly on top of the overpass. Again, the pilot unleashed his 30mm gun on the blocking party on the overpass—absolutely nothing was left on the overpass.

"Nice work, Zero-Six! That was awesome!"

"Roger that, Zero-Three. It looks like we're going to be busy the rest of the way. Each overpass looks as though they mean to stop you; and I suppose with good reason. We're seeing more and more troops gathering to try and stop you guys at each overpass."

"Roger that, just make sure you don't actually knock any of these bridges down; the last thing we need is a complete roadblock from a dropped bridge!"

"We'll try and keep them up for you, Zero-Three."

For the next fifteen minutes, the two Special Forces communications sergeants, working as the JTACs for the motorcade, and Sun Devil Zero-Six, working as the FAC(A) operated in perfect harmony as any of the best philharmonic orchestras could perform. However, as they made the turn onto the Azadegan Expressway, Jericho Zero-Eight watched in horror as one of the Hawgs picked up a heat seeking missile from a man-pad after a strafing run. The shooter had been hiding under the overpass and had been completely missed as the motorcade had completely bypassed the bridge.

"Chaos, Jericho Zero-Eight; Hawg down! Repeat, we have a Warthog down!"

"Zero-Eight, was the pilot able to bailout?"

"Roger that; we can see the parachute. He's drifting away just to the south of us."

"Zero-Eight, take Hawkeye with you and *get that pilot,*" Jackson immediately ordered.

"Sun Devil Zero-Six, Chaos Actual; Jericho Zero-Eight and Hawkeye are en route to the crash site to rescue the pilot. They have priority. We can hold our own for a few minutes."

"Roger that Chaos. We should be able to cover both of you. We have some fast movers on standby just in case. You're not alone, Chaos."

"08, how soon before you can get to the pilot?"

"Chaos, looks like he's drifting down into some type of park or sports complex. We should be there in a couple minutes."

"Jericho Zero-Eight, Sun Devil Zero-Six; our pilot is in that complex. There's a small man-made lake and opposite that, about half a mile to the east, is a soccer field; our pilot is right about in the middle of the two."

"Roger that, Zero-Six; we can see the parachute blowing in the wind. We'll be there in a few."

"Jericho Zero-Three, Chaos; I'm sure you heard— we have a Hawg down and I've split the team, sending Hawkeye and Jericho Zero-Eight to retrieve the pilot. We'll be waiting for them to get back here and join up with us. In the meantime, we're sitting ducks. Keep that CAS coming as that's our only saving grace."

"Roger that, Chaos. I just heard from Sun Devil Zero-Six, the Apaches just showed up and are on station, we have six of them and they're loaded for bear!"

"Awesome! Send one of them with Zero-Eight for any support they might need."

"Roger that, Chaos."

"Archangel, Chaos; we have a Hawg down. I've split up my team—I've got a small unit going to rescue the pilot while we wait at an under pass for them to return with the pilot. The FAC(A) saw the pilot go down and is guiding my team to where he saw the pilot land."

"Roger that, Chaos. Let us know if you need any further support."

"Roger that. The Apaches just showed up so they should take care of any immediate threat we have."

"Hey guys, grab your rifles," Zivah said to Jonah and Luna. "Looks like our pilot already has a welcoming party; going to need to break that up."

"Yeah, looks like we have, what . . . three, maybe four, guys there? Jonah, you take the one on the left and the driver of the Humvee? I'll take the two on the right."

"Got it; let me know when you're ready."

Zivah had now parked their Humvee and both Jonah and Luna were set up. "Okay, Jonah, on my mark . . . three, two, one, fire." And with that, two .338 slugs dropped the two IRGC soldiers immediately around the pilot. A few seconds later, the third soldier and the driver met the same fate as their two compatriots.

"Okay, Zivah, we need to hurry; they obviously know where the pilot landed. Let's get over there, grab the pilot, and get out of here." Jonah ordered Zivah.

"Roger that," she replied.

Twenty seconds later, they pulled up to where the pilot lay in the field.

Luna was the first one out of the Humvee. "Are you okay?" He asked, noticing that the pilot had an obvious broken leg.

"Bailing out at five hundred feet isn't all it's cracked up to be," replied Captain Andrea Parker, wincing in obvious pain.

"No doubt" replied Luna. "Let's get you loaded up and get out of here before the party really gets started." With that, both Luna and Jonah placed Captain Parker in the back of the Humvee as Zivah took off rather hurriedly.

"Sun Devil Zero-Six, Jericho Zero-Eight; we have the pilot and are heading back to the rest of the convoy. She's a little banged up and definitely won't be dancing anytime soon but we got her."

"Roger that, Zero-Eight. You've got an Apache flying top cover for you on the way back to the convoy. They're waiting for you at the junction of the Azadegan Expressway and Highway 71."

"Chaos, Jericho Zero-Eight; we have the pilot and are headed your way; ETA, two minutes."

"Roger that. Nice work, Zero-Eight. How's the pilot doing?"

"She's got a badly broken leg. We need to transfer her to Ferro's rig and let him take a look at her when we get back."

"Roger that; we'll be waiting for you."

"Ferro, Chaos; how's Rossi doing?"

"I've got him stabilized. He's taken a gut shot so he needs to see a doc as soon as possible."

"We won't be able to get him one until we fly out of here so it's going to be a few hours. Jericho 08 has another patient for you as well. You have room for the pilot they just picked up? Sounds like she has a badly broken leg."

"Yeah, I've got room here. Thanks for the heads up; I'll be waiting for them. By the way, how's your patient doing?"

"She's doing fine; thanks for the training, boss," Jackson responded.

"Any word on Ben?"

"He's in another car but word is he's stable. I haven't had a chance to look at him."

"Okay, Ferro, keep me posted."

Sitting back in the lead car, Dani had the chance to finally see Stonewall at his best: the situation couldn't have been more chaotic. In the midst of an unbelievably chaotic situation, Stonewall continued to organize the chaos: He was constantly on the radio talking to his team, talking with Archangel, dividing his team even under extremely dangerous conditions to recover the downed pilot, handling the medical needs of both his team and now that of the pilot, all while continuing to monitor the desperately needed air support that Jericho Zero-Three continued to provide. She had seen Ben in similar situations and he was very good at this sort of thing but clearly, Stonewall really excelled at this—he truly understood the nature and capabilities of a Special Forces team.

As the now reunited convoy headed south on 71, the prospects of the IRGC successfully stopping them began to drop significantly. The Special Forces communication sergeants and the FAC(A) Warthog pilot found their stride again and functioned to perfection: Jericho Zero-Three and Zero-Eight identified their targets and Sun

Devil Zero-Six apportioned the needed response. Arch-angel, following the convoy by aerial feed from an orbiting Reaper, was suitably impressed. By the time the convoy managed to cross the second bypass expressway, Jackson began to feel that they just might pull this off. When they crossed Highway 7, he knew they were home free.

"How you doin'?" Jackson asked Dani.

"Hurt like hell but I don't think it's going to be anything serious; breathing is much easier, as well. You've done that before, huh?"

"Yeah, a time or two. I left that needle in to fully evacuate any air in your chest so don't make any sudden moves. It's taped in so it's not coming out but I don't want it aggravating anything on the inside."

"Yeah, I can kind of feel it. How are you doing, though? You took a couple rounds in the back too, didn't you?"

"Think I've got a broken rib or two; my back's pretty sore, but I'm fine."

"How's everyone else?"

"The medics have stabilized both Ben and Rossi. The pilot we rescued has a badly broken leg but she'll be okay. Ferro's a dynamite medic—I've actually seen him do some minor surgery before. We'll be at the evac site in half an hour. They'll have some medics on board but it's going to be awhile before we can get both of them into surgery—Ferro thinks they'll be okay but won't know the full extent of their injuries until they can open them up. I'll have him look at both the chest tube and that leg of yours once we get airborne."

"I'll be fine; you just make sure they take care of Ben and Rossi."

Half an hour later, the little convoy approached an abandoned airfield. "Batman Zero-Six, Chaos Actual. We are approaching the Bat Cave and have you in sight. Be advised we have four wounded, two critical." Jackson radioed the Ranger commanding officer guarding their hastily prepared airfield.

"Roger that, Chaos. The engines are revved up and ready to go. We can be airborne in thirty seconds after you get here. What's the disposition of your guests?"

"They are a little surprised we managed to pull this off but they are all in good health. See you in a few."

Al Udeid Air Force Base, Qatar

An hour and a half later, two C-130s touched down at Al Udeid Air Force Base, Qatar. Medical personnel had been notified and were standing by for the two critical patients. As soon as the plane reached its terminus, a team of paramedics raced on board and hauled both Ben and Rossi off into an ambulance to an awaiting OR staff who had been advised of their condition. Dani came next and, while her injuries were not as severe as her teammates, the medics hauled into the pre-op waiting room as both injuries needed a surgeon. Ferro had looked at her wounds and bandaged them up while en route to Al Udeid—as gun shots go, her thigh wound wasn't anything too serious and he thought she'd recover from the collapsed lung relatively quickly.

"Did I hear you correctly back there?" Dani asked Stonewall. "We were in the middle of a major fire fight—I mean bullets and RPGs are flying everywhere—and you're quoting Shakespeare?" Dani said looking at Stonewall in of state of utter disbelief.

"What? Who's better than Shakespeare?"

"Oh, I don't know, how about Ridley Scott and Russell Crowe: 'Unleash Hell'—and it's more to the point."

"Maximus Decimus Meridius over Marc Antony in *Julius Caesar*? Are you kidding? Not a chance."

"You really are something, you know that?" Dani said, with an admiring look at him.

"Jim," Jackson spoke into his phone, "a C-17 with your three special passengers took off for Andrews a little while ago. They'll be refueled inflight so they'll be there sometime tomorrow. I'll be heading back to Tel Aviv with Dani. I understand Dr. Bagheri is back in Tehran looking to form a new government after most of the Iranian government was killed in our airstrikes early this morning."

"Excellent; the president will be extremely pleased. I got word on Dani's family for you; they're all fine. Dani's condo, on the other hand, took a direct hit; it's a total loss. How's everyone doing? Understand you had a few casualties."

"Awesome! Thanks for that; I'll let her know. Ah, yeah, Ben, Dani's CO, took three rounds, all three to the right shoulder though two of them were stopped by his vest. Still, his shoulder's pretty messed up. Rossi took a round to the gut just below his vest. Both are in surgery right now. The A-10 pilot we picked up has a nasty broken leg—compound fracture below the knee. Ferro and the other team medic took great care of all three of them though they're going to be out of the game for quite a while. Dani took a round in the thigh, through and through. Fortunately, it didn't hit any major blood vessels. She also took two rounds—one to the shoulder and one in the back—that broke a couple ribs and collapsed one of her lungs. She's banged up and broken ribs really hurt but she won't be down for long. I've got a couple broken ribs myself, and, yeah, they hurt. I'll be heading back to Tel Aviv with Dani on the next flight out of here."

"Good. We want you back in Tel Aviv as I expect we might need you there to help with our liaison with both the Israelis and Dr. Bagheri. Your hotel made it through unscathed so you should be fine."

"Roger that. I'll do what I can."

"Oh, I know that, Tom. Take good care of Dani; she sounds like an awesome girl. You know, I never did get a chance to meet her."

"Well, we'll have to correct that, won't we?"

"That was Jim?" Dani asked as Jackson walked into her room.

"Yes, it was; your family's fine."

"Thank you," she said quietly, looking at Jackson as if he had saved them himself.

"Your condo, on the other hand, took a direct hit, or so I'm told."

"At least my family's safe; everything else can be re-placed."

"How soon can we get out of here? It sounds like Jim wants me to stick around Tel Aviv for a while."

"The docs put some type of valve in my chest to keep the lung inflated so they've cleared me to leave but I'm going to need some help getting dressed," Dani told him as she sat up and let the sheet slip away from her, fully cognizant of the image she portrayed. Stonewall was completely surprised to see that all she had on was a pair of gym shorts that Rossi's wife had picked up for her back at Fort Campbell a few days earlier.

"I know this isn't the image you probably imagined before but right now I'm way too sore to care, or for that matter, too drugged up to care—I'm really sore," Dani continued. "Don't think I'll be rockin' a bikini any time soon," she added with a painful smirk.

Jackson noticed that her right breast and shoulder up to the collarbone was one massive bruise with the flutter valve taped to her sternum. In addition, the nursing staff had completely bandaged her left thigh.

"Considering what we've all gone through in, what, the last eight hours, I think you look amazing."

"Huh; you're only saying that as I don't have a top on. Hand me that T-shirt, would you? I'm not even going to try and put that sports bra on. By the way, how're Ben and Rossi?"

"It looks like they'll be okay. Ben's days in the Unit might be over; his shoulder is really messed up. Rossi should be okay; that bullet did a lot of internal damage, bladder and I think he lost a kidney, so I'm thinking he'll medically retire after this."

"That's good to hear about Rossi; I'm glad he'll be okay, I really like him. Ben's a fighter; if anyone can come back from this, he will. How're you doing?"

"Ah, two broken ribs in the back; they'll take some time to heal but I'll be fine. I know it's only been, what, a week, ten days or so, but, you know, I have this really cool hotel on the beach in Tel Aviv and, from what I hear, it's a great place to spoil someone."

Dani gingerly limped over to him, still holding the T-shirt in one hand, wrapped both arms around his neck, and gave Stonewall the most passionate kiss he'd ever remembered.

"I think that answers that question," Jackson noted, briefly interrupting her kiss.

"Ouch!! Don't squeeze me too hard . . . ."

Made in the USA
San Bernardino, CA
27 January 2017